Praise for

Flesh and Stone

"Vivid characters with complicated emotions help the plot race along, making it an exciting thrill ride!"
—*Romantic Times* (4 stars)

"Riveting from page one . . . A tale to sink your teeth into (literally!), *Flesh and Stone* does not disappoint."
—*Romance Reviews Today*

Carved in Stone

"Taylor's fascinating premise provides an atmospheric setting for an accomplished romance between two strong but prickly and suspicious protagonists. Fans of Christine Feehan's Dark series will find much to like in *Carved in Stone*." —*Booklist*

"Taylor charts a clever and unique new path by unveiling the dark world of gargoyles—an exciting and new world with plenty of opportunities for exploration. *Carved in Stone* is a sexy, sensual, and dangerous romance." —*Romantic Times*

"*Carved in Stone* offers paranormal fans something new, introducing a universe built around supernatural creatures atypical for the genre: gargoyles . . . An intriguing premise . . . A fascinating read . . . Complex and very well thought out. The way this story unfolds offers a smooth introduction to their world and allows us to get a feel for these creatures and their society without being too overwhelmed . . . The way the story finally comes together is effective, with a suspenseful and frightening climax." —*All About Romance*

"There is a whole lot to like here, first and foremost being a truly outstanding and creative story . . . Taylor also has a way of writing about the city of Chicago that gives this story a bit of a crime noir edge . . . Taylor introduces plenty of interesting characters . . . The paranormal subgenre allows authors to be creative, break rules, and stretch boundaries in fantastical ways." —*The Romance Reader*

"Hooks the audience from the onset and never slows down until the final twist." —*Midwest Book Review*

LEGACY of STONE

Vickie Taylor

BERKLEY SENSATION, NEW YORK

THE BERKLEY PUBLISHING GROUP
Published by the Penguin Group
Penguin Group (USA) Inc.
375 Hudson Street, New York, New York 10014, USA
Penguin Group (Canada), 90 Eglinton Avenue East, Suite 700, Toronto, Ontario M4P 2Y3, Canada
(a division of Pearson Penguin Canada Inc.)
Penguin Books Ltd., 80 Strand, London WC2R 0RL, England
Penguin Group Ireland, 25 St. Stephen's Green, Dublin 2, Ireland (a division of Penguin Books Ltd.)
Penguin Group (Australia), 250 Camberwell Road, Camberwell, Victoria 3124, Australia
(a division of Pearson Australia Group Pty. Ltd.)
Penguin Books India Pvt. Ltd., 11 Community Centre, Panchsheel Park, New Delhi—110 017, India
Penguin Group (NZ), 67 Apollo Drive, Rosedale, North Shore 0632, New Zealand
(a division of Pearson New Zealand Ltd.)
Penguin Books (South Africa) (Pty.) Ltd., 24 Sturdee Avenue, Rosebank, Johannesburg 2196,
South Africa

Penguin Books Ltd., Registered Offices: 80 Strand, London WC2R 0RL, England

This is a work of fiction. Names, characters, places, and incidents either are the product of the author's imagination or are used fictitiously, and any resemblance to actual persons, living or dead, business establishments, events, or locales is entirely coincidental. The publisher does not have any control over and does not assume any responsibility for author or third-party websites or their content.

LEGACY OF STONE

A Berkley Sensation Book / published by arrangement with the author

PRINTING HISTORY
Berkley Sensation mass-market edition / December 2009

Copyright © 2009 by Vickie Spears.
Excerpt from *Wicked Enchantment* by Anya Bast copyright © by Anya Bast.
Interior text design by Kristin del Rosario.

For information, address: The Berkley Publishing Group,
a division of Penguin Group (USA) Inc.,
375 Hudson Street, New York, New York 10014.

ISBN: 978-0-425-21304-9

BERKLEY® SENSATION
Berkley Sensation Books are published by The Berkley Publishing Group,
a division of Penguin Group (USA) Inc.,
375 Hudson Street, New York, New York 10014.
BERKLEY® SENSATION and the "B" design are trademarks of Penguin Group (USA) Inc.

PRINTED IN THE UNITED STATES OF AMERICA

10 9 8 7 6 5 4 3 2 1

ONE

Fate dealt Levi Tremaine another shit hand.

He'd never been a particular favorite of the lady of good fortune as far as life in general went, but damn it, he usually had better luck at poker.

He slapped two worthless cards down in the center of the scarred galley table. "Dealer takes two."

No matter, he told himself as he picked up the deck and tapped the edge against the table. Levi had learned long ago to make his own luck.

The White Whale protested the abuse of a rough sea and provided the perfect distraction. Levi feigned a concerned frown and cocked an ear toward the engine compartment aft, as if he'd detected a problem in the rumble of the boat's diesel engine, knowing his crewmates would follow suit. While they looked away, he deftly slipped his two cards from the bottom of the deck.

Mark Morton's Adam's apple bobbed in his thin neck.

He was the newest of the hands on the lobster boat, and so green he'd be virtually invisible in a meadow in high summer. "What? What is it?"

"Nothin'." Levi turned his gaze back to his hand and fanned his cards. Three jacks. That was more like it.

"'Tis just a wee nor'easter, lad," Paddy O'Doole said, teeth clinched on the butt of his cigar. "Nothing to get yer pants in a wad about. Stop worrying yourself about the storm and pay attention to the cards afore you lose the last of your week's pay."

The grizzled sea salt narrowed his eyes across the table at Levi accusingly. Levi met the stare with an innocent, unblinking gaze.

Paddy knew. Levi knew he knew. He should have known better than to throw cards down with the old man. Paddy played the way he lived—with the wisdom of the ages, the luck of the Irish and the soul of a pirate.

"Your bid, old man," Levi said, daring him to call him on the cheat.

Paddy chuckled and chomped on his cigar. Levi relaxed. The old man wouldn't be raising his fists tonight. Not over one hand. Not with the mountain of chips on the table in front of him and another hundred in front of the greenhorn for the taking.

The White Whale pitched and rolled. The single bare bulb dangling above the table swayed like a sailor climbing the gangway after a three-day pass as they made their bids, laid out their hands.

"Damn!" Levi threw his jacks on the table and scowled at Paddy's three queens. The old man's cheeks turned ruddy, and for a moment, his laughter drowned out the crash of waves against the hull.

Levi's jaw hardened at the glint in the old man's eyes. He clenched his fists to keep from drawing his fishing knife and planting the blade in his jacks' leering grins. Now he knew the real reason Paddy hadn't called him on his cheat. The old man had a few tricks of his own up his sleeve tonight.

Paddy scooped the pot to his side of the table with both arms, still laughing. Shaking his head, Levi reached for the bottle of liquid mood enhancer in the middle of the table just in time to keep a hard pitch to starboard from sending the Crown Royal sliding onto the deck. He held the bottle up to the light and waggled it. Between his bad luck at cards and the way this squall was blowing up, he wasn't sure the two inches of amber in the bottom was going to be enough to improve his mood.

The White Whale pitched hard again. The hull muttered and groaned like an old woman toting a load of groceries on arthritic knees. Levi supposed she had a right. The old girl had seen better days and long outlived most tubs of her generation. She was a sturdy enough ship, but she was tired, and she let them know it as sleet pinged against the porthole and another wave battered her bow. Damn storm had blown up from nowhere, with no warning, ruining any chance they had of raiding that sweet line of lobster pots Levi had found this afternoon, laid by some sleek multimillion-dollar corporate tub.

Damn corporations were hogging all the commercial fishing territory, driving the independents—and the poachers, like him—out of business.

Across the table, the cigar dangling from Paddy's lips dropped a load of ash as he dealt a new round of cards. He swiped the debris to the floor with fingers gnarled from years of hauling net and pulling lobster pots. His eyes were bloodshot and the wiry gray brows over them were as unruly as the mess of salt and pepper that stuck out from his head at angles that defied gravity. And combs.

"You in?" he gruffed, looking at Levi.

"I am." The greenhorn threw two chips to the center far too quickly, the eager look on his narrow face announcing like a neon sign that he had a strong hand.

Levi ordered his cards and debated bluffing out of sheer stubbornness, but was saved from his own foolishness when the hatch to the weather deck banged open. A blast of icy North Atlantic air howled down the stairwell, washing away the staler odors of liquor, tobacco and unwashed men.

All three at the table looked up as the captain turned to shoulder the hatch closed against the rush of wind. "Deck's icing over. Seas are twenty-five feet and rising."

"Twenty-five feet?" The kid's throat bobbed. His hands tightened on his cards. "Shouldn't we be heading back to port?"

"We'll be fine, Mark."

Paddy grunted in agreement. "Damn straight. Charlie's in the wheelhouse. Best friggin' lobster boat driver this side of the Continent."

The captain's rubber boots thunked against the deck as they came off. "We'll back off to the edge of the storm just in case."

Levi nodded. "Could work in our favor. Skies clear up in a few hours, and we'll have plenty of time to move back in and pick the pots clean while the fair-weather fishermen are still riding the dock."

Mark-the-greenhorn didn't look convinced, but all three men lost the thread of the conversation when the captain twisted to shrug off the dripping yellow raingear.

Like a creature shedding an old skin for a vibrant new one, the weathered sea captain disappeared, and a lean young woman stood in her place. Despite the foul-weather gear she'd worn, her jeans and sea green sweater were damp, clinging to high, firm breasts, narrow waist and seductively flaring hips. She wrinkled her nose as she brushed rainwater out of her spiky auburn hair, and eyes that matched the color of her top held him mesmerized for a moment. Seeing his opponents similarly distracted, he managed to pull his gaze away long enough to replace a couple of his cards with new ones from the deck.

She arched one thin brow at him, and he shrugged almost imperceptibly before Paddy cleared his throat and he and the greenhorn returned their attention to the game. Meanwhile, Levi was having a time finding his own attention, as it seemed to have dropped somewhere below his navel at the sight of Captain Natasha Cole—Tasha— strolling his way, fingertips jammed in the front pockets of her jeans, hips swaying, and a subtle smile on her face that said he didn't need to play poker to get lucky tonight.

She brushed one hand across his shoulder and wrapped the other around the neck of the whiskey bottle as she passed by.

Levi threw his three aces down on the table and scraped his chair back. "I'm out."

He followed her down the narrow hall past the head to the captain's quarters, then ducked inside and flipped the security latch closed behind him. She stood in front of her dresser, her sweater already off. She leaned over to unzip her wet blue jeans, and the straps of her bra slid down her elegant shoulders. Levi stepped up behind her and unhooked the clasp, then slid the scrap of white lace and elastic down her arms until it fell to the floor.

In the mirror above the dresser, she met his gaze as he wrapped his arms around her, cupped her.

"You're cold," he murmured against her neck, palming the tight nipples.

"Not for long," she said, her head tipping back as his

hands skimmed up her chest to trail along her collarbones, then back down to her breasts. She shivered, and he wondered if it was from his touch or the cold.

He let her go and tossed her the towel hanging over the back of the chair before her vanity. "Dry off. I'll pour you a drink."

While she shucked off her jeans and rubbed down her long, slim legs, he lifted a water glass off the table by her bed and emptied the bottle into it. By the time she straightened up, he was thinking he could use a drink, too. His mouth had gone suddenly dry.

Clearing his throat, he handed her the glass.

"You're not having any?"

"I think I've had enough."

"Not so much that you can't cheat at cards."

He shrugged. "Kid's gotta learn not to be so trusting."

"I see. So you're fleecing him for purely educational purposes." Naked now except for her panties and the pewter necklace he'd had made for her dangling on a leather strap, she sat on the edge of her bunk and rubbed the towel over her feet. He knelt in front of her, took the towel in one hand and one slim ankle in the other to take over the task.

"Just trying to teach him to be a fisherman."

"And Paddy?"

"Huh. That old crab can hold his own in a game of cards." He shrugged. "Not that I wouldn't mind teaching him that he shouldn't be looking at you the way he was looking."

"So you think you're the only one allowed to leer at me?"

The towel in his hands stilled. He didn't have any claim on her, any more than she did on him. Not that either of them wanted a claim. They were solitary people, but they also spent a lot of time at sea, away from the no-strings sexual hunting grounds of nightclubs and street corners.

They fulfilled a need in each other. Eased an ache it seemed neither of them wanted to admit to feeling. But that was all they were to each other. They'd never made any commitments. Never pretended the nights they occasionally shared were anything more than restlessness and easy access.

Slowly, he rubbed the towel down the arch of her sole and dried each perfect toe. "I think no one leers at you that you don't want leering. At least not for long."

Once, when a deal for some of their illegal catch had gone wrong, he'd seen her defend herself. She was an artist with a switchblade and a piece of rebar.

Tasha planted her palms on the mattress behind her and tipped her head back. "Paddy's harmless."

His lips twitched. "He did time for murder."

"Harmless to me, I mean. He was a friend of my father's."

"So you've told me. They must have been quite a pair, the Irishman and the Russian."

"They were. Right up until . . ." She lifted her head and glared at him. "Are you going to talk all night, or are you going to get up here and do some leering?"

"I'm going to do a hell of a lot more than leer, darlin'."

Tasha was also an artist at changing the subject when she didn't want to talk about something, he thought. Still, who was he to argue with a beautiful woman who wanted him in her bed?

She grabbed a fistful of his T-shirt and pulled.

Smiling, he climbed onto the mattress, his knees on the gray down comforter, and pressed her back to the mattress, his chest against hers. "In a hurry tonight, are we?"

She writhed beneath him, her arms clutching him. "Storm's got my nerves on edge. I need—"

His lips stole the rest of the thought. He knew what she needed.

He found her earlobe, her jaw, her collarbone and finally her breast. She arched up into his mouth, gasping and using her hands to plump herself, offer herself.

His body responded to the feel of her flesh against him, her peaked nipples scraping through the fine hairs of his chest. Instinctively his hips ground down against her, a prelude of what was to come.

And come all too soon if she didn't slow down.

One of her hands had found its way inside his jeans, wringing a groan out of him. The other was clamped on the back of his neck, holding him to her breast.

He turned his head to the side for a breath. "Whoa, you really are on edge. Slow down, will you? We've got all night."

She shook her head. "I need to get back to the bridge."

He cocked his head to listen. Outside he could hear the wind screaming across the deck, but the boat wasn't pitching as badly now. Charlie must have steered them out of the core of the storm.

"Doesn't seem so bad now," he said.

She fingered the pewter pendant around her neck as if it were a rosary. "No. Not now."

He wondered at her nervousness. They'd weathered storms worse than this one. And they were out of the worst of it, just waiting for the seas to calm so they could get to work.

Still, her anxiety sparked a warning in him. It was as if his senses expanded, reached farther into the night, searching. For a moment he thought he felt something, something dark and dangerous in the distance, but then it was gone. Probably just his imagination.

Gently he pulled her hand away from the necklace, locked her fingers with his. "Lucky for you, I know the one surefire cure for someone on the edge."

"What would that be?"

He smiled wickedly as he crept backward, down her body, and brought her thighs up beside his ears. "Push 'em over it."

Her smell, a unique blend of seawater and soap and woman, nearly pushed him over. He hooked his arms under her knees, lifted her legs with his shoulders and held her hips down with his hands. He teased her with long, slow strokes of his tongue, then penetrated her with the tip and drew back to suck gently until her body bucked in rhythm with the boat—an ever increasing, ever more violent rhythm, he realized.

So much for being out of the storm.

Tasha's body quivered. The muscles in her thighs and calves hardened, and when she gasped—an agonized sound that definitely wasn't born of pleasure—he realized something was very wrong.

"Damn." He scuttled up the bed and took her by the shoulders, lifted her against him. Both her hands clutched the leather strip holding the pendant around her neck like it was a lifeline. Her eyes lost focus, and she gulped for air like a fish on dry land as her body spasmed.

"Hold on." He rocked her. "Just hold on. Try to breathe. Breathe through it." He'd seen her have seizures before, but never this bad. Just petit mal episodes, she'd said. A mild form of epilepsy. He didn't see anything *petit* about this. *Christ.* "Just breathe."

Her hold on the necklace tightened then relaxed, tightened then relaxed with each wave of agony that seemed to pass through her body. Gradually the spasms receded to shudders and her breathing evened out. Her gaze met his.

"Okay." He let go of her with one hand to run it through his hair. "That was not exactly the reaction I was going for. You all right?"

Reluctantly, he let her go when she pushed against him. "Let me go."

She already had her jeans in hand and was scooping up her sweater when he asked, "Go where? What the hell was that?"

Clutching her clothes against her naked body, she turned to him. In her eyes, he saw something he'd never seen in his whiskey-drinking, knife-wielding, lobster-poaching sea captain's eyes before: fear.

"Trouble," she said. "It was trouble."

TWO

❧

The boat lurched sideways violently, the force of a wave tilting them to an angle that had Tasha swearing silently and Levi clutching the edge of the bunk for purchase. When the deck righted itself, Tasha peeled herself off the bulkhead she'd been thrown into and stumbled across her quarters, snatching up clothes.

"What the hell?" Levi grumbled, reaching for his shirt.

She was putting her jeans back on before she'd even fully regained her balance. *The White Whale* continued to pitch and roll, and the wind outside howled like a tortured animal.

Levi was out the cabin door before her. She followed on his heels, still tugging down the hem of her sweater—she'd left the bra on the floor—and passed him when he stopped in the crew quarters to pick up Mark, who was lying on the floor clutching his head. Blood seeped between the young seaman's fingers.

"What's going on?" Mark's voice trembled. "Are we sinking?"

Levi propped the kid up next to the crew berths. "Stay here. Hold on."

Tasha hurried on toward the hatch, Levi's heavy footsteps close behind her. Neither one of them bothered with rain gear as they climbed up on the weather deck and headed to the wheelhouse. When they got there, Charlie had one arm hooked around a spoke on the wheel and was trying to muscle the boat to port.

"Seas came up from nowhere." He grimaced as he fought the wheel. "And fast. Forty-foot swells."

Levi jumped in to help, eyeing the wild seas outside. "Forty-five, at least."

Tasha looked out the window. Looking for what, she didn't know—until she saw it.

She reached over the men and yanked the wheel back to starboard.

"What are you doing?" the men asked in concert.

"We have to go north."

Levi's jaw clenched as he fought the wheel. "Are you crazy? That'll take us deeper into the storm."

"No, look. There." A wave broke over the railing, rushed into the wheelhouse and swirled icy water around their legs to midcalf. She was shivering from the cold, and her limbs were still shaky from the seizure. Her hand trembled when she raised it to point out the window, and she quickly tucked it in her pocket once Charlie and Levi looked where she directed.

For a moment, even she thought she'd imagined what she'd seen. There was only rain and rolling ocean and the black void of night. Finally there was a brief flicker. A small light in the distance, barely visible through the storm. Then lightning lit the sky, and the silhouette of a boat was clearly—if briefly—visible. A yacht by the looks of it, and a big one.

Levi swore. "Who the hell would bring a pleasure boat out into this?"

"Who the hell cares?" Charlie groaned. "We've got to get out of here, now! If they're smart, they'll be doing the same thing."

"Turn the boat north now, Charlie. That's an order!"

"Tasha—" Levi started.

She sent him a smoldering look. "We're not leaving them. They're in trou—" Before she finished the sentence, the radio crackled to life.

"Mayday, Mayday." The voice sounded breathless, panicked. "This is the *Spanish Dancer* calling any ship in the area. Our coordinates are north thirty-two degrees, sixteen minutes and fifty-two seconds by west ninety-nine degrees, thirty minutes and nine seconds. Request immediate assistance. Over."

Tasha grabbed the hand mike. "Roger that Mayday, *Spanish Dancer*. What is your situation?"

"Oh, thank God. My pilot is injured. He's unconscious. The engines have stalled and I can't get them restarted. I don't know how. We're taking on water."

Levi's brow furrowed. "Without engines, he's got no pumps, and without pumps, he's toast out here."

"We have to help him," she said.

Charlie was still fighting the wheel. "Nothing we can do in this weather. We drive deeper into this crap, we'll be lucky to get out of it ourselves."

She pulled her shoulders back, planted her fists on her hips and met first his gaze, then Levi's, with a hard stare. "Last time I checked, I was captain of this tub. Now turn the damn boat or I will."

The look that shifted across Levi's face might have been

amusement. "You heard the lady," he said, still holding her gaze. One of the few things she disliked about her first mate was his uncanny ability to bow to her authority and yet still make her feel like he was the one in control.

Charlie looked anything but amused, but he turned the boat. Immediately the ride got rougher. It seemed every wave that hit the lobster boat broadside threw her a little farther on her side. *The White Whale* was seaworthy even in the worst of conditions, built to be difficult to capsize, but every vessel had its limits, and though Tasha wouldn't admit it, or give up on some poor stupid stranded pleasure boater, she was afraid *The White Whale* was approaching hers.

Turning, she stepped out onto the weather deck and immediately regretted it as a blast of icy wind and damp cut her to the bone. She wrapped her arms around herself to try to keep from shaking.

Levi stepped up behind her, close enough she could feel his breath on the back of her neck, a tiny puff of warmth in the frigid air, but he didn't touch her. They never touched outside of bed.

"So, you got a plan for what we're going to do if we actually manage to get to this guy before he sinks?" he asked.

She pulled her lower lip between her teeth. "I'm working on it."

She was working hard on it, but so far she hadn't come up with much. What did she know about being a Good Samaritan, anyway? It wasn't her style. Not that she went around kicking puppies and stealing children's candy for fun, but she was generally a you-mind-your-business-and-I'll-mind-mine kind of girl. So far she sucked at changing her ways.

"All right. While you're working on it, why don't you get

Paddy up here on the radio and see if he can talk the guy through getting his engines up and running. Meanwhile I'll pull some lines out in case we have to try something a little more drastic."

"Like what?"

"I don't know. Maybe run a line between the two boats and I can ferry myself over."

She glanced over her shoulder at him. "We'll never get close enough to get a rope to him in these seas."

"We can use the line gun to shoot a feeder cord over to him. He can pull the heavier rope across."

Her lips thinned. She didn't like where this Good Samaritan stuff was going. "Even if we did, it would never hold. The first time a wave pitched us away from each other, the tension would snap it and you'd be in the water."

He turned sideways to slide past her but paused to give her a long, dark look. "I can take care of myself in the water."

Yes, he could.

Levi was a private person, they had that in common. Despite all the time they'd spent together on a small ship, and their intimacy, she knew little about him. But that much she knew.

Thinking about just how well he could take care of himself in the water sent a spiral of thrill drilling down through her. It was the same feeling she'd gotten when she'd crested the first hill, just before the plunge down, the first time she'd ridden a roller coaster. The same feeling as when she'd brought in a poached load of lobster and cut her own deal with a very scary black marketeer. It was a heady rush of fear and exhilaration. Danger and accomplishment.

Everyone had a dark side, but Levi Tremaine's was darker than most. Just looking at him, staring into his eyes as they went from brown to black, making her wonder if she was going to see that other side he so rarely showed, even to her, made her pulse jump and her breathing quicken.

"You just worry about getting us to that boat." He smiled as he moved past her, breaking the moment, and rubbed his thumb across his fingers in the universal sign for money. "I just hope poor little rich boy is grateful when I save his big, shiny toy. Not to mention his ass. Very grateful, if you know what I mean."

Paddy inched his way across the icy deck to the wheelhouse, and for the next twenty minutes she alternated between watching Charlie fight the waves, listening to Paddy grow more and more frustrated as his pupil failed time and again to get the *Spanish Dancer*'s engines restarted and peering out into the dark to make sure Levi hadn't been washed overboard. The direness of their situation sunk into her bones along with the cold, and she gratefully accepted the coat Charlie took off and handed her between curses.

Out in the darkness, Levi was loading the rope gun. He'd already laid out two heavy lines in neat piles so that they wouldn't tangle, or snare a careless crewman's ankle, when they were pulled over to the other ship. The nearside ends were tied in perfect double-figure-eight knots. He was like that—a little scruffy with his cowlicked hair, ever-present day's growth of beard and smattering of tattoos, but in his seamanship, he was meticulous. He was as capable *on* the water as he was *in* it.

Paddy clicked off the radio microphone and rolled his head back on his neck. "Mother o' Christmas, if the man's no' a bloody idiot, then I dunna know who is."

"Keep trying, Paddy. We need those engines."

"I'm no' talkin' about him, lass. I'm talkin' abou' the bloody idiot out on our deck thinkin' he's going to swing himself between two boats on forty-foot seas like Tarzan of the bloody Atlantic." He gestured toward the window, and Levi beyond it.

"Get those engines going, and nobody will have to swing anywhere."

Paddy heaved out a sigh that could have blown over a pile of bricks. "*Spanish Dancer, Spanish Dancer*, have ye found the bloody hydraulic valve yet?"

Leaving Paddy to his pupil, Tasha made her way across the icy bridge toward Levi. She held the rail in a death grip but knew that would do little to help her if she lost her footing when the boat pitched. Gale winds plastered the oversized coat to her small frame, and sleet stung her cheeks like pricks from a thousand tiny needles.

The ocean churned around *The White Whale* like a dark cauldron. Tasha's stomach tumbled as another towering wave slapped against the side of the boat, nearly throwing her off her feet.

She'd never seen a storm as vicious as this. It was almost purposeful in its violence. It seemed to be pulling at them, swirling around them like a vortex.

Her lungs locked up. She couldn't breathe, and for a moment she was afraid she was going to have another seizure, but the moment passed, and then another. She felt no spasm, but she could feel the blood pounding in her head. Her heart beat at the walls of her chest.

This wasn't right. None of it. The sky was too dark, the waves too frenzied. A pressure like she'd never felt before bore down on her from all sides, squeezed her. There was something evil out there, she realized. Something unnatural.

She opened her mouth to call to Levi, to tell him to come in. He couldn't do this. They couldn't do this.

No one could do this. Not with *it* watching. Waiting for its chance.

She was turning this boat around. They would have to talk yacht guy through making his own repairs over the radio.

But even as she looked up with Levi's name on her lips, a massive wall of darkness rose before her. The silver crest towered sixty feet above her if it was an inch, and she knew it would be her death.

When the rogue wave hit, it threw the lobster boat up on her side. The loyal old boat balanced there for a moment like a ballerina on tiptoe, trying to right itself.

Tasha slid across the deck and crashed into the wench amidships. Out of the corner of her eye, she saw a broken piece of antenna strike Levi in the head, and his limp body tumbled into the sea. So, even he might not survive after all. She prayed he would. If any of them had a chance, it was him.

Then *The White Whale* finished her belly roll, and evil crushed her in a frozen, killing grip.

THREE

The last thing Levi remembered seeing was a wall of water towering over him and a broken radio mast flying toward his head. He was disoriented when he came to. He tried to breathe and took in a lungful of water. Choking, he flailed in the current.

Water. He was in the water.

Panic gnawed at coherent thought. He had no idea which way was up, if he was kicking toward the surface or down to his death. His chest burned with the need to cough up the water he'd taken in, to claim air instead. The cold made him feel heavy, lethargic.

Fighting for calm, and for his life, he forced himself to relax. His body would find the surface if he just let buoyancy do its thing—and he survived that long.

When his mind quieted along with his struggles, he heard voices. As always, he recognized the sounds but not

the words. Almasama something-or-other. And someone
named Calli or Callio.

When he'd first begun hearing the voices as a teenager,
he'd searched for their meanings in textbooks, both modern
and ancient languages, but had never found any references
that made sense. Just gobbledygook, he'd told himself.

He'd tried at first, all those years ago, to shut out the
voices. He'd fought them with the same ferocity with
which he now fought for life. Then the visions had begun,
and he had no longer been able to deny that he wasn't like
other people. In fact, a few years later he wasn't sure he
was human at all.

He was a freak. An abomination. He'd tried to deny what
he was, then he'd tried to hide it. He ran away from his life,
from his adoptive family and made his way on his own.

But what he was would not be deprived. He'd been
drawn to the water, to the sea, and the first time he set foot
on a boat, his fate had been sealed.

Tonight he made no attempt to deprive his alter ego. He
welcomed the voices. He focused his whole being on them
and the change that would inevitably come with them.

E Unri . . . sama
E . . . Almasama
Calli, Calli . . . io
. . . alt . . . paximi

The voices grew louder. They repeated their litany, and
the transformation began.

Heat surged through him, bringing feeling back to his
extremities. The darkness that swallowed his vision was
replaced by light. Fires and explosions, a sweltering sun
and a silver moon. He saw times and places he'd never
been. He saw faces he didn't know, and they spoke to him

soundlessly. Some held him tenderly and some tried to kill him. He saw birth and death. Violence.

It all spun before him. The chaos of what he saw and heard threatened to drown him as surely as the sea. He couldn't make sense of it. Couldn't interpret it.

A trail of electrical shocks rained down his body from his forehead, over his shoulders, past his abdomen and groin all the way to his toes. The transformation was almost sexual in nature, like a lover's touch.

He burned as if he were on fire. His blood boiled as his body changed. His limbs shrank and his body elongated. Skin turned to scales. Bones cracked and reshaped themselves painfully. Sinews popped. He wanted to groan but couldn't open his mouth underwater. His body caved in on itself, and a new wave of agony swept over him.

Just as he thought he couldn't take any more, his head broke the surface of the water. He gulped in one last lungful of air before his gills fully formed and lungs became pointless.

Another wave pushed him back underwater, but this time there was no panic, no choking. He unfurled his long body and glided gracefully beneath the swells.

He knew this monstrous body. Knew how to control it. He even knew what it looked like. Once as a teenager, he'd found a secluded cove and crawled ashore to look at himself in the calm water's reflection.

The closest creature he could associate with his monstrous body was the Loch Ness monster. There was a definite similarity to Nessie's head and neck, except Levi had a spiny crest that stood a good foot tall at the top of his head, then tapered down to an inch or two at the base of his long neck. His body was reminiscent of the sea monsters drawn long ago in the uncharted oceans on old-timey maps. He had webbed fins and the tail of a massive eel, with a sharp spike at the end that threw off electrical current when he whipped it left or right. His scales shone with an eerie green and black iridescence.

It was the one and only time he had looked at himself in this form, but horror burned the image deeply into his mind. He didn't know how or why he was what he was. He just knew he was a monster.

Pushing the images of self and the accompanying questions aside, he struggled again to get his bearings. His head throbbed—probably from getting hit by the antenna more than from the transformation. He needed to find *The White Whale*, or what was left of it, and find Tasha, Paddy, Charlie and Mark.

God, he had to help them.

They were his priority, yet now there was another voice in his head, calling him to the boat. Not *The White Whale* . . . the other boat.

He shook his head, shutting out the voice and focusing on the dark water around him. His senses were heightened in this state. Even with the roar of the storm above him, he heard every swish of movement beneath the surface, every gurgle.

The groan of strained steel was unmistakable. Levi turned his head and spotted the hull of his boat nearly completely submerged now, sinking.

A swish of his tail brought him underneath it, and he reached out with his mind again. Focused on Tasha. Her smile, her scent, the softness of her skin despite the years she'd spent out in the elements at sea. He listened for only her voice among all the clamoring of many others in his head.

When he found her, he was afraid it was too late. She was drifting limply in the current beneath the surface. Her skin was as pale as a sand dollar, and her eyes were closed.

A stream of bubbles gurgled from her mouth toward the surface.

He nudged her with his snout, pushing her up, and nipped lightly at her shoulder, trying to get some response from her. Some confirmation that she lived, and to tell her that if she wanted to go on living, she needed to fight.

Don't give up, damn it. Don't quit.

He'd learned over the last two years with her that in addition to the unique ability to shift his body to another form, he had some power to influence her mind. It had started with their sexual play. He would be thinking what he'd like her to do to him, how he wished she would touch him, and the next thing he knew, she would do just that. They had a connection beyond the physical. It was what made sex so good between them. So irresistible. So dangerous.

He experimented a little over time—all without her knowledge—and found that if he held an image in his mind and concentrated on it hard enough, she would see the same thing. He would think about roses and she would suddenly ask if he smelled flowers. He once tried to picture her with longer hair, and the next morning, standing in front of the mirror and frowning, she announced she was going to let it grow.

Thankfully that idea hadn't lasted long. He just replaced it with the knowledge that he found her spiky 'do sexy as all hell.

Now his need to influence her mind was much more urgent. He couldn't afford gentle images. Couldn't afford to fail.

He pictured her mind as an orb floating in the water and punched new images into it. He showed her drowning. Dying. Dead. Then replaced death with life. With her struggling. He showed her waking up, swimming, helping him get her to the other boat. He showed her surviving— but only if she fought for it.

His own head ached with the effort, but he pounded the mental pictures at her mercilessly. This time, he also stung her with his tail for good measure.

Slowly her eyelids opened. Her body jolted as awareness came to her and she realized where she was, what was happening.

He bumped her again toward the surface, shoving the image of her swimming into her mind. Her arms began to flutter weakly. Her legs kicked. Between his efforts and hers, she soon reached the surface, but she wasn't out of danger. Waves crashed down on her, pushing her under again before she could catch her breath.

Levi lifted her again, concentrated on the image of her on his back, holding on to him. Immediately her arms wrapped firmly around his neck. He swam on the surface toward the yacht, fighting the waves, fighting the currents, fighting the whole damned ocean to keep Tasha above water.

Minutes seemed to take hours to pass, but finally they reached the *Spanish Dancer*. Levi hunched his back and tossed her up on the diving platform at the back of the yacht, then dove back beneath the surface and willed himself back to human form. As soon as the change was complete, he climbed onto the platform beside Tasha. They both lay on their backs, arms wrapped in a stranglehold around the ladder to the yacht's main deck. They were battered and bloody, but they were alive.

Looking out at the thrashing sea, Levi knew the same wasn't true for Paddy, Mark or Charlie.

On the deck above them, Roman DuValle, as he called himself now, raised his arms, then lowered them slowly, palms down. As if patted smooth by his touch, the winds began to die and the sea calmed.

Smiling, he looked down on his two new passengers. The girl was unexpected. He hadn't thought she would survive. She might become a problem, but no worries—she could be dealt with easily enough if she did.

Levi Tremaine, however, was everything he'd expected and more. The younger man was weakened now by injury and by exhaustion, but when he'd recovered and Roman had trained his mind, he would be the strongest of Roman's soldiers. He took advantage of Levi's condition to cast a veiling spell to keep him from seeing what Roman didn't yet want him to see—the truth. Soon enough, Levi would learn the true power of his mind, but only after Roman was sure he controlled that power.

Yes, yes. With the son of one of the Old Ones at his side, Roman would be unstoppable. The world would be his playground.

And soon, the games would begin.

FOUR

After taking a long, hot shower, Tasha sat on the berth in one of the yacht's luxury staterooms with her knees drawn up to her chest and two quilts around her shoulders. Even still, she couldn't stop shivering. The storm had let up almost the moment she and Levi climbed onto the yacht, but the sense of foreboding she'd felt just before the rogue wave hit hadn't gone away. If anything, the crushing pressure and sense of doom were stronger than ever.

Telling herself it was grief she was feeling this time, understandable given what had just happened, she fingered the pewter pendant around her neck and told herself she was in shock. It was to be expected. She'd nearly drowned and she'd lost three of her crew, one of them a longtime friend of the family. Paddy's memories and the stories he'd told had been her only connection back to her father.

Grief wasn't a stranger to Tasha. She'd lost others. Anyone who spent their life on a fishing boat learned to accept loss. The sea gave up many treasures, but she also collected her toll.

A knock on the cabin door made her look up. Levi opened the door. The smell of soap and shampoo from his own shower preceded him across the room. Quickly she wiped a tear from her cheek and pretended she hadn't been crying.

He tugged at the waistband of a pair of borrowed sweat pants. "Feeling better?"

"Yeah," she said, but her lower lip trembled as she said it, and she knew she hadn't fooled him. She bit the offending lip to stop a full-blown meltdown. She never showed weakness like this, not even to him.

Especially not to him.

"You?" she asked.

He probed at the bandage on his temple. "My head's still kind of muzzy."

"You probably have a concussion."

"Nah." He shrugged. "It's just a bump. I'll live."

That did it. That one word. How dare they live when their friends were dead?

Moisture filled her eyes again. Again she fought it back. "Too bad Paddy and Charlie and Mark can't say the same thing."

Levi looked uncomfortable, his body tense and his gaze fixed on the far wall. He finally sat next to her, his back stiff. "I'm sorry. I should've gone after th—"

"It's not your fault." She sniffed, her only concession to her pain. "They never had a chance, and you know it. If it wasn't for . . . you know—" She flicked a glance at him and rushed her words. "That thing you do, we'd be dead, too."

His jaw tightened. She knew he didn't like to talk about what he could do. What he could become. Over the years she'd given up asking questions about it. Not that she hadn't been curious, but she had her secrets. She figured he deserved his.

She supposed it was strange that she'd accepted his . . . unique qualities so easily, but she'd known he was different somehow as soon as she'd met him. When he walked onto her boat looking for a job—and not caring if it was legal or not—he'd had a presence about him. It was almost a tangible aura. Power radiated off him so strongly that she believed she'd get a little shock, like a static-electricity charge, if she ever touched him. She'd had this weird picture of him in her mind—only it wasn't him, it was a strange creature, and yet it had his eyes—and she'd followed him. Caught him in the water. He'd seemed surprised that she hadn't run, hadn't screamed. She'd been mesmerized by him. She hired him on the spot.

Two weeks later, she found out she'd been right about the electric shock. His touch sizzled against her skin. From the start there'd been chemistry between them. On their first extended voyage, they'd given in to it.

Since then she'd seen him do his presto-change-o act a couple of times. Mostly she knew he went off by himself when it seemed the need built up and he had to burn something out of his system. But a time or two he'd dived into the water to untangle a line of pots or scout the goods while the rest of the crew was below deck. Once he did it just because she asked him, and because she promised him the best blow job of his life if he let her touch him while he . . . wasn't himself.

It was that danger and anticipation thing again. She couldn't resist the rush. She never dreamed he—or whatever he became—would end up saving her life.

She risked another look his way, let her gaze linger a little longer on his face this time.

He sprang up from the bed and paced across the room and back. "I wish you'd never seen this useless, overpriced, pretentious goddamn tub."

"Me too."

Levi's jaw hardened again. "I think I'll go have a talk with Mr. DuValle." He sneered the name, then spun on his heel and left Tasha alone on her bunk.

For DuValle's sake, she hoped Levi planned on talking with his mouth and not the fists clenched at his sides.

Levi found DuValle in the great room, sunk deep in a leather recliner with a glass of red wine in his hand and his feet propped up in front of a cozy gas fireplace. The flames flickered invitingly—which really pissed Levi off. He didn't want to be on the *Spanish Dancer* a second longer than he had to be, and he didn't want luxury and comfort. Not with his fellow crew and his boat in a cold, dark grave on the floor of the Atlantic.

"How long 'til we make port?" he asked, making no effort at a polite tone.

DuValle swirled his wineglass. "A day, if we can get the engines working."

Anger sloshed in Levi's stomach in rhythm with the fine Bordeaux in DuValle's glass. "Fuck the engines. Call the Coast Guard for a tow."

"Communications are down, too, or so Manny says."

Miraculously Manny, DuValle's boat driver who had been knocked out when he was thrown off his feet in the storm and the engines conked out, had regained consciousness just after Levi and Tasha came onboard. Unfortunately he seemed nearly as inept at fixing the boat as DuValle himself.

Levi cocked his head. "Where did you get that guy?"

"Manny came highly recommended."

Levi snorted. "For what? His skill at foot rubs and polishing silver? Because he doesn't know shit about boats."

DuValle set his wine aside and smiled ingratiatingly. "Perhaps you might be so kind as to educate him."

"Son of a bitch." *Perhaps he might be so kind?* "Where do you get off? Three men died because of you tonight. My crew."

DuValle looked up, his face expressionless. Emotionless. "I'm well aware of what transpired tonight, and your loss. But I wouldn't think you'd be in such a hurry to make port."

"No hurry? How about the fact that I have to go talk to three families. Tell them that Paddy and Mark and Charlie aren't coming home and why. They deserve to know."

"Now, now," DuValle said in that infuriating, patronizing tone of his, "I'm sorry if my rationale seems cold, but I sincerely doubt that any of your crew had families to worry about them."

Levi's anger dampened to wariness. "Why do you say that?"

"I saw the trapline you were no doubt waiting for the cover of darkness to sail into and clean out. The buoys were green and initialed PTJ. I believe your boat was called *The White Whale*, was it not? I assume its color would also have been white."

Okay, so the rich guy wasn't quite as uninformed about seamanship as he looked. It was standard for lobster fishermen to identify their ports with uniquely colored buoys and the boat's initials.

"You're a poacher, Mr. Tremaine. If that is even your real name. I believe the Coast Guard will be asking some

very difficult questions when they find the wreckage of
your boat. There could even be criminal charges."

Levi pinched the bridge of his nose. This headache—
among other things—was really beginning to piss him
off.

"I, on the other hand," DuValle continued, "have only
one question, and it isn't difficult at all."

"What?"

"Please, sit." He stood and gestured toward a matching
leather chair tufted with embossed brass rivets. "Can I get
you something to drink?"

"I prefer to stand, and no."

DuValle inclined his head in a silent "have it your way"
comment, and settled back into his seat.

"You said you had a question."

He lifted one eyebrow pensively. "What do you plan to
do now that you've lost your source of livelihood?"

"Not to mention my friends," Levi added bitterly.

"Yes, and your friends."

"What's it to you?"

DuValle shrugged. "Who knows? Perhaps the two of us
might be able to come to some arrangement."

A harsh laugh bubbled out before Levi could stop it.
"You're offering me a job? I don't think so."

He stood to leave when a sudden pain drove through his
skull like a spike. He dropped heavily into the leather chair
and dropped his face in his hands.

"You don't look well, Mr. Tremaine."

"I'm fine." Levi grimaced, wishing it were true.

"Perhaps you should retire to your stateroom and get
some rest. Do think about my offer, though, will you?"

Levi desperately wanted to come back with some witty,
pithy reply, but all he could spit out was, "Yeah. Sure. I
will."

He needed to get downstairs and lie down before he threw up.

Witty and pithy would have to wait until he could see straight.

Practically giddy with excitement, Roman smiled broadly when his servant and bodyguard, Manny Estes, walked into the great room.

"He's even more powerful than I expected, Manny." He poured another glass of wine and downed a big gulp. "My God, he reeks of power."

Manny shrugged. "I didn't smell nothing."

Roman laughed. "No, my friend. No, I'm sure you didn't, but it is there, I assure you. He is a prize well worth that little knock on the head I had to give you for realism."

Manny touched the lump on the back of his head and winced.

DuValle paced, thinking out loud. "Even without training, he has learned to use his power. He was countering my magic without even knowing it. It took all I had to keep him from dismissing me out of hand. If he hadn't been in the circle, I'm not sure I could have controlled him as much as I did."

Manny looked down at the beige carpet and the navy blue circle woven into it that encompassed almost the whole room. His gaze traced the finer pattern in the middle of the circle that, if one looked closely, formed the five points of a pentagram, and he took a sharp step back, outside the ring.

"Are you sure this is a good idea, messing with him? I mean, if he's so strong, maybe we should just kill him."

"No, oh no. He is far too valuable to waste. He is the single most powerful mind I've encountered among our people in ten generations, and soon, that power will be mine."

The thought of what he would be able to do was as dizzying as the wine. The smile crept back onto his face.

"All mine."

FIVE

While a nor'easter had the upper New England coast in a deep freeze, Chicago was enjoying its first taste of spring. The last of the snow piled beside the freeways had melted into the storm drains, and every here and there, a few shoots of green tried to poke their heads through the cracks in the sidewalks. The first of March, after all, wasn't for delicate petals, but for the hardy weed varieties, thick with stems that couldn't be killed by a little ice or road salt.

With one hand resting lightly on the slight mound of her abdomen, Rachel Cross lowered herself to the floor in the circle of four. At six months pregnant, the baby was showing clearly now—and had already been making his presence known for some time. Even now she felt him shift inside her, and she smiled at his restlessness.

Already he took after his father.

Nathan propped a pillow between her back and the wall,

and she gave her husband a grateful, if chagrined, look. "You don't have to pamper me, you know."

"Yes I do."

"Okay, you do. But I'll make it up to you in about four months. I promise."

Taking his own spot in the circle, her husband picked her hand up in his, leaned over and pecked her on the cheek. "I'll hold you to that."

Teryn, her father-in-law of sorts, sat next to Nathan in the circle. The whole family lineage thing was complicated when it came to her husband's ancient race, she'd learned. They had biological fathers like everyone else, but since they reincarnated, they also had one or more *paytreáns*, or fathers of the soul. Men who had sired them in previous lives and had a profound effect on their everlasting spirits.

In a strange turn of events, Nathan, though he was much younger than Teryn, was the older man's *paytreán*. In his previous life, Nathan had been Teryn's biological father.

Right. Complicated.

Still, whatever the bloodlines, or soul lines, the two clearly shared a special bond. Though Nathan had split from the Chicago clan of *Les Gargouillen*, The Gargoyles, for a time, Teryn had never given up on him and had helped pave his way back in the clan when a crisis arose and they needed him.

That crisis is what brought the four of them together tonight: Rachel, Nathan, Teryn and the newest member of their circle, Connor Rihyad.

While the three of them had already taken their seats in the circle and joined hands, Connor stood by the door, hands in pockets and shuffling his feet. Long dark bangs shrouded his eyes. "You sure I'm not going to mess this up? I know how important it is to you to find your brother."

It was important to Rachel to find Levi. After their parents' deaths, her baby brother had been separated from her by the county children's home. He'd been adopted and she'd gone into foster care, at least for a while. By the time she'd had the resources to unseal the adoption files, he'd reached his teen years and run away from his adoptive family. Though she'd tried for years, she'd never been able to track him down.

Now more than ever she needed to find him, because her search for answers to her parents' deaths had led her to Nathan, and she'd learned the truth about her father: he was a Gargoyle. One of a race of shape-shifting beings created from the villagers of a small town in France by a traitor priest a thousand years ago.

Yep. Complicated again.

The bottom line was, Gargoyle traits were primarily passed down through male lineage. So while she'd led a relatively normal life, Levi was out there somewhere, probably with abilities he didn't understand and couldn't control.

She couldn't imagine what life had been like for him. No wonder he'd hidden himself away.

With Teryn and Nathan's help, she'd been trying new methods to find her brother. Her husband and his "son" had long practiced the ancient magics of their ancestors. The pagan rites exercised long before Romanus and his conversion of the people to Christianity had led her to visions of Levi's whereabouts, but not to an exact location.

She was getting closer, but she needed help, and more magic. Stronger magic.

She smiled up at Connor and patted the space to her left. "You are strong of mind and body, Connor Rihyad, and pure of heart. Together we are all stronger. Nothing you could do could 'screw this up.'"

With a sigh, he took his place, folded his long limbs in front of himself cross-legged and took her hand.

Before Teryn began the incantation, Nathan shot her a look that made it clear he'd rather have her between himself and Teryn, but he made no move to rearrange the circle.

There'd been some bad blood between her husband and Connor in the past. They'd stood on opposite sides of some philosophical issues, but they'd worked all that out.

Or so she thought.

Teryn drew her attention back to the ceremony when he lit the candles in the center of the circle drawn on the floor in his living room, one pillar representing the male, one representing the female, one taper for the goddess and one for the god. Then he picked up a stone bowl filled with salt. "Blessed salt, symbol of earth. Be new, be holy, be pure."

He drew a pentagram in the bowl of salt with the tip of a ritual knife, then passed the bowl around. Each member spread the white grains around the section of the ring around them to seal the circle.

When they'd finished, he picked up a stone bowl filled with water and drew a pentagram in that with the tip of his knife, too. "Blessed water, place of birth. Be new, be holy, be pure."

Teryn passed the water around and each member dipped a thumb into it and spread a swathe across their foreheads.

Finally he was ready to call the quarters. Teryn opened his arms and called the spirits of the north, south, east and west, asking their presence each in turn.

When he'd finished, a breeze kicked up in the room with no open windows. The flame on the incense burner flickered, and Rachel knew they were not alone. Now it was her turn. She had the strongest connection to Levi, a blood connection, so she would be the one to request the grace of the god and goddess.

She picked up the chalice full of wine and lifted it above her head. Her voice rang sure and clear with her invocation.

While once a ritual such as this would have seemed absurd, she had become a believer. She had seen magic with her own eyes, felt it with every flutter of the baby in her womb and each touch of her husband's strong hands.

"God and goddess, tonight we seek that which is lost. The babe, now a man, we must find, no matter what the cost. Our enemies gather for a final attack. Our only hope—to bring Levi back. As blood is to wine, we are of one mind. Help us to see that which we seek to find."

She took a tiny sip from the chalice—barely enough to wet her lips because she didn't want to pass the alcohol on to the baby—and passed the cup to her right, where each member of the circle repeated her incantation and drank of the wine.

When all had finished, she lowered her head, as did the others.

The hum of the house faded, as did the muted light filtering through the blinds. Rachel felt as though she were floating. She had no sense of time or place, only distance. She traveled for miles in this bubble of insight until she was once again over the ocean. She couldn't tell if she was seeing past, present or future, but she knew she was getting closer to seeing her brother, and that was all that mattered.

Her hand tightened on Nathan's. She'd been here before, seen the tiny boat tossed about in the storm, wondered how any vessel could stay afloat amongst the giant waves. Lightning crackled around her, but she stood fast. She wouldn't pull back, no matter how pressing the evil in the vision. She had to see. Had to find Levi.

Long minutes passed as the little boat fought the storm surge. Rachel felt each pitch and roll of the deck. Felt the fear of the deckhands. She strained to get closer. To see more detail.

Her efforts finally paid off. "I see someone! A man, steering the boat."

"Is it your brother?" Nathan asked. His hand tightened around hers.

"I—I don't think so. He's older." She rolled her lips between her teeth and bore down on the vision, willing herself in tighter. Willing herself not to lose it. "There's a woman, too. He's giving her his coat, and another man—" She lurched back as if she'd been stung by a wasp.

Connor's grip matched Nathan's in bone-crushing intensity. "Is it him?"

She nodded, and tears streamed down her face. "It's him. It's Levi."

Emotion so strong welled up inside her that she almost lost the vision. Her brother had been a baby in her arms when she'd last seen him, but when she saw him in her vision, she recognized him on an instinctual level. He had their mother's eyes and her father's cleft chin.

"Oh, he's . . . he's beautiful." Tears streamed freely down her cheeks. So many years she'd spent looking for him. So many years she'd lost. They'd both lost.

Teryn's calm voice cut through the wild surge of adrenaline. "Can you tell where they are, Rachel?"

"No. No, they're still at sea, the same scene the goddess has shown me before, only there's more now."

"More how?" Nathan asked.

"I can see them more clearly now. The woman with Levi has short hair, and the older man has on a sweatshirt. It says—" She struggled to focus through her tears. "It says 'Beth's Best Crab Cakes, Port Elizabeth, Maine'!"

She let go of Connor's hand and clutched Nathan in a two-handed grip. Abruptly the clouds that had obscured her vision dissipated. The lightning that had blinded her and the rain that had pelted her evaporated. The frigid air over the North Atlantic was replaced with the climate-controlled comfort of Teryn's living room.

"He's in Maine! My brother's in Port Elizabeth, Maine, or on a boat somewhere nearby."

"It was just a sweatshirt, sweetheart." Nathan patted her hand and reminded her to breathe, for the baby's sake. "The other man could have gotten it just passing through. There's no guarantee he's there."

"I know he is." She pulled one hand free and wiped the tears from her cheeks, laughing. "I know it. Or at least someone there will recognize him, know him. We have to go to Port Elizabeth."

Nathan sighed and traded beleaguered looks with Teryn and Connor. "We'll check it out tomorrow. See about flights."

"No, we have to go tonight." She couldn't explain the sense of urgency she felt, but she knew it was real. Levi was there. Her baby brother needed her.

"You need to get some sleep, honey—"

She was already on her feet. "I can sleep on the way. We have to go. Now." She shifted her gaze from man to man, finally landing on her husband.

"Right. Now," he said, resigned. "I'll get the car. You throw some things in a bag." He turned and pointed a menacing finger at her as he walked away. "And *eat* something!"

She nodded, but her mind was already on the trip. How could she be hungry when she was about to be reunited with her brother after more than twenty years and, in doing so, save her husband and all their people from an evil force bent on world domination?

Her stomach growled and the baby kicked as if to punctuate the proclamation.

Okay, so maybe a granola bar for the road.

SIX

❧

Her clothes were missing.

Tasha pried her eyelids a little farther open, actually managing to lift her head an inch off the pillow and squint across the room.

Yep. They were gone. She distinctively remembered falling into bed with the pile of soggy, ocean-smelling, seaweed-matted jeans, underwear and sweater mildewing in a pile in the corner near the door.

Her head poofed back into the pillow.

Real down. Nice.

Who the hell would steal her clothes?

Blowing out a deep breath, she sprang up, taking the bedsheet with her, and wrapped it around herself, toga style. She didn't bother to knock at Levi's door.

"Someone stole my clothes! My underwear,"—that creeped her out—"everything."

Levi lay on his stomach, arms flopped above his head

and his face turned toward the wall. He hadn't moved. He looked . . . peaceful.

She raised her voice. "Are you awake?"

Groaning, he rolled over and used his forearm to shield his eyes from the sun streaming in through the porthole. "I am now."

"I said someone—"

"I stole your clothes."

She scrunched her face. "Eww. What do you want with my clothes?"

"I gave them to Estes. Guess he's some kind of man-servant or something as well as the pilot. He offered to wash them. Mine, too."

"Oh." She shuffled her feet and tugged the sheet up. "Well, what am I supposed to wear in the meantime?"

Levi lifted one eyebrow, then groaned as he sat up.

"Are you okay?" It wasn't like him to let an opening that wide go without a suggestive comment.

"Headache," he said, massaging his temples.

"Are you sure you don't have a concussion?"

He rolled up on the edge of the mattress and put his feet on the floor. The covers fell, and she saw he was wearing the sweatpants their "host" had loaned him last night.

Too bad. She might have offered to share her bedsheet.

"We need to get you to a doctor."

"Yeah, well, that's going to have to wait."

He stood, scrubbing his face with his palms, then raked his fingers through his hair. "This tub's engines still aren't working, and communications are out. I don't think the crew here is going to be able to fix them. Looks like it's up to us."

"What?" Heat crept up her neck. "Why didn't you say something last night? Why didn't you wake me?"

"We both needed rest, Tash."

"Rest? We can't rest. We've got . . . stuff to do."

He sighed. "What stuff do we have to do?"

She chewed on her lower lip. "Stuff like . . . like . . . figure out how to get another boat."

The fact that there wasn't much they could do for their friends went unsaid. Paddy, Charlie and Mark didn't have any family, at least none they talked about, and they didn't have any bodies to bury.

"Is that what you want?" His brown eyes darkened, telling her he was troubled when he never would. "To get a new boat and go on just like before. Keep living the way you've been living?"

Her fingers clenched on the edge of the sheet across her chest. "What's wrong with the way I've been living?"

He turned, walked to the porthole and stared out at the horizon. "Nothing. If you like constantly being in danger of getting caught, barely scraping by financially."

Her head snapped up. The heat in her neck rose to her cheeks. "Oh, that's what this is about. Now you've spent the night on a big, fancy yacht, probably eating caviar and sipping champagne with that idiot who got us into this mess, and a hardworking, solid little boat like *The White Whale* isn't good enough for you."

"That's not what I meant." He faced her, scrubbed his face again, and for the first time, she noticed the dark circles under his eyes, the pale skin under the stubble of his jaw. "DuValle offered me a job."

"And you're thinking about working for that asshole?"

"No." He rubbed his hands over his face. "Yes. I mean, I don't know."

"The Levi I know would never consider working for that pasty-faced, limp-wristed, gutless . . ." Running out of steam, she turned her back to him, arms crossed over her chest, but guilt niggled at her despite her huff. She glanced back over her naked shoulder. "What the hell is wrong with you?"

He really didn't look himself. It had to be this place. Him, DuValle and his fancy ship. She wasn't feeling like herself, either, between the grief for her friends and the pressure she'd felt in her chest since she'd first seen the *Spanish Dancer*'s lights in the storm.

She couldn't shake the feeling that something was wrong.

Someone rapped on the door. Levi answered it, and she saw him take a stack of neatly folded clothes. Once Estes had left, he handed her things to her. His hand lingered over hers a moment as they made the exchange. He felt hot to the touch, almost feverish.

She opened the door to go back to her own room and dress, but he stopped her with a raspy question. "Tash, didn't you ever just want . . . something more?"

She turned slowly, almost afraid to look too deeply into his sad eyes, afraid that she'd see that he did want more. More than her and their life, such as it was, on the sea.

"No," she said quietly, and left.

Levi took his time making his way through the yacht to the galley. He was hungry, but his stomach was also a little unsettled. He wasn't sure if the queasiness was a physical ailment or the result of his conversation with Tasha. What had gotten in to him? He wasn't actually considering working for the bastard with the big boat. Was he?

He strolled down the hallway, taking in the crystal chandeliers over his head, the deep carpeting beneath his feet, the smell of polished wood.

It wasn't the furnishings that had him questioning his lifestyle or the choices he'd made. Not that he'd had that many choices given who—and what—he was. It wasn't the money or the air of power that surrounded DuValle. He didn't care about those things.

It was just the resurgence of this idea that he got from time to time that there was something more out there for him. Something he couldn't even name, and yet it pulled at him. His need for it, whatever it was, gnawed at him like hunger.

In the past, he'd been able to quell the restlessness by changing form and disappearing into the ocean for a day, or more recently by working off the energy in Tasha's bed. But this time, the hunger was back with a vengeance. This time, a long swim wasn't going to be enough. Even Tasha wasn't going to be enough.

They'd been together two years now, and that was the first time he remembered having any kind of conversation that didn't involve fishing boats, the weather, or sex. The first time they'd talked about the future or anything remotely emotional.

He realized he'd stopped in the hall, his fists clenched, and he forced his fingers to unfurl.

He'd hurt Tasha a few minutes ago, and he was sorry for that. But he needed . . . something. He felt like he was going to split apart if he didn't find it.

"So tell me, Levi, where are you from?" Roman watched Levi push his scrambled eggs around his plate listlessly. The effort to resist his magic, to close his mind to his intrusions, the seeds he planted, was taking its toll on his young prize. Levi wouldn't be able to keep up his resistance for long. Roman had had their breakfast brought to the great room, and Levi was once again in the ritual circle.

"New York, originally," Levi said without looking up.

"How does a New York boy end up on a lobster boat in St. George's strait?"

"Guess I've always felt drawn to the water."

Roman smiled. That was an understatement. He'd focused his power and his magic on Levi's thoughts, and for just a moment, he'd gotten a glimpse of a skinny, dark-haired boy with a wide smile revealing a missing front tooth as he skimmed across a cove on a homemade catamaran. It had only been a glimpse before Levi's mental barriers had thrown him back, but it was a start.

My God, the power of his young mind! It was . . . exhilarating.

"What else do you enjoy?" This time, instead of trying to see Levi's thoughts, Roman pushed images of his own to his young prodigy. He sent images—just flashes—of the history of their people. He didn't want to give too much away, but he needed to know how much of his legacy Levi remembered. How much of his heritage he'd been able to piece together from images of past lives. If he didn't, he might give himself away when he fed his young pupil new, false information.

A forkful of eggs stalled halfway to Levi's mouth. The silverware clattered back to the plate. His eyes closed, and his breathing quickened.

"Are you all right?" Roman asked.

"Just a headache."

Roman pushed again with his mind, and again Levi's defenses shoved him back, this time hard enough to make him physically flinch.

His nostrils flared in frustration, but in his mind, he laughed in delight. Exhilarating, indeed!

Levi shoved his chair back. "If you'll excuse me—"

"Wait, just a minute." Roman rose before Levi could,

dabbing his lips with a linen napkin before dropping it on his plate. "Let me get you something for your head."

"No, it's okay. I just need to lie—"

"No trouble, really. My mother used to have migraines. She taught me a surefire cure, all natural. A raw egg, a teaspoon of coffee grounds, half cup of orange juice, a little soy protein powder." He glanced over his shoulder to see Levi hadn't left, and took that as a good sign. "There's more, but you get the idea."

He opened the mini fridge under the bar and started mixing. He didn't have any eggs up here, but they way Levi was pinching the bridge of his nose, he doubted the young man was in any condition to notice that. Just to be sure, he pushed a little harder with his mind, drawing a wince from Levi.

The drink finished, he handed Levi the glass and watched as the young man grimaced at the smell but downed the contents.

"Thanks," Levi said as he rose. "For whatever that was."

"You're welcome. I just hope it has the desired effect."

Levi laid one hand lightly over his stomach. "I just hope it stays down. I'd hate to ruin your pretty carpet."

Estes walked in as Levi left the room. He closed the door behind him. "Well?"

"I made some progress but not nearly enough. I believe I'll have better luck while he's asleep."

Manny stared at the door as if he could see right through it. He tipped his head. "You drugged him."

It was a statement, not a question.

"He needs the rest." Roman smiled broadly. "He has a *terrible* headache."

SEVEN

About a half an hour after Levi knocked softly on Tasha's stateroom door and asked if she wanted to walk upstairs and get some breakfast with him, she began to regret turning down his request. More accurately, her stomach began to regret it. The rumbling rivaled that of *The White Whale*'s old diesel engine.

She was going to miss that old boat, her friends. She was going to miss the way things used to be. But that was life—never get too attached to anything, or it was bound to be taken away.

Deciding starving herself in protest wasn't going to do anyone any good, least of all her, she reluctantly set out to find some grub. Hopefully she could sneak into the kitchen and grab a plate of something to bring back to her room without running into anyone.

Especially Roman DuValle.

Doubly especially Levi Tremaine.

Just thinking his name worsened the pressure in her chest.

He wanted more. She just didn't get that. More what?

She'd had everything she needed. A boat, plenty of lobster to catch, a very small circle of friends.

And him.

She peeked around a corner in the hall, and when she saw the coast was clear, continued on her quest for food, and truth.

Who was she kidding? She'd never really had him. She'd had sex. Rather frequently, at that. She'd never had more because she'd never wanted more. She was afraid to want more, because if she got it, it would be all that much more painful when she lost it.

And she was bound to lose it eventually.

The back of her throat burned, and she pressed her lips together and swallowed the tears.

Ahead on the right was a set of double doors. The kitchen? She hurried up to them and peered through the round windows.

Not the kitchen. An exercise room, complete with weights, a stationary bike and a treadmill.

The search went on.

She turned her thoughts to something a little less deep than self-analysis. Levi had asked a good question. What was she going to do now? Work at McDonald's? She had some savings, but she didn't have enough for a new boat, and it was tough for someone who listed her occupation as "poacher" to get a loan.

Besides, she didn't have a crew either.

Back came the burning throat.

She turned another corner and walked down a short set of stairs to yet another hallway. How big was this tub?

The doors down here didn't have windows, and the furnishings looked a little less flamboyant. The crew quarters, perhaps? If so, the kitchen shouldn't be far away. Every ship sailed on the stomachs of its crew, after all.

The hall came to a dead end, though, at a single door marked "Storage."

For heaven's sake. Maybe she could find a carton of power bars or something in there. Or a jar of peanut butter, which she hated. Anything to stop the rumbling.

She opened the door, and her eyes went wide.

No peanut butter.

Cages. Lots of little wire cages. The first row held mice, brown ones and white ones huddled together in masses, sleeping. One little male sat up, a food pellet gripped tightly between his pink front paws, and inspected her as she inspected him, his eyes darting nervously after her every move.

"Hey little guy." She tapped the glass and could have sworn he sighed, shrugged and went back to gnawing on his pellet with tiny white buckteeth.

Larger cages sat behind the row of mice. The first had a solid bottom about four inches deep. She looked inside.

"Frogs?"

Some people liked to keep mice for pets—though she couldn't see the attraction to rodents, herself—but frogs? About half a dozen sloshed through their soggy habitat. Behind them, a warming lamp hung over a cage with some seriously ugly lizards. Yellow and black and scaly. She passed by them quickly, not caring to take in any more detail than that.

At the rear of the room were larger wooden crates, sealed shut and covered with tarps. Pinching the blue vinyl between her thumb and forefinger, she eased one corner up. Who knows what a man who kept rodents and lizards aboard a luxury yacht would be secreting in a dark corner.

When nothing sprang up and shouted "Boo!" she lifted the tarp a little farther and read the marking stamped into the wood.

AK-47.

Guns. Lots of guns. Boxes of ammunition.

Those were all scary enough, but what raised the pressure in her chest, the sense of doom, to a crushing force were the other weapons hung carefully on the wall behind them.

Some of them looked antique. There was a sword that looked like it would be too heavy for her to lift. She could swear the handle was embossed with real gold.

In an open crate, there was one of those ball things with spikes on it hung from a bat by a heavy chain. A mace. She'd thought those were just a creation of the movies, but this one looked to be hundreds of years old.

There were sickles and hatchets and a long, thin dagger hung carefully on display.

Or ready for use.

There was death in this room, old and recent.

Goose bumps prickled her forearms. The hair raised on the back of her neck. The sense of foreboding became so strong that her field of vision began to narrow. Blackness crept in on the sides. She fled the narrow room, muscles trembling, only to run straight into a pair of thick arms. Hands gripped her shoulders, lifting her to her tiptoes. She gasped for air like a fish.

"Ms. Cole. Are you all right?"

DuValle. "Um. Yes." She gasped for air like a fish again. "I was . . . um . . . looking for the galley."

He set her back on her feet. "Deck two. Aft."

"Thanks." She turned her shoulders to slide past him, the feeling of malevolence physically oppressive. Heavy, like the air in the passage.

He stopped her again, this time with a manicured hand

at the base of her throat. He traced the line of the leather necklace over the hollow of her throat to the valley between her breasts, palmed the pendant. His gray eyes studied it, then locked on her, chilling her.

"Interesting piece."

"Thank you." She licked her lips, summoning calm when she really wanted to run. "Levi had it made for me."

"Did he? And what does it mean, this symbol?"

"I don't know," she said. "It's just some design he was always doodling."

What was she doing talking to him? Telling him this? It was none of his damned business. The pendant was special. The only thing Levi had ever given her, the only evidence that there was anything between the two of them other than sex and business. She started to make up some lie, looked up to find his gray eyes piercing her, driving inside her. She felt queasy.

"He said he thought it was a place," she added without understanding why she'd told him that. Levi had admitted it to her in private. In bed. "The symbol for a place."

"I see." DuValle let go of the necklace, dropped his hand. Tasha felt like a fish who'd been cut from a line. Her vision blurred, the light of the hall refracting around her like sunlight through water.

She plowed forward, not quite sure where she'd been going, but desperate to get away.

"Deck two," DuValle called from behind her. "Aft."

Right. The galley.

Her knees wobbled as she hurried down the hallway and out of his sight, then turned toward the bow of the ship. She wasn't hungry any longer. She just needed to get away, far away, before the seizure took her.

*   *   *

The thunder of galloping hooves, the clash of steel and the screams of men were deafening. Levi looked down and saw that he was riding one of the horses, charging toward a huge stone building and the army around it. It was him, and yet it wasn't him.

His mind, but not his body. Not his life.

Not this one, anyway.

He didn't know where the thought came from. Didn't have time to wonder what it meant as he was transported to another scene, another battle. This one was in the woods, more of a quiet hunt. It was dark and there were men all around him. One by one the men began to change. They became beasts of different sizes and shapes. Many of them became bizarre combinations of several beasts, like a nature jigsaw puzzle put together wrong. He would call them monsters, but who was he to fault them?

Levi felt the change taking him as well, but he couldn't. He mustn't. He was a creature of the sea. He would die in the forest.

The macabre band moved forward stealthily, feral eyes gleaming, tongues drooling and fangs flashing. They left the trees behind and climbed a rocky hill to the nest.

Nest?

Levi looked into a cavern in the hillside and saw a ring of boulders glowing as if they'd sat in a fire. In the center sat a creature the size of a small house. Its scaled sides rose and fell in a slow rhythm. Smoke billowed from its nostrils with every breath. Every few seconds, its great wings would flutter, as if flying in its dreams.

Levi's throat went dry.

A dragon.

Suddenly he knew why they were there. They were going to kill it.

They'd been created to kill it.

*   *   *

For the second time that day, Tasha rushed into Levi's
room without knocking. She'd shaken off the vis—the seizure, for the time being. "Levi. We've got to get out of here.
Off this ship. I thought you were fixing the engines, but
you weren't down below. You won't believe—"

She stopped in her tracks halfway across the room.

For the second time that day, she walked in on him sleeping. Only this time, his sleep was anything but peaceful.

The comforter hung halfway off the bed. The top sheet
was twisted around one leg. He twisted against the re-
straint, limbs flailing.

"Hey, wake up," she said, eyes wide.

He moaned and thrashed some more. His face was even
more pale than it had been earlier, and a fine sheen of sweat
covered his chest, matting the springy hair against him. He
coughed, and the cords of his neck stood out as if he were
in great pain.

Worse, his body seemed to be changing shape before her
eyes. His torso lengthened, then shrunk. His arms spread
flat and wide for a moment. His skin darkened and scales
appeared and then disappeared. This wasn't supposed to
happen. Not on dry land—or dry deck. Not like this.

She hurried to his side and shook his shoulders. "Hey, I
said *wake up*. Right now."

His left hand whipped up, knocking her back. In a
flash he had captured both her wrists, flipped her over and
thrown himself on top of her. It was a move he'd made before, but not so violently. This was no lover's game. While
his left hand held her wrists, his right hand closed around
her throat.

She twisted and bucked to no avail. He countered every
move, overwhelmed her. The smell of him that she'd once

found so arousing, leather and musk, now inspired fear. The feel of him moving over her, chest to chest, brought pain instead of pleasure.

His eyes opened but didn't see. They weren't the eyes of the man she'd loved. They were the eyes of the monster he was about to become.

She screamed, and in the moment's hesitation it caused him, found an angle of attack. She jerked her knee up between his legs while he still had legs.

He fell to the side, all the way to the floor and lay clutching himself for a long moment, his eyes closed, breathing hard. His body seemed to have returned to normal. She sat up and backed into the corner of the berth.

When his breathing finally slowed and he opened his eyes, she blew out a long breath. It was Levi. Not the other.

She sat up straighter and crawled cautiously to the edge of the bed, looking down at him. He lowered his gaze to the carpet.

"What the hell," she asked, "was that?"

EIGHT

"What happened?" Levi's throat was raw.

"You tell me."

Tasha sat on the edge of his bed, peering down at him. He sat up, wondering what he was doing on the floor and feeling like he'd gone ten rounds with a gorilla.

"Did you kick me in the balls?"

"Technically I kneed you in the balls."

"Why the hell did you do that?"

"You were trying to kill me."

That took his mind off the pain. His attention snapped to her disheveled clothes and wide, round eyes. "What are you talking about?"

"I came in here because I had to tell you something, but you were having a nightmare. I tried to wake you up and you flipped out."

"Jesus." He ran a hand through his hair. He'd been having a nightmare, all right. That much he remembered. He could still taste the blood and the smoke and the death. "I'm sorry."

He reached for her, but she grabbed his arm instead. "There's something else."

"What?" From the look on her face, he wasn't sure he wanted to know.

"You were . . . changing."

That stopped him cold.

"Jesus," he said again.

She let go of his arm. "Has that ever happened before? In your sleep, I mean?"

"No."

"Maybe it has something to do with what happened last night, having to change to save us."

"No," he said, but he couldn't explain more. He remembered the dream now. Fighting for his life, struggling to make it to the water, where he could battle on his own terms. He knew what he saw, what he felt, but he had no idea what it meant.

"It was just a nightmare," he added, hoping that she would drop it. "What did you want to tell me?"

"Huh?"

"You said you came here to tell me something."

She jolted as if she'd just remembered. "Oh. Yeah. You won't believe what I found."

"Found where?"

"In a storage room downstairs."

Chilled by drying sweat, he reached for the T-shirt he'd thrown over the back of the chair earlier and dragged it over his head. "What were you doing in a storage room?"

"Looking for food." She shrugged. "I couldn't find the kitchen."

He narrowed his eyes at her. "Snooping can get a person in all kinds of trouble, you know."

"Are you going to listen to what I came to tell you or not?"

He lifted one eyebrow.

"I found all kinds of creepy stuff."

"What do you mean, 'creepy stuff'?"

"Like live mice and toads and scaly lizards."

He lifted one eyebrow. "Are you implying that because an animal has scales, it's creepy?"

She flinched. "No, of course not, but . . . well, yeah. When it comes to *pets*."

"I have scales."

"You're not a pet."

"No?" Truth was, sometimes he felt that way. Sometimes he wished she didn't know about him, what he could do.

"Look, I don't think these were pets."

"Why not? Not everyone is hung up on beagles, you know."

She flinched again, and he regretted the reference to a dog she'd confided in him she'd loved as a child. He suspected that dog had been her only friend, though she'd never admit it. She'd learned to sail with him at her side. When he'd finally passed she'd buried him at sea like any good sailor should do.

"He had other creepy stuff, too."

He crossed his arms over his chest. "Like what?"

"Guns. Lots of guns. And old swords and knives and all kind of weapons that look like they were made in the dark ages."

His stomach tumbled as he recalled the weapons in the hands of the army he'd fought with. The weapons he'd carried in his own hands. The way the blood they'd drawn from his enemies had run down his own arms.

Was there some connection?

Couldn't be. It was just a nightmare.

"So maybe DuValle is a collector."

She chewed her bottom lip as she thought, a habit he'd always found adorable. "If it was just the old stuff, I might buy that. But none of this was set up in display cases, or even locked up, for that matter. And some of the guns were loaded."

"He's a rich man on an expensive boat. I can't blame the man for carrying some protection."

"Protection? You sound like I found a glow-in-the-dark condom in his wallet. The man has enough automatic weapons in his closet to take over a small island. This is bad, Levi, very, very bad. We need to get off this yacht. He's into something illegal."

He snorted. "And as a career poacher, your moral compass dictates that you can't tolerate another day on a ship with anyone who might be involved in something illegal."

"We're in danger here, Levi."

"You don't know that."

He had to admit, the sight of Port Elizabeth harbor would be a welcome one right now. Between the storm and loss of *The White Whale* and her crew—his friends— and his headache and the strange dreams, he was a little creeped out himself.

"Okay, so there are some strange and possibly dangerous things going on around here. Short of calling the Coast Guard and getting us all thrown in the hooch, there's not much we can do about it. This afternoon I'll fix the engines, and then we'll be headed home. Until then, we just keep our eyes open and our heads down."

She was quiet so long that he thought she wasn't going to answer. When she did, it was in a quiet voice. "I don't like it."

He sat next to her and draped an arm over her shoulders. "I get that."

"No. No, you don't." She pulled away from him and headed for the door. She wasn't sure she understood the ever-present sense of peril she'd felt since she'd boarded the *Spanish Dancer* herself.

"Damn the woman." Roman slapped his palm on the table hard enough to sting.

It had been working. With the help of a few crushed sleeping pills in his drink, Levi wasn't able to protect his mind, consciously or unconsciously. His thoughts had been open. Roman had planted a few images, and the dreams had started. He'd been able to see how much Levi remembered from his past lives. How much he knew about his people. Their people.

Then *she* had interrupted.

As soon as Levi woke up, the defenses snapped back in place. Roman couldn't even see what was happening by using Second Sight, the ability his people had to cast their vision somewhere else at will, so strong were the son of the Old One's skills.

He knew that girl would be a problem.

Now the question was, what to do about her.

NINE

"What do you think? Drugs, gun smuggling, laundered money?" Tasha craned her neck to get a better look at the bolt Levi was trying to pry off with the socket wrench. Damn, they didn't make 'em the way they used to. They'd have had *The White Whale* up and running hours ago. "My money's on drugs. Everyone smuggles drugs these days. At least now we know how DuValle got his money."

"We do, do we?" Levi asked in his "humor the crazy lady" voice.

"How else could he afford a tub like this?"

"Maybe his filthy-rich daddy left it to him. Maybe he actually earned it in a legitimate business."

"Legitimate businessmen do not take a yacht out into the middle of the Atlantic this time of year. It's not like freaking Cozumel sunshine out there, you know."

"Good point." He set down the socket wrench and lay

back beneath the engine's pumps with his hands behind his head. "Whatever it is, it's best we stay out of it."

"Yeah, yeah. Just keep a low profile and act natural until we get back to Port Elizabeth. I remember."

How could she forget? Levi had practically pounded the words into her head last night as he'd dragged her up to the great room for dinner, where DuValle had invited them for steaks. Both of them. Much as she would have liked to tell the man where he could shove his steaks, she allowed herself to be tugged up the stairs. Don't want to let on to the crazy drug runner with a storage room full of guns— among other things—that you know too much, no, no. Or piss him off.

Matters only got worse when Manny Estes, who was apparently a cook as well as pilot and manservant, set her platter in front of her. Her stomach turned when she saw the steak had been served tartar. To make matters worse, halfway through the meal, DuValle had asked if Levi had thought any more about coming to work with him, and Tasha had barely refrained from dumping her rice pilaf in the bastard's lap.

After that, there hadn't been much conversation. None, really.

So much for acting natural.

She took the wrench Levi held out to her and then he picked up a screwdriver. Twisting her head to get a better look at his progress, she asked, "So what kind of drugs do you think it is?"

"Tasha," Levi warned.

She plopped down on the deck next to him. "I can't help it. I'm bored."

"Really," he said dryly. "I hadn't noticed."

That earned him an elbow in the ribs.

In the grand scheme of things, bored wasn't so bad, she

decided. At least, no one had murdered her in her sleep with one of those archaic weapons. Levi hadn't tried to kill her in his sleep—or had any more nightmares, as far as she knew. And though the sense of something evil she felt so strongly before was still present, it had taken a backseat.

To boredom.

Maybe she'd just gotten used to feeling like she was living in the hotel from Stephen King's novel *The Shining.*

She popped up, paced back and forth a couple of times and was about to ask Levi another question he couldn't possibly know the answer to when the ship's phone rang. She let him get it.

"Yeah, uh, sure," she heard him say, and from the look he gave her when he glanced up, she knew she wasn't going to be happy about whatever he just agreed to.

When he hung up, she waited.

"Well, you want to know what he's up to, you're going to get another chance to find out. We've just been invited to dinner. Again."

She groaned.

Dinner was a much bawdier affair than the somber meal they'd shared with DuValle the night before. Levi even found himself chuckling a time or two as the jokes and stories got more outrageous each time the vodka bottle was passed around. He might have even caught Tasha smiling once or twice.

By midnight, though, her smiles had given way to widemouthed yawns. He stood, swaying a little after having one shot too many of the Russian swill, and pulled her toward the door.

"No, no. You don't go yet," DuValle protested. "The night is young."

Levi glanced at Tasha's heavy eyelids. "I think it's time to call it a night."

Tasha admitted she was too tired to see straight, and DuValle bowed solemnly. "Then good evening to you, my lady. You go to bed. But Levi, my friend. Please stay a few moments." He leaned close. "I have Cuban cigars. The very best."

Levi was torn. He had every reason to hate DuValle as much as Tasha did, but somehow he felt drawn to him. The hell with it. He turned to leave, but a spike of pain speared through his head. Before he recovered enough to walk away with Tash, DuValle clapped him on the back and held him in place. Immediately the pain in his head eased. He looked over his shoulder at Tasha.

"You go," she said, and waggled her fingers. "Have fun."

Fun. Right. He might have fun, but he sure wouldn't be getting lucky any time soon. That much was clear in her glittering eyes.

DuValle did have some fine cigars, though. "Smooth," he said, and exhaled slowly, savoring the flavor and the slight burn in his nostrils.

The foredeck was strangely quiet compared to the boisterous dinner table, and he didn't feel nearly as drunk as he had just moments ago. When Manny came out to join him and DuValle, they scooted closer to make room, and Levi suddenly felt like a hare in a trap. And the fox was close enough to smell his aftershave.

"Nice night," Roman said, gazing up at the stars.

"Yeah. I guess." It was cold, but clear. He couldn't help but think what a contrast it was to the horrendous storm the other night, and of the friends it had taken. Tonight it didn't even seem like the same ocean. The same planet.

"So, you've decided," Roman said. Statement, not question.

"Yeah."

"You're leaving."

"Yeah."

"I don't think you want to do that." Roman puffed out a smoke circle.

"What makes you think that?" Levi wished he hadn't asked. His decision was made. He wasn't any rich man's lackey. And whether he wanted to admit it or not, he didn't like Tasha thinking he was.

"I saw you the other night, you know," Roman continued quietly, puffing on his own cigar. "In the water."

Levi's heart kicked into overdrive. Now he really did feel trapped. "It was dark." He grasped at anything to head off what he feared was coming. "Raining too hard to see your hand in front of your face."

Was this why Roman had really offered him a job? So he could degrade him as a freak? Cage him up and sell him to the highest bidder as some circus sideshow or research subject?

He could go overboard, Levi thought. Backward over the rail. He could make it before they grabbed him. Maybe. He'd be better off in the water.

Roman ground out his cigar on his beautiful teal deck. "Just in case you're thinking about jumping," he said in a very deliberate voice, "remember we have your girlfriend downstairs."

"Anybody touches her, I'll kill you."

"Nobody's going to touch her. We're not here to hurt you, either one of you. We're here to help you. But just you."

"I don't need your kind of help."

"Are you sure?" Roman's eyes glowed too brightly, the same pewter color as the moon. "I saw what you became in the water."

Every muscle in Levi's body tightened. "You saw shit. It was too dark. There was too much rain."

"I didn't see with my eyes. I saw with my mind."

"You're fucking nuts." He looked from DuValle to Manny, who sat quietly, unsurprised. "Both of you."

Roman laughed. "The Second Sight is just one of my special abilities. One you will have, too, once I train you."

"Really," Levi added. "Totally fucking nuts."

"What you're about to see is fucking nuts. But it's real, as is the Second Sight and the many other gifts of our people."

"*Our* people?"

"Watch and learn, my friend."

Roman took a deep breath and dropped to one knee. His head bowed, and when he raised it, his nose and jaw elongated, forming a snout. His ears grew taller and pointier. Tufts of coarse hair, gray and brown and black, sprouted on his face, neck and hands.

Roman grunted and fell forward until his palms joined his knee on the deck. His back arched up spasmodically. His ribs contracted sharply and he gasped painfully for air.

Levi stood transfixed. He knew that pain, the feel of a body transforming. He knew that sound of bones crunching, remaking themselves. He'd heard it. Felt it.

A moment later, where Roman DuValle had knelt, a wolf stared up at Levi.

A wolf with haunting, intelligent silver eyes.

Levi stood stiff, transfixed. He'd had too much to drink. This was some trick of the eye.

A moment later, the wolf transformed again, and Roman DuValle stood in its place.

"You're not alone, Levi."

His breath came in short bursts. He didn't understand. Wasn't sure he wanted to.

"I know what you are." He smiled. "Because I'm one, too."

"Bullshit." There were no others like him. He was a freak. He didn't know what he was.

"More than that," DuValle said softly. Compassionately. "It wasn't an accident, my being so close to your ship. I've been looking for you, Levi. Searching for many years."

Levi had a thousand questions, but only one came to his lips. It was like he was in a trance. "Why?"

DuValle held his hands out, palms up. "Because I'm your father."

TEN

"It's confirmed, the ship was lost. We found plenty of debris, including several life preservers carrying the name *The White Whale."* The Coast Guard officer who sat across the desk from Rachel Cross straightened the papers in his file folder and cleared his throat. "I'm sorry, ma'am, but there were no survivors."

Rachel held Nathan's hand in a death grip. "You can't be sure. He could be—"

"We conducted an extensive aerial search. If your brother was on that boat, he's gone. Again, my condolences."

He offered his condolences, but his eyes held little sympathy. She wondered how many times he'd had to tell families their loved ones had been lost, and the toll it had taken on him.

Nathan stood and pulled her up with him, which was good because she wasn't sure she would have had the strength to stand on her own. "Thank you for the information, Captain Stevenson."

Rachel nodded her appreciation as well and followed her husband outside. "It's not true," she said as they were out the door.

"Rach, you heard the man, they did a search."

"If he were dead, I would know."

"You said you saw the boat capsize."

Thanks to that vision, the memory, and the horror that went with it, would be burned into her mind forever. "That doesn't mean he's dead. We need to set up another circle, right now. Maybe I can see what happened to him, where he went."

"You need to rest."

"There's no time—"

"Rachel, we drove sixteen straight hours to get here. You haven't eaten and you haven't slept. I know how much this means to you—to all of us—but you can't do this to the baby. You've got to rest."

Her hand fell protectively to the bulge of her abdomen. She knew he was right, and it killed her to admit it. "A few hours, then. And we can stop for hamburgers while we look for a hotel."

"Eight hours, and I'll find someplace to get you a nice grilled salmon and some vegetables. You need the protein."

"Six hours, and no broccoli," she negotiated.

"Deal."

Tasha was asleep in his berth, fully clothed and curled up on top of the covers, when Levi got back to his room. She stirred when he sat beside her to pull off his shoes. She glanced at the pink rays of dawn streaming through the porthole, then back at him. "Must've been some party," she mumbled through a yawn.

"Actually, it was."

He wasn't alone. There were others like him. Well, not exactly like him. Roman had shifted into a different creature. But he had shifted.

Levi had thought he was one of a kind. A freak of nature. Never had he dreamed there were others. Lots of others, or so Roman told him.

A million questions had run through his mind. How? Why? What was he? What were they?

Roman had seemed delighted with his questions, but answered few, promising to tell all before they reached Port Elizabeth. Levi had finished the engine repairs that afternoon. They were due in port in less than a day. Suddenly he wasn't in such a hurry. He had so much to learn.

Even the headache that had snuck back as he'd talked with Roman couldn't spoil his happiness. *He wasn't alone.*

On impulse, he leaned over suddenly and captured Tasha's sleepy mouth with his own. The soul-deep joy, the relief he felt at learning there were others like him, exploded into the kiss. He took it deeper, cupping the back of her head in both hands and possessing her with his tongue, then retreating and teasing her into taking him.

They broke apart panting and gasping for air.

She narrowed her pretty green eyes at him and curled one corner of her mouth. "I'm not sure I want to know what happened upstairs with you and the crazy rich guy to bring *that* on."

A bit of his good mood fell away. The one disappointment in the night was that Roman had asked him not to tell Tasha what he'd learned about himself, his people. Roman had been shocked to learn that Tasha knew about him, that she accepted him. But he didn't trust her with the knowledge of their people. Levi didn't agree, but he understood the hesitation. Given time, Roman would come to trust her. He was sure of it.

Until then, he would keep the source of his excitement to himself.

He slapped her on the butt. "Come on, get up and let's go watch the sun come up."

"Now I know you've lost your mind. This is the North Atlantic, not the Caribbean. We'll freeze."

He waggled his brows. "I'll keep you warm."

She snorted.

"You can take the comforter," he offered instead. "And I'll fetch you coffee."

That did it. She threw her legs over the side of the bed. "Let's go."

An hour later, Tasha lay on a deck chair, wrapped in Levi's comforter and soaking up the weak rays of the early morning sun, with Levi snoring softly in the chair next to her.

She'd been only partially kidding when she'd said she wasn't sure she wanted to know what had happened after she left the party last night. While he'd been having a good time with his new buddy, she'd slept fitfully, listening for his footsteps coming down the hall, and dreaming of him surrounded by dark creatures. By evil.

The pressure on her chest had come back with such force that she could hardly breathe. Then there he'd been, tasting of vodka and tobacco and the ocean and kissing her until she melted.

He'd confused her, worried her and aroused her in the span of less than a minute.

She didn't like him getting too close to Roman, but was she really sensing danger, or was she just jealous that he'd found something besides her to be happy about, even if only for a few hours?

Despite the kiss and a shared sunrise, she felt a new distance between them, and it was growing by the minute.

Roman sat across a small square table from Levi, who leaned forward on his elbows, every bit the precocious young pupil, eager for his first lesson.

"How is it that there are people like us around, and no one else in the world—none of the regular people—seem to know it? How many of us are there? For that matter, what *are* we? Do we have a name?"

Roman chuckled. "All in time. And yes, we have a name. We are *Les Gargouillen*."

"French? For . . . Gargoyles? You're kidding, right?"

"Hardly."

"We're not made of stone, and we don't hang around on buildings all day and come to life at night. At least I don't."

"The tradition of the stone images on buildings arose in our honor. We were once revered by all. It's only in recent centuries that humans have forgotten about us, though our images continue to grace their buildings."

Levi shook his head. "Okay, I know I sound like a kid begging for a bedtime story, but how? Why?"

Roman knew the time was right. "It is easier to show you than to tell you."

"Show me what?"

"The history of our race."

"The Gargoyles."

"Yes."

Levi didn't look like he quite believed it, despite the demonstrations he'd seen last night, so Roman explained. His patience would be limitless if it earned him control over Levi's power.

"Our people are not telepathic, but we have some ability to share images between minds. It was first used primarily in battle to telegraph strategy and plans without giving them away to the enemy."

"What enemy?"

"That is for later. For now, I'll show you how our people were created, and why. Relax and open your mind. You also have the ability to shield yourself from my thoughts. You've been doing it quite unconsciously since you came aboard."

"You've been messing with my mind for two days?" Levi's shoulders stiffened.

"Trying to determine if you were ready to know, as well as what you already knew. I assure you, your own thoughts were private. I cannot read your mind."

Levi grunted something that Roman took as acceptance.

"Now relax and open your mind. Think of a blank canvas, and let my mind paint it."

After a few moments, Levi flinched as if surprised. "I see something. I see a . . . a town on the coast. An old-time fishing village." He spoke faster. "I've seen this before, in my dreams."

"This is Rouen, in the country that is now called France. It is where we were created."

Levi flinched violently as Roman showed him the image of the dragon, Le Gargouille, swooping down over Rouen. "I've seen that before, too. Hey, if we're still around, are those things, too?"

"The last dragon was slain many centuries ago. But during this time, this dragon lay siege to Rouen, burning ships in the harbor and snatching children from the streets." Roman illustrated each word with his mind. "One day a stranger came to Rouen, a priest. He promised to give the townsmen the ability to slay the dragon if the people would promise to build a Christian church and give up their pagan ways. The townsmen agreed."

This would be the tricky part, Roman thought. Twisting the truth and altering the true images of the past just enough to serve his purposes, without giving himself away.

He continued. "The priest called the townsmen of Rouen to the forest. There he prayed. He asked the Lord to give them the strength of all the beasts of the world, real and imagined. He asked that He give them the strength to slay the dragon, and his prayers were answered."

He showed Levi the townsmen shifting shapes. Growing fangs and claws and wings. He showed them climbing the steep rock to the dragon's lair, but he stopped just short of detailing the bloody battle. Abruptly he stopped sending images and let Levi's mind fade once again to blank canvas.

His young pupil opened his eyes. "What happened?"

"Thanks to their new strength, the townsmen were able to kill the dragon and free Rouen from its reign of terror. The townsmen made good on their promise, built a church and converted to Christianity. Not long after, they retrieved the dragon's remains and burnt them in the center of town, except the head and neck, already charred by the creature's fiery breath, wouldn't burn. In the end, they hung the head and neck above the door of the new church as a warning to all that creatures of evil would not be tolerated in Rouen. And so began the tradition of decorating the most holiest of buildings, like the chapel of Notre Dame, with the evilest looking of images."

"What about the men of Rouen?" Levi asked.

"They had long since reverted to human form but found they retained the ability to change at will. They became the protectors of all. They were honored by all."

Levi's mouth slanted sarcastically. "Until people forgot."

"There is forgetting and then there is *forgetting*, Levi." Reading the confusion on the young man's face, he explained. "Ours is a proud past. Remember that the next time you walk down the streets of one of our cities. Remember to look up, and you'll find we haven't truly been forgotten. Our history is still there, on the parapets and in the nooks and crannies of buildings on every block. Look up, and you'll see our legacy of stone."

Levi had many more questions and asked repeatedly to be told more about *Les Gargouillen*, but Roman sent him away for now. He needed to proceed slowly, carefully, to avoid tripping himself up. Plus, he simply couldn't contain his glee any longer.

His plan was working perfectly.

ELEVEN

This was the third meal in a row that Tasha had eaten alone, in her room. She picked at the turkey sandwich. She just didn't have much of an appetite. At the sound of footsteps in the hall, she cocked her head. Her instinct was to jump up and go to him when the steps stopped at the door across the hall, and she heard it open and click shut.

But she'd be damned if she'd chase him like a schoolgirl when he'd been ignoring her all day. If he had something to say, he could come to her.

He did just that about five minutes later.

"We'll be back in Port Elizabeth in about an hour," he said.

As if she hadn't been counting the minutes. They should have been back to port yesterday, but apparently they'd taken the scenic route. Levi hadn't seemed in any hurry, and that scared her.

"That's great. We can finally get off this tub."

"Yeah."

He shoved his hands in the pockets of his jeans and started pacing. After five long minutes, she couldn't stand it anymore. "Do you have something to say, or did you just come over here to wear a track in my carpet?"

He stopped suddenly as if he hadn't realized he'd been moving. When he still couldn't come up with any words, she knew whatever it was he had to tell her, it was going to be bad.

She was tempted to help him out. She had a fair idea what he was going to say. She'd be damned if she was going to help a man blow her off, though. Let him suffer.

"About getting off this tub," he finally started.

She looked up and waited.

"When we dock at Port Elizabeth, I'm going to be staying on the boat. I'm taking the job Roman offered."

Zing. Arrow straight to the heart. Not only was he finished with her, but he was hooking up with the man who'd cost them the lives of their friends, not to mention her boat.

Mad enough to not want to look at him, she stood and did some pacing of her own. "It's *Roman* now, is it? No doubt he'll correct that once you're working for him. It'll be, 'yes sir' this and 'no sir' that. Will he dress you up in a little monkey outfit and have you bring him piña coladas on a little silver tray, as well?"

"I'd like it if you'd stay, too."

She spun on her heel to face him. Now *that* she hadn't expected. She bit back the yes that came unbidden to her tongue and raised her only defense—sarcasm—instead. "Oh, so he wants a merry maid to go with his new cabana boy? Sorry. I don't do windows. Or filthy-rich scumbags."

He ignored her jabs, and his sincerity was almost her undoing.

"Why are you doing this?" she finally asked. "What does he have that you can't resist?"

He shook his head and swallowed hard.

"Not talking?" she confirmed. "Then I'm not staying."

Not that she would consider staying in any case. She was a free woman. A strong woman. She would start over again, somehow, with or without him.

"Look," he said. "There are some things I'd like to tell you, but I just can't right now."

"I understand." She didn't have a clue. "Well, it was fun while it lasted," she said in a voice that was far too cheerful for anyone to mistake as real. "The sex was great, but you and I both know that's all it was. It's not like we had a real relationship."

He stared at the hand she held out as if it were a two-headed frog. But then, knowing him, he'd probably seen a two-headed frog.

"You don't have to go."

"Yes, I do." She walked out and was halfway down the hall before she realized she'd made the grand exit from her own stateroom. Sighing, she climbed the stairs to the deck to wait out the hour until they reached Port Elizabeth.

Rachel swallowed the last bite of her dinner and dropped her fork to her plate, wiping her hands together. "There, I'm done. Let's get to work."

She'd not only eaten every bite of her salmon, with all of its healthy omega-3 fatty acids, DHA and protein, she'd also polished off the asparagus and rice pilaf it sat on in record time as well.

Nathan checked his watch. "I think you owe me about four more hours of sleep."

"I napped while you went out to get dinner." Actually

she'd tried very hard to conjure the dream visions she some-times had of her brother, but those were less predictable than the ritual visions that Nathan and Teryn and now Connor helped her create. She had less control of when they came and when they didn't. Tonight they didn't. "I have plenty enough energy for a ritual. A quick one," she amended.

He didn't look happy, but he pulled out the accoutre-ments of the pagan ritual and set the chalice—no wine tonight—and stone bowls in the center of the bed. He filled one bowl with water and the other with salt. Last, he laid out the velvet bag with a piece of lapis lazuli, then climbed up on the mattress and patted the space across from him. "Let's get this over with."

She settled in across from him. Their knees were almost touching, their hands stretched out between them, fingers interlocked.

"Ten minutes, no more," he warned.

"Fifteen."

He sighed. "Twelve and a half."

"Done."

She listened, let her mind drift as Nathan appealed to the god and goddess for their help, called the quarters and finally dropped the lapis lazuli into the bowl of water. She watched the surface of the liquid shimmer, refracting the lights overhead and the color of the stone, and finally made her own appeal to the goddess to be shown that which was lost.

Gradually her vision blurred and the water in the bowl became a much bigger body, the ocean. She prepared her-self for the horror of the storm she'd experienced before, the destruction of *The White Whale*, but it never came.

The day was calm. The waters lapped at the shore with gentle waves, and the sky overhead shone as bright blue as the stone in the bowl. She was transported to this other place, a harbor, though she still felt Nathan's strong grip on her hands, his strength flowing into her.

"What do you see?" he asked.

"A harbor. The one here in Port Elizabeth, I think."

"Is *The White Whale* there?"

"No." That would mean this was a vision of the past, since she knew the boat had already been destroyed, and she had a strong feeling this scene was of the present. It was too crisp, too clear to be otherwise.

"What about your brother?"

"I don't know. I—yes!"

Nathan's grip tightened. "You see him?"

"I feel him."

"How can you tell it's him?"

"I just know." Her breath hitched. There was no doubt in her mind that the spirit whose presence she felt in the vision was the same soul that she'd held in her arms all those years ago when they'd hid out in the closet under the stairs and she'd watched her parents die. Orphaned by their murders, the state had split up Rachel and Levi. Finally, finally she'd found her little brother.

Tears streamed down her cheeks, and these tears weren't caused by the hormonal tides of pregnancy. They were tears of joy.

The joy was short lived, though, as the force of his emotions hit her. "He's—sad. Full of sorrow, and grief. He feels torn between two things he wants."

"Can you see him yet?"

"No. I see . . . someone else. A woman. It's her! The woman I saw with Levi on *The White Whale*! She's walking down the gangway off the yacht. He wants to go after her, but he can't. Not without giving up something else very important to him. He wants her to come back. He hopes she'll come back, but she's still walking away."

Rachel followed the vision a moment longer, then snapped her eyes open and checked Nathan's watch, grinning like a fool. "Seven minutes, forty-two seconds. How's that?"

"It'll do." He cocked his head, clearly mystified. "You know where he is?"

"No, but I know where *she* is. She hailed a cab. I got the address."

Roman stood beside Levi as the woman's cab pulled away from the dock. He clapped a hand over his new toy's shoulder, plotting all the ways he would use Levi's power once he had control over it. "She made her choice."

"Yeah, just like I made mine." Levi's voice was rough, strained.

"Then let's get back to work. I have much to tell you and show you."

"If you don't mind, I think I'd like to take a break."

Roman's anger stirred, disliking the woman even more for distracting Levi even when she was gone. Plus, she knew too much about all of them, but most especially about Levi. It was hard to believe a human woman knew about his true nature and accepted it, but it mattered not. She had to go.

"Of course," he said, trying for a fatherly, understanding tone.

When Levi was gone, he waved Manny over. "Find out where she went and get rid of her. Make sure it looks like an accident." As he walked away he added, "And get me that pendant she wears."

TWELVE

Tasha had trekked up all three flights of stairs to the one-bedroom flat she rented in Port Elizabeth before she realized she didn't have her keys. They were with *The White Whale* on the bottom of the ocean, along with her friends.

Too tired to even contemplate retracing her steps to the ground-floor building-superintendent's office and calling a locksmith to come open her door, she flopped down on the stoop, drew her knees to her chest and buried her face in her forearms. Her chest shook and her muscles trembled, but she held back the tears.

She wouldn't cry over Levi Tremaine, and she wasn't ready to cry over the loss of her friends yet. She was still too raw over their deaths.

Heavy footsteps warned her someone was coming, and she quickly straightened her shoulders. Wouldn't want anyone to think something was wrong with her now, would she? Not Tasha Cole, the invincible.

Maybe whoever was coming would have a cell phone she could use to call a locksmith, but when she caught a glimpse of the face topping the stairs, she knew that wasn't going to happen. It was Manny Estes, and his presence here couldn't mean anything good.

She stood, sliding her back up the door and getting ready to bolt, but her flat was at the end of the hall. The fire escape outside her window wasn't an option, and there was only one other way out from here. Through him.

He sauntered toward her in an unhurried pace, as if he were enjoying the hunt. Now she knew what prey felt like.

Slinking along the wall, she tried to distract him so he wouldn't notice her reach for the knife she always wore in a leather case clipped inside the waistband of her jeans. "Hey, Manny. Did I forget something on the ship?" She had her fingers on it. Just needed to ease it out of the sheath. "Funny. I didn't think I had anything except the clothes on my back. So maybe you just came to visit, huh? Share a cup of coffee and reminisce about old times?"

There. She had it and he didn't seem to have noticed the movement.

She'd learned a long time ago that being defenseless was never a good idea. It was a lesson hard-learned, and she had the scars to prove it.

This time, she didn't plan to be the one coming away with the scars.

He was ten feet away. Eight. Six.

"Not a big talker, huh? That's all right. Conversation is highly overrated in my opinion."

Three feet, and she lunged at him about the same time he made a move for her. She got in the first strike, a deep cut across his forearm that spurted an arch of red blood across the peeling wallpaper of the hall.

"Tsk, tsk," she said. "The superintendent is not going

to like that. I hope you can pay to replace that wallpaper, because I sure can't, having just lost my only source of income and all."

"Bitch," Manny spat, blood seeping between the fingers he had clamped over his wounded arm.

"There we go, you do speak!"

As usual, her mouth got her in trouble. What had looked like cold rage on Manny's face turned hot in a flash. His forehead began to bulge and his whole body pulsed. He dropped to his knees, howling and hissing like a big cat, and in the next instant he was just that. A mountain lion, to be exact, with claws that were so sharp they shredded the hallway carpet with every step the beast took toward her.

She waved her knife at the creature, and it slowed its approach, mewling a clear warning. She and the big cat faced each other in a standoff, and then she heard more steps on the stairs.

"Hey, whoever's down there, call 911!"

The footsteps started running, but toward her, not away.

"No, don't come up here. Just call the cops, quick!"

The idiots didn't listen. A man and a woman hit the top of the staircase and stood there, taking in the scene. They were pretty calm for finding a mountain lion in their hallway, she thought. She expected screaming. Instead, the man stood in front of the woman and began a transformation of his own.

Oh, great. More of them.

This one was fast. She hardly had time to blink before his body had expanded to something similar to the mountain lion, only bigger. A real lion, maybe. An African lion. Only his head and neck were that of an eagle, with a deadly beak and eyes that saw everything at once. His front legs were thin and scaly and ended in six-inch talons. And wings, oh he grew wings that would probably have spanned the length of a bus if he'd been able to extend them, which he couldn't in the narrow hall.

A gryphon, she realized. Half lion and half eagle. She recognized it from the Harry Potter movies.

The absurdity of the situation almost made her laugh. Her life had turned into some demonic version of a children's fantasy series.

She waved her knife again. "Stay back, both of you."

Tasha had almost forgotten the woman was there until she spoke. "Don't. He's trying to help you." She pointed at the gryphon. "This one, anyway."

The giant half bird, half cat turned and hissed at the woman, warning her back with a flap of his wing. Then the two creatures were at it, rolling and clawing and gouging. The gryphon appeared to have the upper hand, and Tasha took the opportunity to make a break for the stairwell.

She grabbed the woman by the elbow as she passed. "Come on, we have to get out of here!"

"No! That's my husband!"

Husband? She looked at the way the woman's hand rested on a mounded belly and knew she was carrying a child. She glanced back at the fight on the floor. Husband?

She couldn't even wrap her head around that at the moment.

The dynamic duo rolled again, and the mountain lion—Manny—gained some purchase. His feline eyes locked on Tasha, and apparently seeing she was about to make an escape, he managed to disentangle himself from the other guy—creature—long enough to make a lunge at her, but he tripped over the gryphon's wing and instead slammed headfirst into the pregnant woman, sending them both rolling head-over-heels down the narrow stairwell.

*   *   *

"This time I want you to push the images into my mind," Roman ordered. "Start with something simple, something familiar like the pencil on the table here, or a tree."

They were back in Roman's stateroom sitting across the same small table where they'd held all their lessons, as Levi had come to think of them. He was thirsty for knowledge about his people, but to be honest, sometimes the sessions were tiresome. They often made his head hurt, and Roman had become more of a taskmaster than coach.

He tried to picture the pencil in front of him, really tried, but only one image locked into his brain. Her face. Her lips, her hair.

Roman snarled. "That's not a pencil."

"Sorry."

"This is a children's game for our people, Levi. You're not concentrating."

"I'm trying."

"You're pining after a woman."

Levi shoved back from the table. "I don't think pining is quite the right word for it."

Barely resisting the urge to go after her was what he was doing. Fighting to keep from reaching for the phone.

If it was really over between them, he at least ought to talk to her one more time, to try to end things better than he had. He owed her that much.

Hell, what he owed her was an explanation. He needed to tell her that he'd found his *people*—or they'd found him, though he wasn't quite sure how that had happened. He needed some time to learn more about himself. About where he came from and what he could do. It wasn't about choosing not to be with her; it was about choosing to understand himself. She had to understand that.

Yet he'd promised Roman he wouldn't tell her, at least not yet. The man had a right to his privacy.

He dragged a hand through his hair and rubbed the back of his neck, then sat down. "Let's try again."

Roman nodded in approval. "Now. A pencil. Focus. You have to focus."

A few moments later, Roman nodded. "Good. Much better. Now let's try something a little harder, moving images, like movies instead of still pictures."

"How?" Levi hardly dared breathe, afraid he would lose his concentration.

"Just think about the pencil moving. Picture it rising from the table and floating to my hand."

Levi furrowed his brow. He cleared his mind of everything but the pencil on the table. Imagining it rising on its own was like lifting weights with his mind. He broke into a sweat.

A moment later Roman swore and scraped his chair back. Levi opened his eyes in time to see the pencil clatter to the table. They both stared at it as if it were a venomous snake.

"How did you do that?" Roman asked.

"Do what?"

"Move the pencil."

"You didn't pick it up?"

"No. How did you do it?"

He frowned. "Am I not supposed to be able to?"

"Telegraphing images of something moving is much different than moving them with your mi—" Roman's head snapped up at the sound of a high-pitched screeching sound in the distance.

Roman's gaze followed Levi's out the window. "You heard that?"

Levi slumped back in his chair. "Am I not supposed to hear whistles, either?"

"We'll talk about this later." The old man rose and headed toward the door. "Right now I need you on the bridge. We're putting out to sea."

"Now? What about Manny?"

Levi didn't get an answer, but he figured his orders stood, so he got up and headed for the bridge. Guess old Manny had been replaced. By him.

THIRTEEN

"Oh my God!" Tasha ran down the stairs. At the bottom, she stepped over Manny, who'd returned to human form when he fell. His head lay at an unnatural angle. She knelt beside the pregnant woman. Her husband, also back in human form thankfully, was beside her before her knees hit the floor.

They both reached for her neck to check her pulse at the same time. Their hands collided. Tasha quickly pulled hers back.

The man raised his head long enough to nod at her, and then he brushed his wife's cheek gently with his knuckles. "She's got a pulse. Rach? Rachel, can you hear me?"

"I'll get an ambulance."

Tasha ran to the superintendent's door and pounded until she got an answer. After quickly explaining the situation—at least the parts she could explain—she waited for the super's wife to pick up the phone and dial 911, then headed back to the stairwell to see what else she could do to help. The super was right on her heels.

When she got to the downed woman, she stopped short. Manny's body was gone.

The super prodded her from behind. "Thought you said there was a man dead and the woman hurt."

The woman's husband raised his head. His dark gaze held a plea.

"He was just unconscious," the man said. "Bastard attacked my wife, knocked her down the stairs and then just got up and ran off."

"Hmmphfff." The superintendent looked scared to get too close to the injured woman. He backed away. "Well, paramedics will be here in a second. She don't look too good."

Tasha couldn't help herself. "Where'd you go to sensitivity school, Mr. Maycox, Callous U?"

With that, the superintendent turned. "I'll go out front and show the medics the way in."

She knelt by the woman again.

The husband checked her pulse. "Thanks," he said, and he wasn't talking to his wife.

"I should be thanking you. You saved my life."

He jerked his head sharply to the side. The sound of sirens filtered in from the front of the building. "We'll talk about it later."

Levi was checking hydraulic pressures and oil gauges when Roman came onto the bridge behind him. He hadn't expected to replace Manny so soon, and hadn't thoroughly familiarized himself with the *Spanish Dancer*'s controls. She was a lot more complicated than *The White Whale*, with her state-of-the-art computer-assisted satellite navigation, sonar, radar—all the latest toys—but he was figuring her out. Slowly. Right now his priority was making sure the ship was in good working order.

Wouldn't want another engine failure, would he?

Without so much as a "Hey, how's it going?" Roman asked, "Are there any other vessels in the area?"

"Don't have a clue." Levi tapped an engine temperature gauge and turned away, satisfied with the reading.

"Check the sonar."

"Yeah." He hiked up one corner of his mouth. "Wouldn't happen to have a user manual for that, would you?"

Roman practically shoved him out of the way and started punching buttons on the electronics console.

Levi watched over his shoulder. "I thought you didn't know how to work this boat."

"I don't know how to fix engines. Computers, I can handle." Roman hunched over the screen, studying it intently.

"Is there a problem?"

"I just want to make sure no one followed us from port."

"Why would someone do that?" Levi watched carefully as Roman shut down the sonar. He repeated the steps to himself silently, along with those used to power up the screen, so he could play with it later. Without the user manual.

"That sound you heard just before we left . . ."

"That screech, you mean?"

"It was The Calling. It's a way of warning each other of danger, or saying 'help' across great distances. With training, we're able to both send and receive a tone so high up on the frequency scale that humans can't pick it up. The Calling you heard was Manny."

His back stiffened. "Manny was in trouble and we just left him?"

"He can take care of himself, and your safety is far more important right now, to all our people."

"My *safety*? What the hell are you talking about?"

Roman's eyes were flat, gray discs, unreadable as he spoke in a tone just as devoid of emotion. "I'd hoped to spare you some of this, at least for a while. To wait until you were farther along in your training."

"Spare me what?"

"Set the autopilot," Roman ordered. He opened the door to the bridge. "Let's take a walk."

Nathan Cross, as he had introduced himself briefly during their mad dash to the hospital, was still sitting on the orange couch where she'd left him fifteen minutes ago, staring at the sheaf of papers on a clipboard the nurse had handed him, pen in hand but not writing anything.

Tasha held the coffee down at eye level and waved it slowly back and forth until he caught the scent and looked up. He set the pen down and took the disposable cup. "Thanks."

"No problem."

He took a long sip and grimaced, then set it down and picked up the pen again. "Goddamn paperwork. They want to know every country she's traveled to in the last year and how old she was when she had the measles." He shook his head. "How am I supposed to remember stuff like that at a time like this. She was pushed down a set of stairs for God's sake. What does childhood measles have to do with anything?"

Her heart went out to him. His fear for his wife and unborn child was etched deeply into the worry lines at the corners of his eyes and mouth. His dark hair was tousled and his clothes were dotted with blood spatter.

She took the clipboard from him, chewed her lip as she studied the form. "Your wife have any health issues?"

"Besides being pregnant and falling down a flight of stairs?"

She gave him a look.

He ran his hand through his hair again. "No."

"She's about thirty?"

"Close enough."

"On any medications?"

"Prenatal vitamins. Nothing else."

She checked the medical history form and found that he'd filled out the information on the pregnancy in detail. Everything else was blank.

She made quick work of the forms, circling yes or no in all the right spots, checking all the proper little boxes, then handed the clipboard back to him. "There you go, all done. It'll be two weeks before some clerk gets around to entering all that stuff in the computer where the staff can access it anyway. Until then, if the doctor needs to know something, he'll ask."

She walked the admission forms up to the desk and handed them to the duty nurse.

When she returned, Nathan was studying her over the rim of his coffee cup. "I was kind of surprised you were still here when the doctor finally kicked me out of the ER."

"After what just happened, I think right here, near you, is the safest place for me to be."

He glanced side to side, as if making sure no one was close enough to overhear. "You weren't afraid of what you saw."

"Hell, yes, I was. Full-blown freak-out, hair-standing-on-end, piss-in-your-pants afraid."

He almost smiled. "But you weren't surprised by it. You've seen . . . something like that before?"

"I've seen a lot of things." She didn't know how else to answer. How much to say. They were both dancing around the same big pink elephant in the middle of the room.

"On the yacht you came into the harbor on this morning?"

Her gaze snapped to his. "How did you know that?"

"I know a lot of things."

"Do you know why that man tried to kill me?"

"I might. Do you know a man about your age, dark hair, dark eyes? Used to work on a lobster boat."

"Half the men in Port Elizabeth fit that bill."

"His name is Levi, but he could be going by something else."

She schooled her face to show no reaction. She hoped. "Why are you looking for this guy?"

She expected the game to continue and Nathan to respond with the same bland expression, neither willing to give away all they knew. Instead she got genuine concern and a long appraisal, as if he were deciding whether or not to trust her. Finally, he blinked first.

"He's Rachel's brother, and he's in a lot of danger."

She was about to ask what kind of danger when the ER doctor walked up. Questions would have to wait as Nathan sprang to his feet, his attention focused solely on the man in pea green scrubs.

"Your wife has a mild concussion, Mr. Cross, but she's conscious and coherent, and there is no sign of subdural hematoma. Her left shoulder is sprained and she has quite the collection of bumps and bruises, but she's going to be fine."

Visible relief washed across Nathan's face. "And the baby?"

The briefest of pauses in the doctor's answer gave away his concern. "Him, we're not so sure about. It's wait and see for now."

FOURTEEN

Levi strolled along the deck with Roman, his enjoyment of the warm midday sun negated by the stiff north wind that wound beneath the collar of his coat and down his back. He kept his mouth shut, waiting for Roman to start his story, but the older man seemed in no hurry, pausing to prop his elbows on the deck rail and gaze off at the watery horizon.

"So what is this thing that you hoped to spare me from?" Patience had never been Levi's strong suit.

Roman sighed, and a part of him seemed to drift off toward the horizon to a time long ago and a place far away. "I told you, we're a proud race, and honorable people. We were created a thousand years ago to protect out towns-people. We live our lives in anonymity, still carrying out our original purpose, helping humans as we are able, protecting them. Contributing as productive citizens. At least most of us do."

"And the rest?"

"I'm sad to say that over the years, some factions have splintered from the traditional congregations of *Les Gargouillen*. They believe their heritage makes them somehow better than humans. They use their strength and their gifts to incite fear. To terrorize the very people they were created to protect."

Roman's voice was filled with heartrending sorrow over what he proclaimed as their people's dark turn, but the sentiment never reached his flat eyes.

"Our power, the ability to use our gifts, varies from man to man. Some of these traitors to *Les Gargouillen* are very powerful, but they fear the rise of someone stronger."

Roman laid a hand on Levi's shoulder. "You are the son of one of the Old Ones, my friend. One of the original souls transformed by the priest at Rouen. You alone have the power to crush them. They can't let that happen."

"Me? I can't even do the moving picture thing."

Roman smiled. "I haven't seen one of our kind levitate an object with just his mind in over six hundred years."

Levi's stomach had twisted as Roman's story went on. Evil Gargoyles bent on world domination. Ancient protectors of the human race—who also happened to be Gargoyles—trying to fight them off. It all sounded a little too science-fictiony to him. Too black and white.

"Who are these guys out to kill me? Where are they?"

Roman's hand tightened on Levi's shoulder. "They are many. And I'm afraid they are very near. While I was concentrating on training your mind, I neglected to keep my senses tuned to intruders. I believe they've been watching. They may be watching even now."

Okay, now Levi was feeling seriously on edge. "They can do that? I mean, we can do that?"

"It's possible, through the Second Sight."

Levi frowned.

"It is an advanced skill," Roman added. "But one I am sure you will master quickly. In the meantime, I will take precautions for both of us. The Second Sight can be blocked by another Gargoyle if he is diligent enough. Come inside, I'll tell you about it."

Levi shrugged away from Roman's hand. "Yeah, that sounds good. Maybe later. Right now, you know what I'd like to do? I'd like to take a swim."

A long, hard, cold swim in the middle of the friggin' Atlantic Ocean, to clear his mind.

He knew the words now, though he still didn't know their meanings, if they even had any meanings. Knowing the words made the process less painful, he found, and made the transformation—or Change, as Roman called it—complete much more quickly.

> *E Unri Almasama*
> *E Unri Almasama*
> *Calli, Calli, Callio*
> *Somara altwunia paximi*

Before the last verse ended, he was over the rail and in the frigid North Atlantic. Over an hour passed before he forgot about whistles that only Gargoyles could hear and pencils that moved by themselves and bad guys that could change into monsters that wanted to kill him, righteous martyrs that wanted to save the human race—without telling the human race.

Funny, but all his life he'd dreamed that there were others like him in the world somewhere. Now that he'd found them, all he wanted was to get away from them for a little while.

*   *   *

Tasha stood self-consciously in the doorway, watching Nathan and Rachel's reunion. The love they shared spilled over into the very air around them. It choked Tasha, watching them whisper to each other and stroke each other's faces and hold hands, and it warmed her at the same time. She remembered her mom and dad acting that way a few times, but that had been a long time ago. So long ago that she wasn't really sure if they were real or just a little girl's imaginings.

This, what Nathan and Rachel shared, this was real.

For a moment, watching them, she almost wished . . .

No. She slammed the door on that thought. She was what she was. A loner by both choice and necessity.

Rachel Cross looked over to her. "Come on in. I'm Rachel."

She eased closer to the foot of the bed, her hands clasped together in front of her. "Tasha Cole. I'm sorry about . . . what happened."

"I'll be fine." She looked down at the bedsheets and laid a hand over her abdomen. "We both will."

Tasha nodded. She hoped it would be true. She really did.

"Well, at least we now know my brother has good taste." Rachel squeezed her husband's hand then gazed back at Tash. "You're lovely."

Tasha looked down at her battered deck shoes, the faded jeans and oversized green sweater she'd been wearing for days—at least they'd been washed again before she left the yacht—and wondered if they'd been giving Rachel the good drugs. Probably not, with the baby and a head injury to complicate matters, so maybe she was just a good liar.

Or a really good person.

"Tell me about my brother, please."

Tasha's shoes squeaked on the tile when she shuffled

her feet. "Yeah, can I ask you about that first? Levi never mentioned a sister."

"I'm sorry, I thought you knew," the woman on the bed explained. "Our parents were killed when he was just a—" Her hand stalled where it had been circling her belly in a light, comforting rub. Her fingers trembled before she took a deep breath and continued. "A baby. My brother and I were adopted separately. Because the adoption records were sealed, it took me years to find out where he'd been placed, and by the time I did, he wasn't there anymore. He'd run away. I've been looking for him ever since."

"No. He never . . . he never told me."

"Maybe he didn't know himself. His family may not have told him he was adopted," Nathan offered.

Rachel smiled. "In that case, he's got quite a surprise coming."

"I'm sure he'll be thrilled." Tasha thought he would. A few days ago, she would have been sure of it, but he'd changed since he'd met Roman DuValle.

"Nathan tells me you know about Levi's special abilities."

"Yes." Her shoes squeaked again. This time she planted her feet and made them stay still. She studied Rachel. "Are you . . . like your husband?"

Nathan chuckled and squeezed his wife's hand, answering for her. "No, that's kind of a guy thing."

"Oh." She wasn't sure she wanted to know any more than that. "You said Levi was in danger."

The air in the room grew heavier. Rachel let out a deep breath. "Yes. There are people out there—people like Nathan and Levi—who want him for his power."

"Levi is very special, even among our kind, but he's grown up outside of our society. He doesn't know the history of what's happening," Nathan added.

Creases folded around the corners of Rachel's mouth. "I can't imagine what it must have been like for him, not understanding his abilities, thinking he was alone."

Tasha had some inkling. She knew his haunted eyes.

"Do you know where he is now?" Rachel asked.

"Not exactly."

"But he was on the yacht with you."

She hesitated, unsure how much to trust these people she barely knew. She did know, though, that on the *Spanish Dancer* she felt cold and in constant threat. Here she felt warm. Welcome.

"Yes," she admitted.

Rachel sat up straighter, her excitement visible. "Do you know the name of the ship, the harbor and slip number where it's docked?"

She gave them the information.

"They'll be long gone," Nathan warned his wife. "Romanus knew the instant his hit went bad. He would have pulled up stakes and set sail within minutes."

"I can find them," Tasha jumped in. "I know a lot of ships' captains in this area. Someone will spot him."

Nathan and Rachel smiled at each other. "That would be a big help, thanks," Rachel said.

"What will you do once you find him?"

"Get a message to him. Help him get out of there," Rachel said, and cleared her throat.

Nathan lifted a glass of water with a straw in it from the nightstand and held it for his wife to drink. "It won't be easy. Romanus will have filled his head with lies, tried to turn Levi against us. And you can bet he's heavily armed."

She nodded. "Automatic rifles, and . . . some really wicked-looking old stuff."

Nathan's faced darkened. "You saw all this?"

Tasha nodded.

"We can't afford a gun battle," Rachel said. "Levi could get hurt."

"I could get a message to him," Tasha said before she even realized the possible consequences of what she proposed. "I could tell him what you told me. He would believe me."

"It's too dangerous," Nathan warned.

"Levi won't let them hurt me."

"You don't understand," Nathan said. "These people have powers you've never dreamed of. They can manipulate minds, plant false memories, watch you even when they're miles away. They can communicate with each other, at least on some level, without speaking, they can manipulate the weather and—"

"Wait!" Tasha cut Nathan off. "Manipulate the weather?" Suddenly she felt dizzy. She felt sick. "Oh my God, the storm. The night *The White Whale* sank. I knew it wasn't natural. The whole thing felt . . . evil. Is it possible this Romanus guy sank my boat, killed my crew just to get to Levi?"

"Not just possible," Nathan said. "Probable. He would have known Levi could survive in the water no matter how rough the seas. He probably even thought it was an amusing test to make sure he was the real deal."

Tasha's chest locked up. "I'm going."

"It's too risky," Rachel said.

"With you or without you," Tasha clarified. "The son of a bitch killed three of my crew. I'm not letting him have another. And there *will* be paybacks for the others."

"See," Nathan teased. "She already sounds like one of us."

Rachel didn't laugh.

Nathan looked at his wife a long time before he spoke. "Teryn and I could help her with some veiling spells to keep Romanus from poking around in her dreams."

"Uh, did you say *spells*?"

They both ignored her. "This is not a good idea, Nathan."

"We could give her some slightly enhanced memories to throw them off the track if anyone gets curious about what happened at her apartment building."

"Listen to me." Rachel enunciated as if she were speaking to a child. "Not. A. Good. Idea."

He squeezed her hand. "It may be our only chance."

"There you go." Tasha cracked her knuckles, having no idea exactly what she was getting herself into, but knowing it felt more right than anything had in days. "Haul out the cauldron, cook me up, hook me up, zap me up with the memory maker. Wrap me up in some protective veils and let's do this. Roman DuValle is going down."

FIFTEEN

Levi had taken to swimming every evening, just about dusk, if only to alleviate the boredom. The *Spanish Dancer* was a sweet ship, smooth as a baby's bottom under his hands when he was at the controls. The problem was, it was so damned automatic that there wasn't much for him to do but stand there. He was used to working a boat. Cursing her and sweet-talking her and begging her. Hauling rope and throwing net, sometimes wanting to kiss her and sometimes wishing he could kick her right in the pistons.

Good boats were like good women. If they were too easy, he got bored with them fast.

That's why he and Tasha had lasted more than two years—she was never easy and never boring.

Levi gave his mighty tail a swish and glided along, with an underwater current pushing like a strong tailwind. A school of yellow fish in his path broke to either side.

Don't worry little fishes, the big bad sea monster is not going to eat you today.

Not unless you somehow end up in a frying pan back on the *Spanish Dancer*.

A burst of air that sounded surprisingly like a sigh gurgled out of his gill slits. Sometimes he was tempted to head out to sea and just keep going. Better yet, to turn toward shore and go find Tasha.

Exploring his skills, mental and physical, was fascinating, but the lessons required extreme concentration. Last week he'd mastered the control to access memories of some of his past lives, and he'd been fascinated by his life as a sailor in the 1850's royal navy, and as a river rat in Scotland before that.

No wonder he resembled Nessie, the Loch Ness monster. Maybe she was his mama.

Absurd as it was, the thought made him smile and lightened his mood enough that he could face going back to work. The last couple of days, on his way back, he'd slipped into this little fantasy that Tasha would be waiting for him when he got there.

Stupid, he knew. God, he was a sap, but these days, any little sliver of hope that kept him going was a good thing. He'd gotten so used to picturing her standing there on the deck, waving to him as he climbed on board, that when she was actually there this time, he almost wrote her off as a figment of his imagination.

Only she wasn't standing alone, and she wasn't waving. Roman DuValle had her by the arm and was dragging her toward the diver's ladder on the aft end of the *Spanish Dancer*, where a Zodiac raft was tied at the water level. The trawler that must have launched the Zodiac trailed the *Spanish Dancer* a quarter mile back.

Tasha struggled to escape, and DuValle tightened his grip, nearly pulling her off her feet.

Levi ducked underwater to avoid being seen by the two men in the raft—fishermen he knew from the pubs in port, she must have talked them into taking her out looking for the *Spanish Dancer*—but swiped his tail just beneath the surface hard enough to send a plume of sea spray over the railing, sending the raft rolling hard enough to knock the men inside overboard, and drenching Roman—and Tasha.

Tasha sputtered, and when she saw him climb onto the deck, narrowed her eyes at him accusingly, then glanced to the side to see that the men were safely climbing back into the Zodiac, none the wiser. "Was that really necessary?"

Levi stood between the two of them, Tasha and Roman, feet spread shoulder width apart and arms hanging loosely, but ready, at his sides. With exaggerated deliberation, he turned his back on Roman and focused on Tasha. God, she was a sight . . .

"You okay?" he asked, each word sharp as a scalpel.

"Fine."

She'd no sooner than finished the clipped response than he spun. He had more questions for her, but those would wait until he could talk to her in private. Until the memory of Roman's hands on her faded. Until his heart stopped thundering with fear for her and his fingers weren't unwillingly clenched into fists. For now, he turned his focus on Roman like a fine-beamed laser. "What the hell is going on?"

The bright red spots were already fading from Roman's cheeks. Didn't take the bastard long to regain his composure.

Roman pulled his back up straight and patted down the soaked collar of his thousand-dollar, tailor-made linen dress shirt. He, too, looked over the side of the ship at the sailors flopping around in the raft, but Levi doubted the man was concerned about their safety.

"Perhaps we should take this conversation somewhere . . . more private."

Perfect. Levi was feeling just wound up enough to enjoy going mano a mano with Roman. His animosity was quickly building toward rage. Funny, just days ago he'd given up everything of the life he knew to follow Roman, to learn who and what he—*they*—were. Now a restlessness had set in. The feeling that something wasn't quite right, but he couldn't put his fingers on what.

He nodded toward Tasha. "Wait for me in my stateroom."

"Oh, really?" Her eyes flashed, water still clinging to her long lashes. "Are you sure you didn't mean 'off to my bed, wench'?" She waved her arm grandiosely.

He hooked one eyebrow. "If that's what you want me to mean."

Her lips rounded into an O. For a moment he honestly thought she was going to kick him in the shin.

Like mist burning off the water under a morning sun, his ire faded, replaced by humor for her, and cold determination for the man behind him.

"Wait for me downstairs, please."

He saw the debate raging in her head. Saw her decide. She gave him a clipped nod, waved at her buddies in the Zodiac to signal them it was okay to leave, and stared at Roman through narrowed eyes as she passed by him on her way to the hatch leading to the living quarters.

When she was gone, he followed Roman to the great room, shaking off the need for physical battle his body had so recently craved and preparing for the battle of wills he knew lay ahead.

* * *

"She can't stay." His back to Levi, Roman used a set of silver tongs to pick two cubes out of the ice bucket and drop them into a crystal tumbler. He measured two shots of scotch and poured them on top for himself, then two in an empty glass. The old man had finally figured out he liked his whiskey neat.

"She doesn't have anywhere else to go," Levi countered. "She lost her boat and with it her only way of earning a living. All while she was saving your ass, I might add."

He thought the little guilt trip added a nice touch.

Roman took a sip of his drink and handed the glass without ice to Levi. "This isn't about my ass. It's about your dick."

Levi's fist clenched around the glass.

"I have to give you credit, though. She's a feisty one. I'll bet she's good—"

Levi was on his feet in one smooth move, his nose about a quarter inch from Roman's, his breath hot on the man's face. He didn't say anything. He didn't have to.

Roman raised his glass in salute and took a step back.

Ding! Ding! Round one to Tremaine.

Levi sat again, and Roman took his usual place in the opposite chair. A pounding started behind Levi's eyes. Why was it every time he entered this room, his head ached like he'd just woken up after a three-day binge?

Roman chuckled, swishing his glass so the ice clinked against the sides. "I really have been negligent in having the Gargoyle version of the birds and the bees talk with you."

"I think I'm a little beyond that."

"No, you're not. You see, one of the things I left out of the story of the first transformation at Rouen was that the priest wanted more than just the few of us there in that one village. He wanted a population that would grow and thrive to protect humans everywhere. So he created us with two directives: to protect humans and to propagate."

Levi downed the last swig of his liquor. "Is this little fairy tale going somewhere?"

Roman leaned forward and propped his elbows on his knees. "I'm sure he had no idea his simple words would result in the intense sex drive bred in us today, but as women became less inhibited and therefore more available through the ages—" He shrugged. "Well, it is what it is. You're young. You don't want to tie yourself down to just one woman. There are lots of fishes in the sea, as the cliché goes."

"Keep trying there, Roman." Levi pushed to his feet and set his glass in the bar sink. On his way back, he paused to spin one of those perpetual motion desk ornaments and watched the glittering silver rings go round and round. Like this conversation. "I'm sure you'll eventually hit on some reason I might want to send her away."

He was kind of liking this turn of the tables. Until now, Roman had been the one in control, the one making the decisions. Now Levi was beginning to see he had power over the older man, too. The bottom line was, Roman needed him more than he needed Roman. He knew what he was now. He knew what he was capable of doing, though his skills needed a lot of sharpening.

He knew he wasn't alone in the world.

"She'll distract you from your training," Roman complained. "You're making such progress! You need to stay focused."

Levi almost laughed. "I'm sure I'll be able to keep that intense sex drive of mine in check for at least a few hours a day."

"All right, then think about her."

"I am thinking about her. A lot."

"She could be hurt. I told you we have enemies."

"Enemies I have yet to see, despite the fact you keep claiming they're watching us."

"Just because you haven't seen them doesn't mean they are not there. They would go through anything, use anything, to get to you. Including her. She could already be compromised, either knowingly or unwittingly."

"A minute ago you were worried they might hurt her to get to me. Now you're accusing her of being a spy?"

"Ah!" Roman swung his arms up in a gesture of surrender. "You have no idea what you're up against."

"You're the one who keeps telling me I have all this power. We're safe for now, out here in the middle of the ocean. I'll keep learning. I can protect her."

Roman hung his head. "She's a liability."

"Then she's my liability." He was through. He headed for the door.

"Levi—"

He spun on his heel. He needed to get out of there before his head exploded. "I chose you over her once, Roman. I won't make the same mistake again. Either she stays, or I go. Your call."

A sigh of defeat was the only answer he needed.

One down. Now he just had to go toe-to-toe with Tasha and it would be a clean sweep.

Heading down the hall to his room, he steeled himself for his toughest opponent of the day.

"All right, Tash. Quit talking crap. Why are you really here?"

Damn him, he hadn't been back in his room more than a minute, and he'd already called her bluff.

She put on her best southern belle affectation and fluttered an imaginary hankie as if cooling her cheeks. "Whaw, whatevuh do you mean, kind suh?"

"You didn't come crawling back here to kiss my ass and make up. I know you better than that."

Double damn. Nathan had warned her to go slow, not to reveal too much too soon. He'd impressed on her that DuValle might be messing with Levi's mind, and he might not believe anything she told him, like how Manny had tried to kill her and how Levi's sister and brother-in-law had saved her. She needed to get some idea what bill of goods Roman or Romanus or whoever he was had sold Levi before she blurted out the truth. But he wasn't giving her much choice. He wasn't going to accept anything except a straight answer.

That didn't mean she couldn't call a few bluffs of her own before she gave it to him.

She jutted her chin toward the top of his head. "I came to see how far gone you are."

"What?" The single word cracked like a whip.

"You know. If you still had balls or if he'd cut them off. How your knees were holding up with all the—"

"Sorry to disappoint." He cut her off before she finished the taunt and loomed over her. "But I'm still just the pilot of this multi-million-dollar tub. The only thing I *service* is the ship."

"Mmmm." She spun away from him with a flamboyant turn, wiggled her behind a little and stretched out on her side on his bed.

"You didn't come here to have sex, either."

She winked. "Well, not *just* to have sex, anyway."

"What do you want?"

"I missed you." Her heart kicked as she said it. Too much honesty was not going to help here. "And I wanted to

find out what kind of bullshit lies DuValle has been feeding you."

Levi's jaw ticked. "He owns the boat. I drive the boat.
That's the extent of his bullshit lies."

She leaned in close, her lips an inch from his, and traced
her finger along his jaw. "Now who's talking crap?" she
whispered.

She spun away. When he opened his mouth to respond,
she cut him off. "I want to know what kind of hold DuValle
has on you to keep you here."

"Besides a good job, a clean place to sleep, plenty of
booze and three meals a day—gourmet?"

"I don't think that's it. I know you better than that.
You're a survivor. You don't need his money or his fancy
yacht. It has to be something bigger than that."

"And what would that be?"

She turned serious. "He's hiding something, Levi, and
he's playing dangerous games."

"Oh, please. Not the drug dealer/gunrunner tirade
again."

"No, those things wouldn't keep you here, either. I think
Roman offered you the one thing you couldn't refuse."

He folded his arms over his chest. "Oh, do tell. Please."

"He offered you an explanation. An understanding of
what you are, what you can do."

He swayed back. His breathing went quick and shallow.

"How the hell did you come to that conclusion?"

"I've come to a lot of conclusions in the last few days,
Tremaine. Like the fact that you're not one of a kind. There
are more like you. Lots more."

"How the hell do you know that?"

She continued answering his first question, ignoring the
second. "Like the fact that your new mentor is using you."

"He hasn't done anything but help me. He's teaching me—"

"He's feeding you a bunch of lies. Everything he's teaching you is wrong, a fairy tale orchestrated to make you trust him."

"I've seen for myself—"

"You've seen exactly what he wanted you to see—images he fabricated and used his Gargoyle powers to *teach* you about your history out of the kindness of his black heart."

Levi did a double take, shook his head. "How do you know any of this?"

She drew a steadying breath, ready to make her final argument, and hoped he was ready to hear it. "The same way I know that Roman is not the noble protector of the human race he claims to be. He is a magician—a master of dark magic who—"

"He's my father."

Her breath stopped. Who was she kidding? Her *heart* stopped. "*Son of a bitch!* That's what he told you?"

He sat—nearly fell—to the edge of the bed, pinching the bridge of his nose, his face furrowed in pain.

She eased down next to him. "He's playing you, Levi. Everything he's told you is a lie."

He shook his head. "I've seen. I've felt the power. He's taught me to use it, to do things I never thought—"

"I'm not denying that you have power that's hard for a mere mortal like me to understand. I'm just saying he's put his own spin on it." She trailed her fingers over his shoulder. He really didn't look well. "And he's not your father."

He turned his bowed head toward her. His eyes were bloodshot, pained. "How do you know that?"

She laid her head against him, felt the comforting rhythm of his heart. "Because I've met your real family."

SIXTEEN

"*What do you mean, my real family?*" Levi's heart kicked the walls of his chest, and he jumped to his feet, immediately regretting it when a wave of dizziness hit him. The headache was back with a vengeance.

What kind of game was she playing? Who had put her up to it? And who the hell had cracked his skull with an axe?

"You might want to sit back down," she said.

Instead he paced the length of the room. Hands clasped in front of her, she sighed from the berth. "Okay, I'll sit. This could take awhile. You have a sister."

"Who told you that?"

"She did. You mean you knew?"

He nodded. She slapped the mattress and pulled one knee up to rest her chin on it. "Well see, now we're getting somewhere."

"When I turned twelve, my parents told me I was

adopted. That my biological parents had died in a fire and that I had a sister, but they didn't know anything about her. I tried a few times on those Internet websites to find her but never got any matches."

"Turns out she was looking for you, too. But by the time she found out where you'd been placed, you were gone."

A lot of bad memories rose unexpectedly. The confusion of those tween and teenage years when things started to happen with his body that weren't part of the normal puberty process. "I ran away when I was fifteen."

"So I heard. How come you never told me?"

"We never did a lot of talking."

"Mm."

No. They were usually occupied either fishing or . . . doing other activities that involved a fair amount of heavy breathing but not a lot of talking. Maybe Roman wasn't telling fairy tales with that whole sex-drive thing after all.

"Did you ask Roman about that?"

The question pulled him out of memories of some of the times they'd spent not talking. He raised his head, trying to follow her line of thought. "About what?"

"How he's here when he supposedly died in a fire."

Levi frowned. "No." How could he not have asked about that?

Probably because the headaches muddled his brain.

Tasha's expression brightened. "By the way, your sister is married to a really nice guy named Nathan, and they're going to have a kid in a few months."

"My sister is pregnant?"

"That's usually where kids come from. She had some trouble a few days ago, and they thought she might lose the baby, but they're going to be fine. She was spotting some, but it was just some broken blood vessels, not a tear in the placenta like they thought at first."

"That's good." He didn't have a clue what she just said. "I guess."

"Very good. Maybe you could go visit her when we get back to Port Elizabeth, or something."

His hackles went up. A new possibility took root in his mind and wouldn't die.

"How do you know you aren't the one being played, Tasha?"

"How so?"

"These guys—people like me—have ways of finding out a lot of things. They could have found out about my sister and decided to use it against me." Roman's warning that their enemies would use anyone to get to him rang in his ears, along with his warning that Tasha could be compromised. "They could have gotten any poor preggo girl, put her in the hospital with some sob story about almost losing her baby in order to get me there. It could be a trap."

"It's not a trap, Levi."

"How do you know?"

"Because I—" She shook her head. "I just know. They're good people. I liked them! And they saved my life."

His gaze jumped to hers. "Saved your life?"

"When Manny tried to kill me."

Levi swore, looking away. "Roman said there are some of our kind who would do anything to keep me from learning more about what I am. Maybe Manny worked for them, was some kind of spy."

It didn't make much sense, but the pressure in his head seemed to ease as he thought it. Almost as if it was pushing him to that conclusion.

Doubt clouded Tasha's green eyes.

Levi sat heavily on the bed and scrubbed his face with his palms. He didn't know who to trust, including her, and he hated that. "Come 'ere," he said and pulled her into his arms.

"What are we going to do, Levi?" she murmured against his shoulder. "Everything is so friggin' messed up."

He kissed her forehead and tugged at the hem of her sweater. "Tonight, we're gonna do some not talking."

Levi decided he'd like to return the "gift" of Second Sight for a full refund. Which would mean he'd pocket exactly nothing, he reminded himself.

Over the last couple of days, Second Sight training had become the bane of his existence. He'd rather scrub the head.

Roman frowned at him. "Concentrate on the shiny surface of the silver tray, there, where the light reflects off of it the brightest."

"Yeah, yeah. Let your vision blur until the light becomes a tunnel. I got that part. But when we get to the part about thinking about the place you want to see, my tunnel keeps zinging off wherever it pleases."

Maybe what he needed was some proper motivation. Something a little more exciting to see than the perpetual motion machine Roman had left spinning on a table downstairs for him to practice on.

Tasha had said she was going to the exercise room when Levi came up for his training . . .

He took a deep breath and blew it out slowly, then went through the steps one at a time. Concentrate on the shiny surface. Blur vision. Let the light become a tunnel. Think about the exercise room. The exercise room.

The tunnel bounced around like a Mexican jumping bean at first, making him nauseated. But when it landed, lo and behold, there she was! Or there he was, as if he were standing right in the room watching her.

She was lying on the padded bench in bike shorts and a spandex tank top. Thank God for spandex. The pewter pendant he'd given her lay in the hollow of her throat. It pleased him that she still wore it. It meant something.

She palmed the weight bar she held just over her breast-bone. A pretty serious cache of iron hung on each end.

She drew in a breath, her lovely chest rising, a fine sheen of sweat visible in the valley that disappeared beneath her top. Then she blew the breath out and pushed the bar away from her body.

He really should remind her she ought to have a spotter for that exercise. He'd volunteer. The view would be even prettier from directly above her.

As if on command, the perspective of his Second Sight shifted until he felt as if he could reach down and touch her shoulders. It was strange and cool at the same time, know-ing he could see her but she couldn't see him.

He'd tell her later, just so he didn't feel like such a perv.

She lowered the bar and repeated the exercise. He loved the way her lips curled a little with the effort and veins stood out in her neck, looking perfectly edible.

He must have shown some sign of pleasure, because Roman suddenly crashed the party.

"What are you looking at? You are not focusing on the perpetual motion machine in the galley, are you."

Before he could stop himself, he accidentally shot Roman a flash of the scene playing in his mind.

"I told you. I *told* you!" Roman strode in a circle, flap-ping his arms like a strange mechanical bird. "She's been here two days, and you've already lost focus. You've lost all focus!"

Levi grinned, breaking the line of sight to the exercise room. Reluctantly. "I did it, Roman. I had a good stable connection. I could see everything, perfectly."

"Yes, yes. I know exactly what you were seeing perfectly."

"Hey, it worked, didn't it? You should be happy."

"Happy. Be happy." Roman stalked off.

Pleased with his success, Levi decided to try again. This time, the connection was much smoother.

Tasha was getting off the bench, toweling herself off. She leaned over to wipe down her legs, and he sighed in pure pleasure paradise.

He'd accomplished his goal and gotten a sneak ogle. He really should leave her alone now. But he watched a second longer.

She leaned over again to put the towel in a canvas bag. When she straightened up, she had something in her hand. She looked around as if to see if anyone was watching, then flipped open a small electronic device.

"Shit!" Levi was out of the chair and rounding the corner to the exercise room in thirty seconds.

She froze when she saw him charge through the door. He never slowed down, covering the room quickly and grabbing the device from her hand.

She lunged after him, reaching. "Give it back!"

He stiff-armed her and studied the device in his other hand. "Text pager? Out here?"

"It's satellite, not cellular based." She continued trying to reach around him. He easily held her off. "It works anywhere."

"Cool."

"Give. It. Back." She stopped fighting, breathing hard. "Please give it back. It isn't mine. I have to return it eventually."

He found the menu button and flipped through the options until he found the inbox and outbox. He wanted to see who she'd been texting.

And what she'd been saying.

Unfortunately, both were empty. Either she hadn't used it yet or she was meticulous about deleting the messages.

"Return it to who?" he asked, slipping it into his pocket.

She chewed on her lower lip.

"Roman was right. You are spying on me."

The knowledge hit like a hammer blow to the chest.

"I am not spying."

"Then who were you texting?"

She chewed on her lip again. "Your sister."

"And how is that not spying?"

"She just wanted me to check in with her. She wants to know if you're okay, Levi. She wants to talk to you, to meet you. She's searched for you her whole adult life—and wait a minute. How did you know I was sending a message?"

Her eyes widened. "*You* were spying on *me*! Using one of your Jedi mind tricks."

His breaths were coming slower now, deeper. "It's not a trick; it's called Second Sight, and I wasn't spying I was . . ."

Great. How did he explain what he'd been doing?

A change of subject was definitely in order. "Do you know what Roman would have done if he'd found you using that?"

"No."

"Well . . . me neither. But you wouldn't have liked it, I know that much."

She at least had the good grace to look contrite. "What are you going to do?"

Hell if he knew.

"Right now, what I think I'm going to do is lock you in our room and . . . go for a swim. A very long swim."

"You wouldn't." She crossed her arms over her chest.

He lifted her chin with one finger. "Watch me."

Rachel turned her new satellite text pager over and over in her hand.

Nathan sat down on the bed next to her with the sandwich he'd brought her from the deli on the corner east of the motel. "She hasn't checked in yet?"

"Not yet."

He took a bite of her tuna sandwich and then passed it over to her. "Do you think she's okay?"

"I don't know. Maybe they found the pager. Maybe she just can't get away from them long enough to use it without being seen."

"Should we page her?"

He licked a bread crumb off his lower lip. "No. If it went off when someone else was around, she'd be busted."

"Maybe we should call Teryn and perform a ritual. Try to see if she's okay."

"No way." He lay his hand over the mound that held his son and pretended he could feel the heartbeat. "The doc may have released you from the hospital, but you and Junior are still recovering. Besides, Romanus might detect our magic, and it would be as sure a giveaway as the pager."

"So she's really on her own then."

"We have Connor as close as we can get him in a boat without being detected." The cavalry, Teryn, Connor and his wife, Mara, had arrived the day after the accident to help look after Rachel and to strategize what to do about Tasha and Levi.

"But, yes," Nathan finished. "Basically she's on her own."

SEVENTEEN

Sitting on the edge of their bunk, Tasha measured each heavy step as Levi paced the length of the room and back again. They'd called a truce for now, but sooner or later, they were going to have to resolve the issues between them—namely trust, or the lack of it. She'd expected Levi not to trust Rachel or Nathan at first, but she'd never thought he would doubt her.

"There's only one way to solve this, you know?"

"What's that?"

"You need to meet them yourself, your sister and her husband."

"Oh, yeah. I'm going to walk right into that setup."

"What if you pick the place and time. You could make any arrangements you want."

"Fine. Have them come out here."

She rolled her eyes at him. "Any arrangements except that."

"Look, even if I wanted to, it wouldn't be easy." He waved at the plastic pager case on the table. "It's not like there's a Stop-n-Go on the corner where we can meet. We're at sea. We'd have to wait until we got back to port."

She threw her hands up. "Jesus, this isn't a yacht. It's a floating prison!"

"There's a lot at stake here, Tash, including his life and ours. He's says all the security is for our own safety."

"Mmm, I bet he does." She crossed her arms. "And you buy that?"

"No," he said and sat next to her with a sigh. "I'm not saying I believe Roman is the evil magician trying to brainwash me that you make him out to be, but I admit, I think there's more going on here. He's not telling me everything."

At last, an admission that Roman DuValle might not be the shining bastion of hope for the Gargoyle race that he pretended to be.

"But he's not kidding about the danger, Tash," he warned. His face twisted. "He showed me scenes from a battle a few months ago. These others he's so worried about attacked a group of his people. They were . . . massacred."

"Nathan tells me these images can be fabricated. Or at least manipulated."

He shrugged. "I know only what I saw. But I know it's not something we want to get caught in the middle of. Or cause. We need to be careful."

"We will be. Just tell me you'll think about it."

He blew out a deep breath. "I'll think about it." His brows drew down. "When we get back in port."

She barely contained a gleeful squeal, settling instead for throwing her arms around his neck and giving him a big smack on the kisser.

* * *

Levi sat in his usual seat at the round table in the great room, staring out at a matte blue sea. Even the sun had seemed undecided what to do the last few days, appearing on and off to light up the water like crystal, then sliding back behind a mask of clouds.

The rhythm of the ocean was hypnotic, and he let his mind drift. Indecision rolled through his thoughts in waves as constant as those slapping the side of the ship.

Roman DuValle had shown Levi that he was not alone. He was teaching him what it meant to be one of *Les Gargouillen*, and Levi was devouring that information like a starving man at a buffet dinner. His skills were getting stronger every day. He didn't want to give that up. Didn't want to go back to being alone.

But he was seeing only one side of what Roman painted as a very bleak picture. Levi had no way to verify anything Roman told him. It wasn't as if he could get on the Internet and search "Gargoyles" to get the straight story. He had no way of knowing if Roman was telling him the truth or feeding him lies.

On the other hand, he had no reason to believe Roman's intentions were anything other than genuine. Roman had shared his knowledge freely, helped Levi develop abilities he hadn't even known he had and asked nothing in return.

Yet.

Roman was his teacher, his mentor. But Levi stopped short of calling him his friend. He couldn't help but feel like there was another shoe somewhere, and one of these days it wasn't just going to fall—it was going to kick him in the ass. Tasha's doubts certainly didn't help the feeling.

Maybe they'd both just gotten so used to being dealt bad

hands by fate that they couldn't believe it when a little good fortune came their way.

Or maybe Roman just wasn't ready to let on yet what he was really after.

The older man slid a sheet of plain white paper across the table toward Levi and turned it over, watching his reaction intently. But watching for what?

"What does this mean to you?" Roman asked.

Levi shrugged at the symbol sketched in heavy pencil on the page before him. "Nothing."

"You had it made into a necklace for your girlfriend."

Levi's hackles stood. "She's not my gir—" He caught himself. Well, hell. He guessed she was his girlfriend at this point. The thought struck him odd. Their relationship had never veered toward the Friday-night dates and flowers on Valentine's Day cliché. It was more . . . visceral.

He sat back in his chair, studying the symbol again. "It's just something I used to doodle as a kid."

"Where did you first see it?"

"I don't know that I ever *did* see it."

Roman raised his eyebrows like gray wings. "Perhaps not in this life."

A knot coiled slowly in Levi's belly.

"I've told you our people reincarnate, Levi."

"Yeah, if they have a kid and do the whole propagate-the-species thing." They had skimmed the edges of that conversation a number of times, but Levi hadn't pushed his mentor for too many details. He hadn't gotten used to the idea of having a girlfriend yet. He definitely wasn't ready to start considering the need to father a child.

"You've lived many lives, in many places, my friend. You see them in your dreams, don't you?"

He swallowed hard, remembering the thundering hooves,

the wind whipping the sails of great ships of old. "Sometimes."

"Perhaps this symbol meant something to you in a previous life."

"I have no idea."

"You will. Our children are taught how to recover the
memories of those past lives. To preserve our history."

"Yeah, well they didn't offer that class in my grade
school."

Roman smiled so wanly that his lips were almost flat.
"You can recover them now. Stare at the symbol. Relax
your mind. Let it bring you to it. To its origin."

The paper blurred before Levi. The air in the room grew
heavy, hot. His own breath rasped in his head as if a large
animal were whispering in his ear.

"What do you see, Levi?" Roman's voice spilled across
the table like syrup, slow and quiet.

"A forest." God, it was working. He felt different, knew
he was himself, but he wasn't. He was another version of
himself. One bigger, older. More tired.

"What else?"

"Rocks, a cliff. A lake at the bottom with a waterfall
tumbling into it." He raised his mental gaze and squinted
at the bright light, felt the last tepid rays of the day wash
across his face. "The sun setting over the waterfall."

"What else? Go deeper." Roman's voice trembled. Levi
couldn't remember ever hearing such urgency in one of
their lessons.

He took a deep breath, blew it out slowly and seemed to
float along on the current of air he loosed. Over the water,
up, up the rocks.

The temperature changed and his skin grew tight in reaction. The light faded to black.

"What? Where are you?"

"I don't know. A dark place. I hear the water running nearby. It's cold. It's damp." Levi flinched and opened his half-lidded eyes wide. He was back in the stateroom across the table from Roman.

He frowned, his heart still beating too hard, his breath coming too fast.

"What happened?" Roman's words shot out like darts now.

"I don't know. I . . . I lost the connection."

"Concentrate again. You must focus."

"No." Levi skidded back his chair and stood, dragging a hand across his face.

"You must!"

"No!" Spears of pain shrieked through Levi's temples. Wincing, he marched to the bar and helped himself to a shot of whiskey. The fire in his throat eased the pain in his head. "No more lessons tonight." He set the glass down with considerably more control than when he'd picked it up.

"Tomorrow, then."

Conciliatory? From Roman? What the hell was so important about a dumb symbol?

But he knew. He felt the chill in his veins. The dark place, it was a place of power. Power so immense it was a presence in and of itself. Unfathomable. Incomprehensible to his human mind.

But not his Gargoyle mind.

"Maybe," he allowed. He wasn't sure he ever wanted to go back there.

He strode toward the door, intent on getting a couple of Advil and hitting the sack, but he stopped. He'd come to this lesson with a purpose tonight, one other than learning magic tricks. He couldn't leave until he fulfilled that purpose.

He turned at the door.

"Why now, Roman?" He sure as hell wasn't going to call the man *Dad*. "Why did you come looking for me now, after all these years?"

Roman steepled his hands. "I've been looking for you for many years, using every power I have. I only recently found you."

"How *did* you find me?"

"I've spent years developing the skills to extend the Second Sight. To reach out beyond even the limits of one of *Les Gargouillen*'s senses."

"Why? If you wanted me with you, why pretend to be dead all these years? Why let me be adopted?" The bitterness in his own words surprised him. He'd thought he'd gotten over that hurt, that sense of abandonment, a long time ago.

"I told you, I was trying to protect you. You were young, and you would have been a great prize to our enemies if they knew about you. I never planned to let you go forever. I planned to come for you, but—"

"But when you did, I was already gone. I ran away."

"Yes." Roman's sigh almost sounded genuinely sad. Almost. "I'm sorry for that. I know it must have been difficult for you, growing up and not knowing—"

"Difficult not knowing why you heard voices in your head and dreamed of lives you'd never lived? Difficult watching your body change into something not human, not being able to control it? Yeah, you could call it difficult." Levi's laugh sounded like a wire brush on tin. He smoothed his hair, subtly checking to see if his hand was shaking. "Hell, don't worry about it. I got over all that years ago. Why doesn't really matter, I guess. What I want to know is how specifically you found me. How did you know where *The White Whale* was, and how did you know I was on board?"

He had this nagging feeling that there was so much more his kind were capable of that Roman wasn't telling him. Didn't want him to know. He felt like a warrior caught blindfolded in the middle of a raging battle. He didn't know which direction to heft his sword.

Sword? He'd taken this past lives thing a little too far.

"I've told you that our kind can sense each other. Usually the range on that sense is quite limited—a hundred yards or less for most of us. But your mind is so strong that I sensed your presence from miles away. I knew immediately who and where you were, it was all there to be seen in your untrained mind. I knew I had to find you."

"So that you could train me."

"So that you wouldn't live your life without knowing what you are, and so that you might become an ally."

Ah, there it was. Roman's true purpose. "You want me to join your fight."

"I want you to know the good of what our people can be. What you choose to do about the bad is up to you."

"So once I learn all you can teach me, I can just walk away if I want?"

Roman flattened his palms on the table. "You can walk away from this ship, if you like. But you can't walk away from what you are. Eventually one of the others will find you, as I did, if they aren't stopped. Eventually you'll have to decide which side you're on."

Levi had a feeling that decision might be coming sooner than even Roman knew. And right now, he didn't have enough information to decide what color shirt to wear tomorrow, much less cast judgment on who was good and who was evil in the world.

He wanted to leave, but he still wasn't done.

Roman studied him. "Your mind is troubled."

Troubled. Yeah. That would be the word.

"Well, spit it out."

"I do have one more question." He met Roman's serene gray eyes with his own pained gaze, jammed a hand in his pocket and turned the satellite pager over and over in his palm. "After you . . . *left*. What the hell happened to my sister?"

Roman bought some time to consider his options by digging the box of cigars out of his desk and lighting one up. Handling his young protégé had become a tricky matter, and a matter of some concern. Levi grew stronger every day. It was a continual source of frustration that even without training, Levi's ability to shield his mind was so strong. Roman couldn't divine what was going on in that stubborn head. And maintaining his veil over the truth, so that Levi couldn't see into his own mind, grew more difficult with each training session, even in the spiritual circle of the great room. Soon he would be beyond Roman's control at all.

He needed to make sure he had Levi firmly in his court before that happened.

He sighed heavily and swirled the amber in his glass. "Sadly, I had to let her go. For her own good."

"Let her *go*?"

"She was adopted as well."

"You found me. You can find her."

Roman shook his head. "No. It would be too dangerous for her. The females of our kind don't possess the powers the males inherit. Think about it. We were created in a time before feminist activism. It would never have occurred to our creator that females could contribute to the protection of the human species. She would have been defenseless against our enemies. A target, and a liability."

"Liability?"

"If our enemies got her, she could be used against us. It was safer to let her go." He added a wistful note to the last, but at the same time he pushed one more brutal wave of control into Levi's mind. The younger man's face paled. He reached out to steady himself against the doorjamb.

"You don't look well, Levi. Perhaps you should rest."

Levi nodded but stood his ground. "One more thing," he said from between clenched teeth. "We're running low on just about everything. Pretty soon we're going to have to head back to port to resupply. And I don't know about you, but I could use a little shore leave."

Roman tucked the cards into a drawer at the bar. "What a coincidence. I was going to suggest we head to port tomorrow. Right after we run a little errand."

"An errand in the middle of the Atlantic?"

"We have a few guests coming on board. I'll give you the coordinates in the morning. Once we have them, we'll head to Cape Sim."

"Why Sim?"

Roman smiled pleasantly. "We have friends there. And it's time you met a few of your brethren."

Levi was gone, clutching his stomach as if he might vomit, before Roman got a good look at his reaction. The boy was too full of himself, thinking he could pull something that blatant over on Roman. He was up to something.

Never mind. Levi would learn his lesson. This one would be a lesson in motivation. Why he needed to commit to allegiance with Roman.

He spread a dollop of caviar on a cracker.

He would let Levi play out his little scheme, see what he was up to.

Then he would give Levi a taste of just how deadly an evil Gargoyle could be.

EIGHTEEN

❧

"Where do you think you're going?"

Kolyakev, the tall Russian with unruly black hair, stepped in front of Levi from his guard position at the top of the gangway. At least one of the two Russians who had come aboard from the freighter the *Spanish Dancer* had met at the coordinates Roman had provided Levi the day before yesterday had been on watch at the entrance and exit to the ship since they'd moored that morning.

New recruits to the cause, Roman had explained. They were the only others of his kind he had met other than Roman and Manny. He'd sized them up as he watched from the forecastle as they climbed on deck, and he had written them off as muscle. He wouldn't learn much from them.

Except, perhaps, whether the foreign muscle was keeping watch to make sure no one got on the ship without permission, or to make sure no got off.

He pulled Tasha closer to his side, his arm draped around

her waist, and took his sunglasses off so he could look the man in the eye. Kolyakev didn't intimidate him. He was a big guy, but he was a little soft in the middle. "Not that it's any of your business, but I'm going to the boat shop."

"What for?"

"Piston casings. I'm afraid our friend Manny didn't take very good care of his engines. The casings and about a dozen other parts are shot to hell."

Kolyakev shrugged his soft round shoulders. "Call a mechanic."

"I am a mechanic. And I have no desire to sit around three days waiting for some dickhead shore lover to work us in to his schedule. Look, I told Roman I was going to do some maintenance while we were in port. It's a done deal."

Kolyakev looked uncertain at the mention of his boss's name. "You wait here," he finally said. "One of us will come with you."

Levi rolled his eyes and pulled Tasha closer. "Great, then after we get the casings and I take my girl for a stroll down the boardwalk, maybe buy her some cotton candy and get our lips all sticky, you want to come along for that, too? Maybe we can find a bench big enough for three and you can sit in the middle."

Kolyakev still looked undecided. Levi took on an irritated tone. "Look, it's broad daylight and there are people everywhere out there. What do you think is going to happen? Some big, bad Gargoyle is going to come swooping out of the sky and carry me off?"

The dark-haired man brooded over that another moment, and Levi continued to stare him down until grudgingly, the man moved out of the way. "You don't wander too far. Come right back."

"Yes, mother," Levi said as he and Tasha passed by.

It was about a half mile out of the marina, then another

hundred yards or so to the dilapidated tin building that housed the local marine parts store. Levi ducked in and bought a couple of piston casings just for show, then took Tasha's hand in his and headed toward town.

He offered to hail a cab, but Tasha said she'd rather walk, and he agreed. The breeze was cool and the crisp air seemed to blow away a haze that had grown thicker around him every day he'd been aboard the *Spanish Dancer.*

They reached the center of town about thirty minutes later and stepped into the hubbub of the busy boardwalk. It was a tourist trap to be sure, with T-shirt vendors every twenty feet and ladies at folding tables selling genuine handmade Atlantic seashell jewelry they'd probably ordered from Taiwan hawking him to come and buy the pretty earrings for his lady. After the relative quiet isolation of the yacht, the mill of people seemed abnormally noisy to him, chaotic and distracting. But it was the perfect place to set up a meet—open, good visibility, a nice crowd to disappear into if he needed to.

They strolled in silence for a while, hand in hand, soaking in the sights and sounds, the smell of fried fish and brine. He checked his watch every few minutes and timed it so that at precisely four thirty they stood just north of the cotton candy stand with the neon palm tree flashing yellow and green that he remembered from his last visit here.

He stopped and studied the stand and the people nearby, reaching out with his senses, searching for any sign of danger, of deception.

At first he felt nothing, but as he recalled what Roman had taught him and sharpened his senses, their presence registered gradually, like an airplane, a speck in the distant sky slowly coming into view.

"There they are!" Tasha pointed, and he pulled her hand down. "They got the text!"

He saw them then, the woman with dark hair falling over her shoulder in thick waves and a man next to her. Even through her thick coat, the bulge of her pregnancy was evident. When she saw him, her hand clutched over her heart, and for an instant his mind brushed hers. Not enough to decipher images, just a sense of two Gargoyle minds acknowledging each other for what they were. But how could that be?

Women weren't supposed to have any of the Gargoyle abilities, according to Roman, yet he recognized her as one of *Les Gargouillen*. Different than the others he knew, not as strong as the man beside her, his arm draped protectively around her shoulders, but definitely Gargoyle.

He was still trying to decide what that meant when he felt a sudden, powerful presence behind him. More Gargoyles. Thinking it was a trap, that someone was moving in behind him while his *sister* blocked his escape from the other direction, he whirled, tucking Tasha behind him and backing toward the edge of the boardwalk.

"What?" she asked. "What's wrong?"

A black Ford Expedition trolled slowly down the paved road off to the side of the boardwalk. Tinted windows kept him from seeing how many were inside, but he sensed several distinct minds.

One of the electric windows rolled slowly down. Levi stiffened, ready.

Roman poked his head out and waved them over, all smiles.

"What are you doing here?" Levi asked when he reached the truck.

"We have dinner plans, remember? With our friends? I thought I'd save you the walk back to the boat and pick you up on the way."

Levi stared at Roman a moment, trying to read his

expression. Had the man known what was going on and interrupted the meeting intentionally, or did he just have exceptionally bad timing? It would be easy for a Gargoyle to miss the touch of his sister's gentle mind, but surely Roman would have sensed the presence of her husband if he'd been paying attention at all.

Finding no answer in the matte silver eyes or complacent smile, he climbed into the car, pulling Tasha in after him. Gregor, the second Russian, was behind the wheel, and Kolyakev sat in the third seat behind him.

"No cotton candy?" the Russian asked in a deadpan droll.

Levi just turned his head away. He looked up to the cotton candy stand as they pulled away, but his sister and her husband were nowhere in sight.

Roman's friends lived in a cottage on the bluffs that overlooked Cape Sim harbor. The outside seemed effeminate for four men, with its light blue paint and scrolled cornices, but the inside was stereotypically bachelor. The couch and chairs were dark leather, the coffee table deep cherrywood. A massive entertainment center, complete with a big-screen television and video game console, overwhelmed a tiny living room.

The house was tidy, but she wouldn't call it homey. There were no pictures of family, no rumpled afghan in the corner of the sofa, no trophies from long-past bowling tournaments, no slippers kicked off at the door. Just tables and lamps, a small stack of firewood piled neatly next to the marble hearth and a plain clock gracing the mantle.

The place was functional . . . yet stark.

It also had the same heavy feel as the *Spanish Dancer*. Tasha had gotten so accustomed to the thickness of the air on the ship that she hardly noticed it anymore, but after just an hour off the yacht, walking the boardwalk with the breeze coming off the sea to lighten her step—and her heart—the oppressive air in the house weighed on her more than ever.

Levi didn't seem to feel anything, though. He'd been openly wary when they'd first arrived, but the four men who lived here had drawn him out of his shell over dinner. He seemed especially taken with the youngest resident, Calvin, who they'd been told was sixteen, but who looked more like thirteen with his fair skin, light hair and guile- less smile.

"So, Cal," Levi asked during a break in the dinner con- versation. "You got a girlfriend?"

Calvin's cheeks turned red. "No, sir."

"You kidding me?" Levi swallowed a forkful of green beans. "Good lookin' guy like you? Why not?"

"Umm . . ." Calvin looked to his dad for help, his cheeks gaining a notch on the color spectrum. Poor boy was never going to be able to hide a reaction with a complexion like his.

Calvin's dad was named Marshall, she remembered. He reached over and laid a hand on his son's forearm. The table went quiet.

"Not all human women are as . . . understanding as yours about our differences," Marshall said. "It can be dif- ficult for a boy."

Levi studied Cal thoughtfully. "Yeah, I guess I kinda forgot what it was like at that age."

Tasha wondered what Levi had been like at that age. Probably tall and rangy, like him. All gangly limbs and at- titude. But she couldn't imagine him blushing.

She wondered if he'd had girlfriends, and decided he had not. He'd been an angry young man with a big secret when she met him. He'd had women. He was too sure of himself the first time they'd made love to have been a virgin. But she doubted he'd have let anyone get close enough to him to call her a girlfriend.

Hell, he'd never even called *her* his girlfriend.

Calvin looked over at Levi again, and she thought she saw a hint of hero worship in his eyes. "So you ran a fishing boat before you met Mr. DuValle?"

Levi cut her a sideways glance. "Technically Tasha ran the boat. I was just the first mate."

"And you were a poacher? You stole other people's fish right from under their noses?"

"Calvin." Marshall cut his son off.

The boy's eyes sparkled with excitement. Their lives must have sounded like a pirate tale to him.

"It's all right." Levi smiled.

Apparently taking that as encouragement, Calvin continued. "You didn't know you were a Gargoyle. You never heard of us?"

"No. I didn't grow up with others . . . like us." He arched one eyebrow. "Although I did begin to suspect I was different from most people the first time I sprouted a tail."

Calvin giggled, then laughed outright. The rest of the table soon followed suit, all except Tasha. She hadn't found much to laugh about growing up thinking she was a freak.

"We've got to tell you, then," Calvin said when the chortles died down.

"Tell me what?"

Calvin shrugged. "Tell you what it's like to be a Gargoyle."

Levi looked almost as taken with Cal as Cal was with him. Who'd have guessed her big, tough sea monster was a sucker for kids?

"I'd like that," he said.

Roman scraped his chair back. "Why don't we retire to the living room for the storytelling."

"Good idea." Marshall stood and gestured to the other room. "You first, Levi."

The other men and Calvin left the room after Levi and Roman. Since no one bothered to look back to see if she was coming, much less invite her, she kept her seat at the table, surveying the mess of dinner plates and platters and sticky silverware.

What, did they expect the little lady to stay behind and do the dishes?

Well, bugger that!

Wadding her linen napkin up, she left it at her place and slipped out the back door. Leave the men to their guy-talk. She'd rather get some fresh air anyway. The meal, pot roast, potatoes and beans, had been wholesome, yet unsatisfying. Like the house, it left her a little queasy.

About a hundred yards beyond the back door, the Cape Sim bluffs fell to the sea. Hugging herself and wishing she'd taken the time to get her coat, she wandered toward the sound of the sea.

Tonight hadn't gone as planned. She'd been sure that once Levi met Rachel, he would see the truth. But that hadn't happened.

Very convenient, Roman showing up at exactly the right—or wrong—time.

Now how was she going to get Levi and his sister together? If anything, after tonight Levi seemed even more ingrained with Roman DuValle and his cronies.

Levi was smart, though, and he'd begun to question Roman's real intentions. If he'd had the doubts to set up one meeting with Rachel and Nathan Cross, he would set up another.

Tasha sat near the edge of the bluff. Probably too close,

but she didn't care. She was feeling a little dangerous to-night. She had that tingly feeling, like something was going to happen. She just hoped it wasn't another seizure.

The sound of the waves lulled her, took away some of her disquiet, until she realized that the sound she was hearing wasn't just surf slapping against rock. There was another rhythmic sound mixed in. A heavy whoosh and thump. Several thumps.

She looked down the coastline, searching for the source of the sound. Against the clear night sky seven black shapes appeared—no, eight! She couldn't see them well enough to make out their shapes other than odd bodies and long wings. The whooshing grew louder. She could feel the heavy thumping vibrate in her ears.

They were coming in fast, and without bothering to question how she knew, she knew they were coming in to kill.

NINETEEN

Levi practically pulled Tasha off her feet, yanking her through the back door. She'd tried to shout a warning, but he already knew. They all knew. They'd sensed the others' approach.

Levi had nearly gone crazy when he'd run into the kitchen to get Tasha and found her gone. For a moment he thought she'd been taken already, that he'd lost her. Then he'd seen her running toward the house from the bluffs, and had seen the dark shapes of the beings in the sky behind her.

"Holy Christ!" Her momentum carried them both into the wall. He held her there for a moment, their bodies pressed together, hearts frantically lunging for each other. "Are you all right?"

"Something's coming!"

Some*thing*. Not some*one*.

Her green eyes were wide. Shocked.

"I know." He ran his hands over her shoulders. There was no time for more. "Get in the living room. Get under cover."

"Levi. Come on. We must go." Roman's voice boomed through the house, calm authority in a sea of chaos. But what the hell was he talking about. They couldn't leave now.

"It's too late," Levi called back, on Tasha's heels as she hurried into the room where the other men were gathered. Two of them had already changed, one into a hyena-looking creature with six-inch fangs and a single upturned tusk in the middle of its snout. The other towered over his companion, raking the air with the claws of a bear while screeching through the beak of some sort of predatory bird. The third man, Stephen, checked the magazine in an automatic pistol.

There's the smart guy, he thought.

"Do you have any more of those?" he asked. His sea monster form wasn't going to be much use in the living room of a cottage. He needed some other way to defend himself.

Stephen shook his head, and Levi swore.

Outside, a horn honked.

"We must go, Levi," Roman said. "That's Gregor with the car."

Levi lifted his head, listening. The sound of wings was close. "No time. It's too la—"

Glass shattered, and a blast of cold air and rage roared through the room. A large shape looking more like a two-hundred-pound rat than anything else Levi could put words to flew in through the broken window. The Gargoyle took out Stephen before the poor man could raise his gun. Razor claws shredded the shirt across Stephen's chest, and one talon got his neck, spewing a fountain of blood onto the carpet.

Levi tackled Tasha and rolled with her across the floor to relative safety—for the moment—behind the couch. Roman sank to all fours and became the wolf, snarling and snapping at the air around the flying beast, but not able to get a good hold.

More Gargoyles sailed into the room, flying creatures of every species. The bear-bird leaped up and snagged a giant crow out of the air. They crashed to the floor in a tangle of fur, feathers and claws. He couldn't see what happened to the pig, but the squeal of a dying swine could be heard in the din, and Levi knew Paulo had lost his battle.

Tasha squirmed beneath him. Levi adjusted his weight to let her breathe. When he lifted his head, he saw Stephen's gun, the barrel sticking out from under the front corner of the sofa. He crawled forward, reaching, and wrapped his fingers around the butt of the weapon just as a dark shadow loomed overhead.

"Shit!" Levi rolled and fired in one motion, putting three rounds through the heart of the bat about to behead him. The flying rodent fell still, laying over Tasha's legs.

"Get it off me! Get it off me!" She kicked and squirmed, trying to free herself.

Levi leaned over and helped her roll that bat away, then put one more bullet between its beady rodent eyes for good measure.

Armed and ready now, he took her hand and together they crept to the edge of the sofa. To his left, Roman was still snarling and snapping at the air, fending off the crow. The pig lay gutted on the hearth, but the bird-bear, though bleeding from multiple wounds, had his thick arms wrapped around a flying horned thing Levi couldn't even name and his fangs sunk into the creature's throat. A moment later, the horned bird slumped motionless to the floor.

Marshall, in human form, used the break in the action to pull a panic-stricken Calvin, who was slipping half-in, half-out of his Gargoyle hyena form toward the kitchen. Levi covered the kid, wounding another bat as it joined the fray. Then Roman was beside him, growling and tugging his pant leg as if to drag him toward the back door. Kolyakev was shoving him the same direction from behind.

The back door slammed open, and Levi whirled, gun raised, but it wasn't one of the flying murderers. Gregor stood on the stoop, hair flying and eyes wild. He had blood on his hands. "We're clear for the moment. But we've got to go *now*."

Levi moved back toward the living room. "We can't leave the others. We've got to help—"

With a nod from Roman, Kolyakev grabbed him from behind, catching him in a headlock before Levi could duck. He dropped the gun.

Tasha jumped on Kolyakev's back, pounding his shoulders with her fists. "Hey! Hey, what are you doing? Let him go!"

Kolyakev shook her off like a fly, and Gregor joined the struggle, grabbing Levi's legs.

"What the fuck?" Levi yelled and kicked, but it was no use. The two bigger men had him out the door and were shoving him in the backseat of the car, and there was nothing he could fucking do about it.

From the house, he heard screams. One a man and the other higher pitched.

"Jesus!" he screamed. "The kid. They've got the kid!"

He made one more try to lunge out the door, but the Expedition's engine roared, and instead of diving out, he barely had time to pull Tasha in before the tires slung gravel and they tore out of the drive.

A thud on the roof had everyone looking up, but Gregor fishtailed right, then left, throwing the Gargoyle clinging to the roof off onto the side of the road.

"Back to the boat, Gregor," Roman ordered, then gave Levi a hard look. "When we get there, we're putting out to sea. Immediately."

Rachel Cross lay in her husband's arms in a dark hotel room, wishing it was morning. Wishing she could do something, anything, now to find Levi.

She'd seen her brother tonight for the first time in more than twenty years, since she'd been a child and he'd been an infant. Since the night their parents were murdered.

He'd looked every bit as strong and handsome as she'd imagined him to be. She'd been so close. A few more minutes and she could have talked to him. Held him. Told him how long she'd looked for him, how hard. She could have cried on his shoulder for all the years they'd lost and laid his palm across the mound that held his nephew, yet to be born.

Those dreams had been crushed in the blink of an eye when Romanus had rolled up. How had he known? What had gone wrong?

"You have to face facts, Rach," Nathan rumbled in the dark. "Levi may have told Romanus about the meeting. It could have all been a setup."

"No." She was sure. Sure of her brother. "He was as surprised as we were. Did you see the look on his face?"

"Are you sure you didn't just see what you wanted to see?"

"Positive."

Nathan shifted, sighed against her neck and traced his palm over their baby. "It's time for you to go back to Chicago."

"No." She stiffened, rolled her head to look at him. His eyes were closed, his face a mask of pleasure as he stroked their child.

"I'll keep trying to make contact," Nathan said. "But it's too dangerous for you here. Romanus is too close. I might not be able to protect you." He patted her tummy. "Both of you."

"And you and Teryn and Connor and Chase and Hunter are all here, too. We protect each other."

He sighed against her neck. "Have I ever won an argument with you?"

"No." She combed his hair back with her fingers. "But I might let you sometime next week." He peeked at her out of one eye, and she grinned. "If you let me stay."

"A day. Maybe two. No more."

She opened her mouth to counter but was stopped by a high-pitched whine that made her wince. The noise seemed to be coming from all around her, and from inside her own head, and was joined by several others.

She and Nathan bolted upright in bed.

"The Calling," he said.

She got up and was belting her robe when Teryn rushed in from the adjoining room. A moment later Nathan had thrown on a pair of jeans and let Connor in while the man's fist was still raised to knock.

"Trouble," Connor said.

Rachel looked from one man to the other, dread a fist clenched around her heart. "What if it's Levi? What if he's in trouble?"

Nathan shot Connor a look that Rachel knew contained a message between the two men. Damn Gargoyles and their secret mind games.

"We'll check it out," Nathan said.

"I want to go." She had to go.

"No way," Nathan said in a tone that brooked no argument.

"He's my brother!"

"And you have no idea if he's even involved in whatever is happening." Nathan raked his hand through his hair and then grabbed a shirt from the dresser. "Teryn and I will go. We can get there quicker by air."

He turned his attention to Connor. "I don't care if you have to tie her to the bed, you make sure she stays here."

"Done," Connor answered.

Nathan took a half a second to acknowledge how drastically his relationship with Connor had changed. Six months ago he wouldn't have trusted the man to take his garbage out. Now he was leaving everything that was holy to him in Connor's care.

Connor had earned that trust.

"We'll call you as soon as we know anything," Nathan said. Then with a nod to Teryn, the two men sprouted wings and took to the sky.

TWENTY

Tasha sat in her stateroom with her face buried in her shaking hands for a long time, trying to understand what she'd seen tonight. Trying to forget it.

She hadn't led a sheltered life. She'd seen brutality before. She was no stranger to violence. But, my God, the carnage . . . Those poor people.

Shuddering, she stood. She had to find Levi. He had come out of the car with fists flying, but Gregor and Kolyakev had half shoved, half dragged him down the dock, their eyes on the sky as if they expected another attack any minute, and he had finally given in and grudgingly put the ship out to sea when they'd argued that if the evil Gargoyles found him, they found her.

Levi, she reminded herself, grounded herself. He hadn't come back to their room after they'd left port. She had to find him. If she was in pain from what they'd seen tonight, his suffering would be far greater.

She found him on the bridge, alone, thankfully, standing like a statue before the wheel.

"Are you okay?" she asked, stepping quietly up beside him.

He answered her, but his body was motionless, his face expressionless. It scared her. "I can't get that kid's face out of my mind."

"There's nothing you could have done."

His head snapped toward her, and she was glad to see the anger flaring in his eyes. Even anger was better than that emptiness. "I had a gun and nine more bullets. There's a hell of a lot I could have done. Damn those goons for dragging me out of there. That kid needed us. He needed help, and we fucking left him to be slaughtered."

"Guess Roman isn't your hero anymore, is he?" She regretted the words the moment she spoke them.

The rage in his eyes turned cold. "Is that what you think this is all about? That I'm infatuated with Roman and I follow him around like a little puppy dog, begging for bones?"

She cast her gaze away.

"Believe me, I never thought he was the pope," he continued. "I just don't care what kind of secrets he's keeping or games he's playing. Hell"—Levi threw his arms wide— "I don't care if he's fucking Ted Bundy in a miniskirt. All I ever wanted was to know what I am. *Why* I am. He's given me that."

He laughed, but it was a sickly sound devoid of humor. "You know what? You know what is really crazy? Now that I know, I wish I didn't. I wish I'd never heard of *Les Gargouillen*. Now that I know what *my people* are capable of, I wish I could go back to just thinking I'm some freak of nature. A one-of-a-kind cosmic joke."

She dared to reach out, touch his arm. The muscle

bunched under her fingertips, but he didn't shove her away. "Levi, you are one of a kind. But you're not a freak. Or a joke."

"No, no. I guess not. There's sure as hell nothing funny about what happened tonight."

"No."

He pulled her to him, wrapped her in an embrace. After a long moment, she felt some of the tension in him drain away. The emotion was still there, but now it was merely simmering beneath the surface instead of boiling over.

"God, I was scared they were going to hurt you," he said against her neck. His breath was warm and moist and reminded her what it was like not to feel the bone-aching chill of fear that had settled in at first sight of those flying . . . things, and showed no signs of warming.

She rubbed his back. "We were both scared."

Cupping her elbows, he set her back a few inches. "What if they followed us, Tash? What if we led the bastards right to the house?"

She didn't understand at first. "What if who follow—" His meaning dawned on her, and she shook her head sharply. "Your sister and her husband are not responsible for this."

"Then who is?"

"I don't know. But I know it wasn't Rachel and Nathan."

He let her go and turned back to the instrument panel and the wheel. "I wish I had your faith."

"You will, once you've met them."

"How is that going to happen now? We're back at sea, and after what happened tonight, I don't think Roman is going to be willing to dock again anytime soon."

She stepped up behind him and wrapped her arms around his waist. With her hands splayed across his chest, she kissed the back of his neck. "I don't know how, but I know you'll make it happen. You have to, because no matter what you wish, Pandora's box has been opened. You know about the Gargoyles. Now you need to hear the whole truth about what, and who, you are."

He picked up one of her hands and kissed the palm, then slipped from her grasp and engaged the autopilot. "I don't know about the whole truth," he said as he turned to leave the bridge, "but I know that what I need tonight are some answers."

*Romanus was waiting for Levi in the great room, sip-*ping a glass of wine and thumbing through a tattered copy of Milton's *Paradise Lost* when his young pupil stormed in.

"You're disturbed," he commented and got up to pour Levi a drink.

"Disturbed?" Levi raked a hand through his hair, pausing a moment to tug at the roots. "I watched four people get ripped apart tonight, one of them was just a kid. Yes, I'd say I'm a little *disturbed*."

"I told you this battle was a vicious one. Our enemies are swift and deadly. They have no conscience, no compassion. They have no heart." He mixed a little something extra in Levi's glass, but Levi set the wine aside without drinking it.

"I need to know what the hell happened tonight. Why were those people attacked?"

"They were Gargoyles who followed the traditional path. They protected humans and abided the laws of their congregation. That is reason enough for the others to want to destroy them." Romanus sat and propped his feet on the ottoman.

"Why did you run?"

Roman looked up, his brows arched. "I did not run,

Levi. I protected you. Because if you had been killed, many more like them will die. Your power is our one great hope. You are our only chance to destroy the others and restore *Les Gargouillen* to the honorable race they were created to be."

Levi sat heavily. "What if I don't want to be anyone's great hope?"

Roman went and got Levi's wineglass, brought it to him and Levi drank. "Picture that boy's face. What was his name? Calvin. Picture Calvin. If he were standing before you now, could you ask that?"

Levi bowed his head, and Roman knew he'd scored a direct hit.

"I need to see," Levi said. "What happened to them. My Second Sight is still a little shaky." He raised his head and said the words Roman had waited so long to hear. "Will you help me?"

Levi rubbed his temples while he waited for Roman to come back with some things the man said they needed. A dull throb had started behind his eyes, and he knew from experience it was likely to expand into a bass drum beat before the night was over.

Roman walked in with an armload of stuff and began setting it on the carpet in the middle of the room, then sat himself down cross-legged next to the goods he'd laid out.

Levi walked over and looked down. "What's all this?"

"Tools of the trade, my friend."

He eyed the assortment of junk. "What trade would that be?"

"Sit." Roman pointed at the carpet on the other side of his treasure trove.

Levi did as asked, albeit dubiously.

Roman straightened his back and took a deep breath, signifying a lecture to come. Another lesson. Great. He really wasn't in the mood tonight.

"These items, arranged in this way, form the ritual altar for a pagan ceremony."

Levi's jaw dropped. "You're kidding, right?"

Roman raised one eyebrow.

"Okay," Levi said. "Are we going to sacrifice a virgin now, too? Or does that come after the dancing leprechauns?"

"Mock me if you must, Levi. But what you have learned here so far is only a fraction of the powers of the universe. As Gargoyles were created by magic, so some of us have studied that magic and use it to expand our abilities far beyond what was given to our people so long ago."

"You're serious about this, aren't you? You think a couple of candles, a gold cup, a bag of rocks, some incense and a bowl of"—he stuck a finger in the bowl and tasted the coarse white grain—"salt are going to give us some kind of superpowers?"

"Those very things have already given you powers you would once have considered super." Roman rearranged the objects between them, scooting each one a little left or right, a little closer or farther away. "Look around you."

Levi saw nothing he hadn't seen in the room a hundred times.

"See the ring in the carpet that goes around the outside of the room? Notice the thin pentagram woven inside? You're sitting in a ritual circle, as you have been for each lesson I've given you. What you've learned so far takes young Gargoyles years to master. Yet you've learned in mere weeks."

"I thought that was because I had all this power because my father was one of the original souls of Rouen."

"That is partly the reason. Also contributing was the fact that I enhanced your learning through magic."

Levi wasn't sure he liked the idea of Roman casting some sort of spell on him, but he didn't argue. He was not in an arguing mood, not anymore. In fact, he was feeling downright agreeable. Must have been the letdown from the adrenaline rush.

"This stuff can help me see the house?"

"That and much more."

"All right." Levi settled himself more comfortably on the rug. "Let's get on with it, then. Show me."

"Patience, Levi. Patience. There is a structure to a ritual. A rhythm all its own."

Levi listened while Roman talked him through the welcome, the calling of the quarters, the naming of the deities and the request. The sound of Roman's voice was hypnotic, and he found himself more and more relaxed, so much so that Roman had to call his attention when it was time to participate.

"Place a stone in the cup and ask the deities to show you that which you wish to see."

Hesitating only a moment, he took a rock out of the red velvet bag, felt it warm in his palm, then dropped the stone into the cup. "Show me the hou—"

Roman held up his hand, palm out. "*Ask* to see it. The deities do not respond well to demands."

Levi started again. "Please, could you show me the house where we were earlier? Show me what happened there tonight."

"Good," Roman said. "Not exactly poetic, but specific. Now use the Second Sight and picture yourself going there. Keep your mind open and let the deities, and me, help you."

Levi practiced what he'd been taught, focused on the house, and found himself zooming over the water at a dizzying speed, coming up on the bluffs, the little cottage.

"Show me what happened to the people there," he said, and quickly added, "please."

With a flash of bright light, he was in the house, standing among the shattered glass, broken lamps and blood. Looking down on twisted bodies, their expressions frozen in horror.

Levi's stomach rebelled. Breathing deep to keep his dinner down, he found he could move. He could walk through the house as if he were there, hear the glass crunch under his feet, see the blood spatter on the walls, only it was like he was seeing the cottage and the destruction there through a long tunnel. The details were fuzzy and the light too bright.

He heard a sound in the other room and turned toward the kitchen. Could someone still be alive? He'd last seen Calvin in the kitchen.

His heart thundering, hoping against hope. Across the living room, stepping over Stephen's dead corpse, to the door. He put his palm out and pushed.

The noise hadn't been Calvin. The kid lay on the floor in a pool of congealed blood, his dead eyes looking up at his killers. The smell of copper tingled in his nostrils.

Squatting beside the boy's body were a gray-haired older man . . . and Nathan Cross.

White light exploded in Levi's mind like a flash grenade. It was as if his anger were a tangible thing, a being of its own, and that being stood in a house of mirrors, reflected and magnified a thousand times.

He was right. They'd done this. They had been setting him up, trying to get their hands—or claws, paws or hooves—on him. And they'd used Tasha to do it.

Suddenly the light grew even brighter, blinding, and the two men leaning over the dead boy flew backward, away from the body, and hit the wall behind them with a sickening crunch.

TWENTY-ONE

As his rage rose, so rose the power within Levi. It bloomed in him like a living thing. This was what Roman had been talking about all this time. This was his legacy. He felt like he could scale skyscrapers. Crush mountains with his bare hands. He felt untouchable.

In his mind's eye, he saw the two men rise from where they'd fallen against the wall. The older man held an arm over his ribs, and Cross lifted him to his feet by the elbow.

"Teryn, we have to get out of here," his sister's bastard husband said.

Teryn. He didn't know if it was a first name or a last name, but it was one he would remember, so he could get it right on the grave marker. Along with Cross.

"What is happening?" Teryn asked, looking around as if trying to see his tormentor.

"Romanus," Cross answered, pulling the other man toward the door.

Not Roman, you son of a bitch. Me. Levi fucking Tremaine.

The walls of the house began to shake, and the men stumbled. The kitchen chairs and table began to bounce and shake, clacking against the floor.

Levi followed his two prey into the other room, flung them back from the front door with his mind.

"If Romanus was able to attack us like this, he would have done it long ago," Nathan said, scrambling to his feet.

Teryn shot him a worried look. "Levi, then. He's the only one powerful enough."

Damn straight. He could feel the power surging through him, from the magic, from Roman, from the very air he breathed, charging every cell. He was drunk with it, and while some part of his brain recognized that he was out of control, that the power was controlling him instead of vice versa, the majority of his brain wanted more.

Every cell in his body hummed with energy, and still he wanted more.

With his mind, he flung Nathan and Teryn to the floor, on their backs. He held them there, visualizing a choking grip on their necks.

Their legs flailed. Their arms tried to pry the invisible grasp away.

The older man faded first, his lips going blue and then his skin to gray. Levi let go of him and doubled his efforts on Cross. He lifted the man's head, still choking. Nathan's eyes were bloodshot, his face graying.

The magnitude of what he was doing shocked him for a moment, but then the image of Calvin came to mind unbidden and added fuel to his furor.

Cross's eyes were open, and he was looking at Levi almost as if he could see him. Levi wished he could. He wanted Cross the see the man who would be his death. Would be Calvin's retribution.

Then Levi realized what Cross was trying to do. The man was trying to send images. Levi caught a glimpse of his sister, a flash of a gymnasium of some sort, with little boys flying through the air in various Gargoyle forms. Rookery. They called it the rookery.

Levi had never mastered blocking, locking another's visions from his mind, but he lashed out against Cross's tampering. He meant it to be a forceful mental slap, but apparently he had little control over this newfound power, because what he got wasn't a slap, it was a full body blow that sent Nathan Cross's head snapping backward and hitting the floor with a bone-rending crack.

Levi felt dizzy for a second, and then everything went black.

Tasha pressed the damp washcloth to Levi's forehead, and pinched him on the upper arm. She probably ought to let him rest, but he'd been out for hours.

"Come on, Sleeping Beauty. Time to wake up. You're scaring me here."

He stirred. Encouraged, she pinched him again. Harder.

"Ow." He tried to slap her hand away, but it was a weak effort.

He shifted to roll to his side, and she pinned his shoulders to the mattress. "Oh, no you don't. I said it's time to wake up."

One eyelid slowly cracked open, then the other. His gaze moved around the room in jerky swipes. "What the hell happened?"

"That's what I've been trying to ask you."

He sat. The washcloth slid off his forehead. He retrieved it from his lap, tossed it on the desk across the room and rubbed his palm over the front of his T-shirt. "How did I get down here?"

"Gregor practically dragged you. He said you passed out upstairs. Then he dumped you on the bed and you were out again. I haven't been able to wake you. What happened?"

He scrubbed his face. "I was talking to Roman. I asked him to help me with the Second Sight thing. I needed to see the house. I needed to know for sure—"

He lowered his head and she didn't have to ask what he'd needed to know. Or that he'd gotten his answer at some point during the night.

"He set up some kind of ritual—"

"A what?" She sat on the edge of the bed and tucked one leg under her.

"Some kind of damn ceremony that is supposed to be magic, make the Second Sight stronger. All I know is that I started feeling really weird. Kind of woozy at first, and then . . . things got crazy."

As if things hadn't already been crazy enough. "Crazy how?"

He swallowed hard. "I could see the house, the broken windows, the furniture turned over, the bodies, everything. It was just like I was there. I wanted to find Calvin, to see what had happened, so I went to the kitchen, and I saw *him*."

She shook her head, not following. "Who?"

"I was right, Tash. He must have followed us from the meeting point. He was one of the Gargoyles that killed those people, Calvin. He was still there, in human form, admiring his handiwork."

"*Who*, Levi?"

"Nathan Cross."

No. He had to be wrong. She couldn't be that mistaken about someone.

"Are you sure what you saw was real, Levi? That it wasn't some dream, or an image Roman provided?"

"Why would he do that?"

"I don't know. Why would any of this happen?" She held her hands out to her sides. "There's got to be an explanation, and only one person can give it to you."

"Nathan Cross."

She nodded.

He said, "I doubt I'll be getting anything from Nathan Cross."

"Why not?"

He looked up at her, despair so deep it was hard to look at in his bloodshot eyes and creased face. "Because I think I killed him."

"You're definitely going back to Chicago. First thing in the morning."

"You could use a few stitches."

"After I put you on an airplane. Maybe."

Groaning, Rachel let her husband straighten up from where he'd been bent over the sink while she cleaned the cut on the back of his head. She rinsed the bloody washcloth, wrung out the water and hung the cloth on the bathroom faucet to dry.

"You can't be sure that it was Levi. How could he have learned to use his power like that so quickly?"

"With a little help from Romanus, apparently. We were lucky they didn't kill us."

Teryn nodded from across the room, where he leaned on the bureau with his ankles crossed and his arms folded over his chest.

"Maybe Levi didn't want to kill you. He's not evil and you know it."

Nathan lifted one eyebrow at his wife. "You didn't see the furniture flying around the room, lightbulbs popping. It was very *Exorcist*."

She turned her back on him, stomped to the bathroom vanity, then with no purpose for being there, stomped back. Nathan stopped her pacing by taking her in his arms and kissing her forehead.

"No one is giving up on Levi just yet, sweetheart," he said. "But you have to face the fact that Romanus may have poisoned his mind against us. We may never be able to turn him to our side."

"We've got to find him, Nathan. We've got to find him and get him back, whatever it takes."

He rocked her in his arms and murmured comforts in her ear, but as much as she loved her husband, Rachel found little solace in his arms today.

For more than twenty years she'd searched for her brother, worried the whole time for his safety, his life. Now that she'd found him, she was worried for his very soul.

TWENTY-TWO

For the next couple of days, Levi alternated between withdrawing so far inside himself that he wasn't sure he could find his way out and generally being pissed off at the world. The images from the ritual seemed to be seared into his eyes—Calvin's bloody body, Nathan and the older man Teryn, standing over the boy, Levi's hand at their throats, squeezing by sheer force of the mind.

He could still see the blood vessels bursting in the whites of their eyes, hear what miniscule wheezing breath they were able to draw.

Worst of all, he could feel how the power had raged through him, and how he'd liked it. He'd been drunk on it, out of control.

He'd gone too far.

Levi had killed before. He'd led a hard life, lived on the dark side of society. But then it had been self-defense, survival of the fittest, and in his days living on the streets, he'd been pretty damned fit. This had been . . . calculated. It was pure revenge.

And for just a moment, it had been sweet.

He picked up the wrench and tightened the fittings on the manifold one last time before sitting up and wiping his hands on a greasy rag. He hadn't been kidding about Manny Estes neglecting the *Spanish Dancer*'s maintenance.

Working on the engines the last few days had given him a quiet place to retreat, be alone with his thoughts. God knew, he wasn't fit company for anyone else onboard. Working with his hands, carefully dissecting, cleaning, repairing and refitting had given him something productive to do. As he put the ship back together, each day when he'd finished his repairs, the pieces of his life began to click back in place as well.

He felt like he'd been gutted the other night, stripped to the bone. Slowly, painfully, in the quiet of the engine room, he rebuilt himself.

Sighing, he stood and surveyed his work. The engines hummed, almost musical, and he imagined them singing their gratitude. She was a happy boat now, he decided.

He turned to leave when the door opened behind him. He was surprised to see Roman step in. The man wasn't exactly the type to dwell in the bowels of his ship—might get grease on his pretty pressed-linen trousers. Levi didn't think he knew where the engine room was.

"There you are," Roman said. He left the door open behind him. "I've been looking for you. How are the repairs coming?"

"All done," Levi admitted. He tucked the hand rag halfway into the back pocket of his jeans.

"Good, good. Then we can get back to work."

Levi's stomach soured. Just the thought of another

lesson, or God forbid, a ritual, made him sick. "Maybe tomorrow."

Roman reached out to rest a hand on Levi's shoulder, but Levi instinctively pulled back.

"Walk with me, Levi." He turned and left the engine room without waiting to see if Levi would follow.

Figuring he had to go upstairs sooner or later anyway, Levi fell in step with Roman.

"I know your experience the other night must have seemed . . . overwhelming."

"That's one word for it," Levi said dryly.

Roman clasped his hands behind his back as he walked. "Magic is often like that when it comes to us. It rages like fire in the blood. It seems too strong, too big for mere mortals."

"You ever think maybe it is too big for us? Maybe we shouldn't be dabbling in stuff we don't understand and can't control?"

"You have to try again."

"I don't think so."

"With each ritual, you will learn to manipulate the magic more, rather than it manipulating you. You will learn to control it."

His skin crawled. He wanted no part of Roman or his rituals, and he told him so.

"I may have pushed you too hard, too fast," Roman conceded. "You weren't prepared for the force that is at your fingertips. But understand this. I pushed you out of desperation, Levi. The others are growing in numbers every day. They're getting bolder, as you saw at the cottage. Crueler."

Roman stopped in front of Levi and turned so that they stood face-to-face in the narrow hall. "You were alone, not knowing who or what you were. We took you in, we've made you part of something. You have family now, brethren. Don't turn your back on this."

The man knew how to get under his skin, Levi gave him that.

"I'll think about it," he said, more to end the conversation than because he had any intentions of playing along with Roman's little head games.

"You do that," Roman said. Then turned to leave and looked back over his shoulder. "Just don't take too long."

Or what? Levi wondered.

"Well, look what crawled out of its cave." Tasha soaked in the sight of him from her exercise bike, legs pumping. He looked tired. "Haven't seen much of you for the last few days."

"Yeah, sorry about that." He slung the towel on his shoulder over a bench and picked up a couple of free weights. "I was in a mood for some time alone."

"Oh, you were in a mood, all right."

He cut a look at her.

Maybe she should take it easy on him, coddle him and coo over him, and tell him that everything would be okay, but it wasn't her way, and he'd never been the type to appreciate that kind of cosseting. They both preferred the direct approach. Direct as a slap to the face.

"If you're done sulking, maybe we could start working on a way to get out of this mess."

He curled his left arm, then the right. His biceps bulged invitingly at the strain of the weights in his hands—he did have a great body—and the veins stood out in neck, whether from the weight lifting or in irritation at her, she wasn't quite sure. "Which mess would that be?"

"The one where we're stuck on a boat with a crazy man performing satanic rituals and messing with your mind."

He curled each weight again. "The rituals aren't satanic. Pagan maybe, I think."

"Whatever." She stopped the pedals and slid off her bike. A trickle of sweat ran from her collarbone down between her boobs. "The question is, what are we going to do about him?"

Levi put the weights on the floor and sat on the bench. "The question is what are we going to do about you?"

"Me?" She wasn't sure where he was going with this, but she was pretty certain she wasn't going to like it.

He sighed. "I just want out of here, Tash. But more than that, I want *you* out of here. I can swim away anytime, be gone before they could stop me. But I can't figure any way to get you off the ship. At least not a way that doesn't risk you getting hurt."

Her heart sank. "Is that what you've been doing these past couple of days? Trying to figure out how to get me off the yacht?" She snapped her towel at his thigh. "You're not getting rid of me that easily, buster."

"Nothing easy about it. You could hold on to me and I could pull you, like we did the night of the storm, but we're a hundred miles from land."

"And this is the North Atlantic. I'd freeze before we got anywhere near shore."

He nodded.

She chewed her lip. "You still have the text pager. We could send Rachel coordinates, have a boat meet us and you could swim me just far enough to get away from the *Spanish Dancer* and meet up with it. I could last that long in the water in a wet suit. Maybe."

Levi looked up at her from under heavy eyelids.

"But you still don't trust her," Tasha guessed.

"Given that I just killed her husband, I don't know how likely she is to help us."

"You don't know that he's dead. You said so yourself."

He agreed, but he still wouldn't consider Rachel an option without knowing for sure. They didn't even know if she was still on the east coast.

"Okay," she said. "So we can't leave and we can't stay. We need a third option."

Levi almost smiled. "I'm open to ideas."

"Hmmm. I'm fresh out of those." Out of the kind of ideas he was talking about, at least. Seeing him back from whatever dark place he'd been hiding inside himself since the ritual disaster, actually speaking in complete sentences and almost smiling, was definitely giving her some other kinds of ideas, though.

She walked two fingers up his bare thigh from his knee, stopping at the hem of his gym shorts. "I suggest we go somewhere more private where we can give the matter our"—she dragged her fingertips over his groin and pulled him to her by his waistband—"full attention. Like the shower."

He leaned in close, his lips a whisper away from hers. "It just so happens I do my best thinking in the water."

Through the tunnel of Second Sight, Roman watched them from the great room. Damn Tremaine and his stubborn righteousness. They were wasting time. The longer he delayed in executing his plan to bring an end to Nathan Cross, Teryn and his Chicago congregation, the more likely the whole charade he'd staged for Levi was to fall apart. He already sensed distrust in his young pupil.

He watched Levi and the girl kiss, lips moving, hands touching, and snarled, then forced himself to relax.

Maybe after he laid the bitch, Levi would be in a better mood.

If not, Roman would have to provide a little more motivation, make the war on the Chicagoans a little more personal for him.

The girl might actually prove useful after all.

TWENTY-THREE

Tasha opened her eyelids and stretched, her limbs deliciously sore. Whatever dark place inside himself Levi had retreated to the last few days, the man was definitely back. The shower had been hard and urgent, their bodies pounding like the water, reacquainting themselves and claiming each other.

In the berth they shared afterward, they'd made love at a much more leisurely pace, taken their time climbing the peak, stopping to explore all the scenic nooks and crannies along the way, but in the end, the freefall of climax had been just as exhilarating.

They'd actually taken a few moments in between rounds of sex to brainstorm ways to get off the ship but hadn't come up with anything that didn't end up with one or both of them dead.

He was already gone this morning, taking an early shift on the bridge as usual, probably. Which left her to her own designs—always a dangerous thing for someone with her penchant for trouble.

The first few days after the massacre at Cape Sim, she'd been traumatized, worried for Levi and grieving for the men who had died. But as the shock had worn off, boredom had set in. Levi had provided temporary relief for that last night, but the prospect of an entire day of doing nothing but stare at the ocean—again—was almost too bleak to ponder.

What she needed to be doing was figuring out a way to help Levi. She was out of her element—magic and rituals? What the hell was that about?

Deciding moving was better than sitting still, she got up, dressed in her usual low-riding jeans, a sweater and deck shoes, and ran a brush through her hair, pulling the spiky strands upright where they'd been flattened on the pillow.

She wandered the halls for a while. Not seeing anyone around, she found herself outside the door to the great room, debating whether to go inside.

Early on during her adventures on the *Spanish Dancer*, it had been made clear to her that this was the king's domain. Prince Levi had an open invitation, but peasant girls such as herself were not welcome.

She twisted up her mouth and reached for the brass doorknob. "Screw them."

The plush carpet crushed beneath her feet. The air smelled like old leather, cigars and a touch of incense.

Across the room she examined the booze set up at the bar. All top shelf, of course. In the refrigerator below were stacked cans of club soda and tonic water, a bowl of fresh-cut lemons and a bottle of wine. Nineteen sixty-four French Bordeaux, according to the label.

Tasha ran her fingertips along the edge of the cherry

desk next. The desktop was polished to a high shine, and immaculate of any folders or notes or anything else that might tell her something about Roman DuValle other than that he was an anal-retentive neat freak.

On impulse, she pulled open a drawer. The nail file, yellow highlighter and pack of matches were no help. Checking each drawer in turn, her disappointment grew. The man either was very careful about leaving his things where anyone else might see them, or he had no personality.

She was betting on the latter.

Behind her was a small built-in bookcase. She scanned the titles, mostly contemporary thrillers with all the right classics thrown in to reinforce Roman's status as one of the upper crust.

Below the books was a cabinet with louvered doors. She pulled on the knobs and bent down to peer inside. More wine, mostly, in dusty bottles. Tsk, tsk. Not so neat in here.

She started to rise, but something white behind the bottles caught her eye. She moved one or two aside and saw a box.

Biting her lip at her find, she pulled out the wine and slid the box to the front, hoping it wasn't Roman's stash of porn magazines or something equally as disgusting.

She found more books. At first disappointment had her shoulders slumping, then she noticed the titles on the books. She dug through the small stack. *Spells and Enchantments of the Dark Ages. Pagan Rituals and Deities. Dark Magic, Light Magic.*

She smiled.

Maybe, just maybe, she had the beginnings of an idea.

Levi stood on the bridge, staring out at the glare of the sun on the sea. A band of gulls circled overhead, div-

ing and dipping into the waves. In the distance, a black oil
tanker broke the even line of the horizon.

He didn't know how long he'd been standing like that,
racking his brain for some way to get Tasha off the ship. He
even considered trying to take over the ship. He could manipulate the Russians with his mind, take them down one
by one and hold them captive. But what then? He couldn't
exactly motor into port with a pair of Russians and a gray-
haired man bound and gagged below decks. And what if it
didn't work?

The Russians he thought he could handle with his mind,
and Roman he could take physically if he caught the man
off guard. But Roman was sharp, his senses acute. If he
sussed out the plan before he got him, Levi was screwed.

No, it was better if Roman continued to think of Levi as
his eager and pliable pupil for as long as possible.

He mentally listed the options again, adding reasons for
ruling each one out. At Tasha's idea of getting Rachel to
help, he paused.

Had he really killed her husband? The truth was, he
didn't know. God, she would hate him then, before she'd
ever met him, even if he really was her brother.

The light reflecting off the water grew more intense.
Levi's vision started to blur, to tunnel.

It surprised him. He hadn't called the Second Sight,
but he could feel it forming. He didn't fight it. It probably
wouldn't work anyway—he wasn't very good at this without Roman stabilizing the connection, but if it did . . . Well,
he would finally know.

The tunnel grew longer. Levi's senses ranged, almost
as if of their own free will. He focused on the feeling he'd
gotten in Cape Sim, when his mind had briefly brushed
Rachel's. Quiet strength. Inner calm. Love for her husband
and devotion for her cause.

He formed the picture in his mind. Her dark hair blowing, her cheeks glowing.

And he found her.

Her mind was fuzzy, caught in that state somewhere between sleep and wakefulness.

He could see her. She lay on a plaid couch with a crocheted blanket thrown over her hips. One hand was tucked under her head and the other lay protectively over her stomach.

Levi delved deeper into the vision. He could feel her breath warming the inside of her upper arm. He could feel her baby kick against her palm and the reassuring stroke she gave it.

He let himself sink past the physical sensations to the images of her dreams. He couldn't influence what she saw—he wasn't that good and didn't have that close of a connection with Rachel. But he could watch.

At first he saw her flying on the back of a Gargoyle, a gryphon, half eagle and half lion. He felt her smile as she buried her face in the place on his neck where feathers turned to a mane of fur. Felt her laugh as the gryphon twisted left and right in a series of aerial acrobatics meant to amuse her.

She smiled in her twilight sleep and another hand joined hers over her abdomen. A bigger hand, rougher, it pulled her back against a hard male chest, and she snuggled in close to her husband.

Levi let out a breath. *So, not dead, then.*

Before he had time to figure out how to feel about that, he smelled smoke and felt fire. Joy flashed to terror in Rachel's mind, and suddenly she was a child again, not more than six or seven, huddled in the dark. Her bare feet were cold on the hardwood floor and her nightgown twisted around her knees.

He felt the moisture, heavy in her lashes and warm and wet on her cheeks. There were angry voices outside, and shadows on the wall where the door to wherever she was hiding cracked open. The shadows clashed and rolled together. Grunts and scrapes of bodies across the floor added sound to the shadow show.

He felt something move in her arms and looked down to see she held a baby.

"Shh, Levi." She rocked him urgently. "Shhh."

Outside the dark room, two gunshots popped off. There was a roar, and then one of the shadows on the floor rose up, no longer human, but in a silhouette of a winged creature with a long neck and tapered body.

Clutching him, young Rachel leaned forward and pushed the closet door open in her dream. She looked up through her tears. *Daddy?*

The door to the bridge swung open, letting in a bracing blast of air. "I've got it!"

It took Levi a moment to realize it had been Tasha's voice, not Rachel's. He found himself swaying at the abrupt loss of the Second Sight, and he held on to the polished wooden wheel of the *Spanish Dancer* for support.

She studied him from across the deck. "Are you all right?"

"Yeah." He blinked hard. "Just kind of zoning. You've got what?"

Tasha glanced around as if making sure there was no one else in the small room. "An idea."

His mind still wasn't firing on all cylinders. "An idea for what?"

She planted her hands on her hips. "Are you sure you're all right?"

Understanding pried through the haze of fading memories of his sister. "Oh, that kind of an idea."

She crooked a finger at him. "Follow me."

Back in their stateroom with the door locked behind them, she pulled her gym bag from under the berth, unzipped the top and pulled the sides apart so he could see inside.

"Books," he said, not getting her excitement.

"Magic books," she clarified. "Some of them black magic. Look at the titles. They look really old, too."

Levi's stomach turned. They also looked really well used. "Where did you get those?"

"From the great room." She flipped through the biggest tome. "I was up there looking around, trying to trigger some idea and I stumbled across them."

"You mean you were snooping."

"Please. Snooping is such a harsh word." She turned a dazzling smile up to him. "I prefer 'poking around.'"

He cut her a look. "Anyway, what do you want with these things?"

Personally, he didn't even want to be in the same room with them.

"I was just looking at them when it came to me. We can't figure out how to get off this tub because we're playing by our rules. We need to play by his rules."

He sat, tentatively picked up one of the books. Inside was a drawing of ritual items placed in much the same configuration Roman had used the other night. He closed the cover. "His rules?"

"This stuff." She swept her hand over the pile of books. "He's got the upper hand right now because he knows all this stuff."

"Not to mention has several lifetimes of practice."

"But you're supposed to be some super Gargoyle, right? Bastion of power and all that."

"I don't know about that."

"Oh, come on. If what you've told me is true, that's why he wants you so bad. You're like the plutonium for his A-bomb."

"So what does any of that have to do with the books?"

"We need to read up on this stuff, figure out what kind of tricks he's been turning, learn what he knows, do a little practicing ourselves." She looked completely pleased with herself. "Then we beat him at his own game."

TWENTY-FOUR

"*I'm telling you it wasn't a dream. He was there,* watching me through the Second Sight or something." Rachel cut the crust off her peanut butter and jelly sandwich and took a bite. Nathan looked at her dubiously from across the kitchen table while Teryn fiddled with his cheese toast. Connor Rihyad and his wife Mara listened intently on either side of him.

At Nathan's insistence, they'd returned to Chicago the night before. She'd wanted to stay on the east coast, but they'd had no leads on Levi since the glimpse they'd caught of him on the boardwalk, and the elders needed to know about the attack in Cape Sim.

Nathan and Teryn had gotten there too late. The dead were still warm on the floor when they arrived, but the attackers had gone. There'd been no sign of Levi, or any reason to believe he'd been hurt, thank the Lord.

It had been a long trip for Rachel, and she was tired,

so she'd napped on the couch midmorning when she'd felt Levi's presence. She recognized the mind that had brushed hers in Cape Sim. She would know him anywhere now.

Nathan frowned. "He's getting very strong if he was able to trace your mind all the way here after just that one brief contact."

Connor spoke up. "And if he can trace you, he can find all of us here and that means Romanus will know, too. This place isn't safe for anyone, the women, the children."

Second Sight didn't come with a locator beacon. Most Gargoyles couldn't trace minds to a particular location at all—quite the opposite. It was the location they focused on, regardless of who might be there.

A few especially strong among them could find a mind within a distance range, especially if they knew the mind well. Nathan had always been able to find her no matter where she went.

She could never get in any secret shopping, darn it.

Connor swept the crumbs of his sandwich off of the table in front of him and into his napkin. "You're right. He's not just getting strong, then. He's getting dangerous. If he can see what's going on in here, we have to assume Romanus can, too, through him."

Teryn agreed. "We need to cast some protective spells, at the very least. Something to block the Second Sight."

"No!"

They all turned to her.

"He's trying to make contact. We've got to let him. If anything, we've got to gather a circle of our own and open up to him, let him know that we hear him. It's the only way we have to communicate with him."

"Honey." Nathan laid his hand over hers on the table. "He nearly killed Teryn and I. For all we know, he's the one who killed the Gargoyles at Port Sim."

"No."

"What's to stop him from doing the same to you, or any-one else here, for that matter?"

"I can't believe he meant to do that." She squeezed Na-than's hand. "My brother is reaching out to me. I'm not going to turn him away."

*Levi sat across from Tasha on the floor of their state-*room. "You sure we should be doing this? This isn't like some kids playing Magic 8 Ball. This is serious shit. Be-lieve me."

He couldn't shake the feeling that they were inviting doom.

"I've been reading up. It sounds simple enough." She chewed on her thumbnail and paged through one of the books spread open beside her.

"One day of reading does not a pagan priestess make, darling."

She looked up. "Did you just call me *darling*?"

"Sarcasm."

"Fine, sweetie pie."

She narrowed her eyes and went back to her book, ar-ranging the junk she'd scavenged from the ship's stores that afternoon. She had collected a reasonable approximation of the ritual objects Roman had used.

Finally she seemed satisfied with everything's place-ment. "Okay. How do we start?"

"I thought you were the expert."

"I can only read so fast. I got the stuff and made the circle and everything." She glanced at the lasso of nylon rope that surrounded them. "You're the one who's actually been through the process."

"All right, all right." He took a deep breath and thought

back to the night he'd rather forget. "I think we started with some kind of welcome or something."

Sitting cross-legged, she rested her hands on her knees and closed her eyes. "Okay, so something like . . . thank you all for coming tonight. We hope you enjoy the ceremony and find we haven't butchered the rites too badly."

Levi had to cover his smile with a cough. "Not exactly like that, but let's move on. Next he did this thing, calling the quarters."

She flipped through another book, frowning.

"I'll give it a shot," Levi said. He raised his arms toward each cardinal direction as he called it by name. "Guardian of the south, bringer of fire, light and warmth, we ask for your guidance tonight in our quest. Guardian of the north, mother earth from which all life springs forth, grace us with your presence this evening."

He had to think harder for east and west, but he was pretty sure they were air and water, respectively.

He opened his eyes. "Now we ask for what we want."

"Just like that?"

"Just like."

"The book says we can see past, present or future. Let's start with something easy and ask to see the present. What Roman is doing right now."

"No!" He straightened his back as his hackles stood. "Some practitioners can sense when magic is being used on them, according to Roman. We don't want him to find out we're fooling around with this."

"Okay." She chewed on her lip. "Something else, then. Nowhere near the ship. Let's ask to see the boardwalk, the cotton candy stand where we were supposed to meet Rachel last week."

"Okay." He squirmed deeper into the carpeting, centering himself. "Focus on the place. Picture it in your mind."

He centered his thoughts on the blinking palm tree. He was there in seconds, could see the people walking by, the bored vendor resting his chin in his palm behind the cash register. It looked like a slow night. "I've got it. Can you see it?"

"No. Nothing."

He steadied that part of his mind fixed on the cotton candy stand and also tried to project the image to Tasha. "Hey, I see it! There's a guy in a red-checkered shirt walking by, and a lady digging through her purse, not watching where she's going."

"Yeah, that's it." He let go of both connections and opened his eyes. "But that wasn't magic. That was just the Second Sight and me projecting images. I can do that without all of this gobbledygook."

Her shoulders slumped. "Crud. Maybe we should try something you can't normally do, then. Like see the past."

"All right." He called the deities again and made a new request. "If you favor, please show us Natasha Cole in her awkward teen years. One of those really embarrassing moments."

"Hey!"

"Concentrate . . ."

The image wasn't as clear this time, and it didn't come as quickly, but as if through a fog, he could see a girl walking down a row of fishing docks at night. A single mercury lamp on the street corner lit her way.

She was wearing a pair of low-riding jeans and a midriff top that rode up when she fished a crumpled piece of paper out of her pocket and checked the writing then the slip number on the nearest mooring.

"No," he heard Tasha mumble in present time.

Beyond her in past time, shadows slipped in and out of the dark. She turned a slow circle as if waiting for someone, watching for them, a shy smile on her shiny painted lips that matched her nail polish.

"No," she said again, this time stronger. The vision wavered, and he opened his eyes to find her chest heaving, her fists clenched. Her head and arms started to jerk, like she was having one of her attacks.

She swiped her hand over the altar objects, sending them flying. The vision disappeared. He grabbed her arm, snapped her out of it.

"No," she said again, and this time there were tears in her eyes.

TWENTY-FIVE

Other than the day their friends on The White Whale
had died, Levi had never seen Tasha cry. He'd never seen
anything phase her all that much, good times or bad, and
they'd seen a lot of bad together. The sight of her tears
wrenched his heart, as did her brave attempt to wipe them
away and pretend nothing was wrong.

He scooted over and gathered her in his arms. "It's okay.
It's okay. What happened?"

"Mmm." She sniffed. "Just. Hey. Ugly teenager years.
Not something I want to relive. Ever. Best day of my life
was the day I turned twenty and got to drop the 'een' off
the end of my age."

He stroked her face dry with his thumb. "Not wanting to
relive the teenage years, I'll give you. But ugly? No way."

"Are you kidding? Did you see that lipstick job?"

He scrubbed his thumb across her bottom lip now. "I
thought it was kind of cute. Along with that short top."

"You would."

"Hey, I was a teenager once, too, you know."

Her shoulders relaxed finally, and she turned her face up to him invitingly.

It was the kind of invitation he couldn't refuse. At least when it came from her.

He took her lips with his, nibbling at the full centers and licking at the corners. She responded with a quiet gasp and settled deeper against him. He felt her unfolding around him, opening herself up to him in a way she never had before. It was like he was inside her skin.

And she was inside his. She took the kiss deeper at the exact moment he needed her to. She touched him in all the places he wanted her to, his temples, the base of his neck, the quivering muscles above the snap on his jeans, her fingertips light, exploring, one second, then wringing a groan out of him the next.

She arched back, and he knew she wanted him to pull her sweater off before she asked.

"God, yes." The cable knit landed on the desk across the room, and Levi rolled her to her back, burying his face in the valley between her breasts. He pushed himself up long enough for his fingers to find the front clasp of her bra, and she lifted her breasts to him, rosy nipples already peaked with pleasure.

The memory of the first time he'd seen them flitted through his mind. After days of electric looks flying between them on *The White Whale*, they'd finally tumbled into the captain's quarters with clothes flying. When those breasts sprung free, so high and firm and shaped like perfect candy kisses, she took his breath away. He could die in those breasts and think he'd gone to heaven.

Her pleasure zinged through him as he suckled one, and she shuddered right along with him when his T-shirt went the way of her sweater and she scraped her fingernails down both sides of his spine.

Her heartbeat quickened with each touch, and it was like her pulse beat in his veins. Her need joined with his to send the blood pounding to his groin, his hips surging forward, seeking friction.

They'd had plenty of hard, fast sex before, but this struck him as different. She was practically climbing him, trying to get her legs over his, and his hands were shaking so hard he could barely find the tab on the zipper at his fly.

It wasn't until his foot kicked over the bowl of salt that he realized what was happening.

"Wait," he said.

"No." She reached up to finish the job on his zipper.

"Slow down."

"I can't."

Her slim fingers slid beneath his boxers and wrapped around him. He saw stars. Whole solar systems rushing by.

He captured her hands in his, still holding him. "It's the ritual. We didn't close the circle. We didn't end the rite."

She glanced over each of his shoulders in turn. "You mean the deities are watching us?"

"I mean our minds are still linked." He groaned, barely able to stand the glove of her fingers sheathing him. They were being swept away in a flood of memories. First bike rides, first kisses, first times.

"Don't you feel it? It's like I'm in your head, I'm part of you."

It wasn't just physical sensations, either. He could feel her emotions, her fears, her dreams. They swelled inside him. This was a part of her he'd never known. Sex had always been about the physical pleasure with them. Who could make the other one feel better. Now he was sensing a whole gamut of deeper feelings. Emotions. He could see in her eyes that he was an open book to her, too.

Instinct screamed for him to push back, to pull away before it was too late. There was a reason they never shared themselves on this level. They were both wounded, limping through life like a couple of stray dogs protecting an injured leg even years after the scars had healed.

To let one another experience what they felt for the other beyond the physical pleasure was equivocal to baring one's throat to a circling wolf. You'd better hope the wolf wasn't hungry.

She moved her hand a fraction, and he felt a tentative tendril of her emotion, her love, reach into his mind like the first tender shoot of a new plant burrowing through the soil.

"Aw, hell."

He came down on her, came inside her in a swift thrust, and rode wave after wave of hopes, desires, dreams and disappointments passing between them until he couldn't sort out one feeling from the next. Bits and pieces of her life flashed by too fast for him to make them out, like the sidewalk outside the window of a speeding car. His existence became a blur of color and heat and soft, scented skin, and then the world flashed to bright white, and there was no thought at all.

"Who'd have thought the pagans were into such kinky sex?" Tasha glanced over her shoulder at him as she set the ritual tools on the floor.

He brought the two ends of the nylon rope together to complete the circle. "I doubt that's what they had in mind when they came up with these rites."

"How do you know? Were you there?" she teased.

"I might have been."

She'd forgotten about all those past lives of his. Maybe he had been there.

"Well what about all those orgies they used to have in the woods?"

"What about them?"

"They used to do their magic sky-clad, you know. Without clothes." She waggled her eyebrows. "Maybe we should try that."

"How long do you think it would be before we were jumping each others' bones if we did that?" He sat in his usual spot and gestured for her to take her place.

"All right. Ritual now, sex later."

They'd been practicing magic for three nights now, when the waters got still and the ship got quiet. The spot of star shine twinkling in through the porthole and flickering candles created a mood that often led them straight from the circle to the bed when they were done. But in the meantime, they'd made progress.

They could now see the past, at least recent history, with some regularity, though Levi had shied away from her younger days. They hadn't had any luck with the future, but they were able to manipulate their environment. They could stir a breeze in the closed cabin, warm a glass of cold water, even light the candles on the floor with only their minds.

The problem was, none of those parlor tricks seemed likely to help them out of their situation with Roman. Levi was playing along, maybe even mildly amused by their newfound skills, but she knew he felt it, too. The monotony. The hopelessness.

And still they went on. They spoke the welcome and called the quarters.

"What do you want to work on tonight?" he asked.

She sighed. "How about sprouting wings so we can fly off of this ship?"

He didn't answer.

"Couldn't you turn into one of those bird things instead of a sea monster, just once?"

"Sorry. It doesn't work that way. I've only ever been able to shift to one form. How about we try for the future again. See if we can see a time when we're not stuck on this god awful—" His head snapped up, eyes searching.

"What?"

"I felt something."

"Like what?"

"Like a touch. Someone brushing their hand across my face."

"There's no one here."

"I know, but—" He picked up her hands in his. "Open your mind, just like you would for any other ritual. Think about being a . . . a television antenna."

"Oh, now that's flattering."

"Just do it. Concentrate on picking up any signals that might be passing by around you."

She understood when Levi called for the deities and asked them to help him turn their vision back on those who would watch him tonight. She slowed her breathing until her chest rose and fell in synch with Levi's. Sure enough, a moment later she began to see a fuzzy picture. Staticky and flickering, but a picture nonetheless.

"What is that?" she breathed.

"You mean *who* is that."

All she saw was a large room with walls of big stone blocks and pictures of stout men in period dress lining the walls. The room was dimly lit with only a few candles mounted in holders around the exterior walls. A cool draft flickered the flames.

After a time, Tasha's eyes adjusted to the dark, and she saw she'd been wrong about the room being empty. A lone figure sat on the floor in meditation position. When she lifted her head, Tasha saw it was Rachel Cross.

She seemed to look right at them, and Levi was looking back. Some sort of silent communication passed between brother and sister she was sure, though she had no way of knowing what.

The moment was broken when a large wooden door banged open. Nathan Cross stormed in. Tasha couldn't hear him, but she could see the single name on his lips as he spoke it.

Rachel!

Then the connection was lost, and Tasha was once again sitting on the floor of the stateroom with Levi, no strange stone monoliths in sight.

She opened her mouth to ask him exactly what had just happened, but before she could get the words out, a knock sounded at their door. She pinched out the candles and swept the evidence of their activity under the berth.

Levi opened the door to a scowling Gregor. "Mr. DuValle wants to see you on the bridge. He said right away."

TWENTY-SIX

Levi debated dawdling awhile before reporting to the bridge just to make the point that he wasn't Roman's lackey, jumping at the man's beck and call. But if Roman was on the bridge, then it was possible something was wrong with the ship. He decided to go.

Roman looked haggard, his hair for once not neatly combed and the back collar of his shirt only folded half-way over.

"What's up?" Levi automatically scanned the gauges behind the wheel. Nothing looked out of whack.

"I need you to lay in a new course."

"For where?"

"Closest port. We'll be leaving the ship in dry dock and going inland. I have a house on Lake Superior, so there'll be a place for you . . ." His sentence trailed off with a wave of his hand.

Levi didn't care about the lake. He was still caught up

in the fact that they were getting off the boat. He could hardly contain his enthusiasm behind a straight face, but he was also wary of this sudden change in plans. "Something wrong?"

"Everything is wrong." Levi had never heard that kind of snap in Roman's voice. "They're gathering, Levi. Gathering to strike. They grow stronger with every day we waste."

"How do you know that?"

"I've seen it."

"You performed a ritual."

"As I have every night for the last six. Alone. Hoping to catch a glimpse of their plans. Get some warning to our people." He cut Levi down with bloodshot eyes. "I could have used your help."

"Yeah, about that. Guess I've . . . had a lot on my mind. Maybe tomorrow . . ."

Or when hell freezes over. But Roman seemed on edge, and Levi didn't want to risk pushing him over without knowing more about what was going on.

Roman seemed to calm a bit and pulled his shoulders straighter. "I fear the ship is no longer secure. We've been out here too long, they've had too much time to track us. And with only the four of us on board, we wouldn't hold up to even a small attack."

"Five souls on board," Levi calculated. "You forgot Tasha."

"Yes, of course, five. I meant four of our kind who could fight."

"Don't worry. If it comes to a fight, Tasha will hold her own."

Roman dropped the conversation like an anchor and looked anxiously out the window. "When can we be in port?"

Levi checked their position on the GPS. "Tomorrow midday."

"Make best speed then. And let's hope it's enough."

"What the hell were you thinking, performing a ritual alone?"

Nathan watched his wife's back stiffen in her chair. He'd definitely gotten her dander up. And she was a dangerous woman when she was this determined.

"I was thinking that if my *husband* had been willing to help me, I wouldn't have *been* alone," she answered haughtily.

"Do you know how dangerous that was? For you and the baby."

"You've played the baby card enough, Nathan. You know I would never do anything to put Edward at risk."

"I thought we decided on Samuel."

"Did we?" she asked sweetly. Edward was a family name on her mother's side, and she knew damn well Nathan hated it. It made him think of Eddie Munster.

And she'd managed to both distract him and threaten him at the same time.

Dangerous, dangerous woman. Life was never boring with her around.

"He caught you spying on him, didn't he? He saw you."

"Yes," she admitted. "He must have formed his own circle, because when I looked at him, he looked right back."

Nathan swore. "How much did he see? What were you thinking about at the time?"

"Relax, Nathan. Nothing about the congregation, or where we've stashed the children away. I know how careful we have to be."

He trusted her on that. Rachel might not be a male Gargoyle, with all the powers that came with that, but she was a daughter of one of the Old Ones, and she possessed more traits than any other female in recent history. She couldn't make the Change, but she could hear the Calling, and share and receive images with the rest of them. What abilities she hadn't inherited from her Gargoyle father she'd learned to perform by magic.

His wife had become quite the little pagan.

He squatted down by her chair. "Promise me you won't do that alone again."

She arched one brow. "Promise me I won't have to."

"I'll help you, and I'll get Teryn and Connor to agree as well, but only on my terms. Never alone and only with the proper protection spells in place, deal?"

"Deal." She held out her hand. "Now take me to bed."

The last day and a half had been a whirlwind, it seemed to Levi. They'd no sooner parked the boat than they were on a commuter airplane out of Bangor to JFK, then aboard a jumbo jet to Milwaukee and finally in a rented truck, another black Ford Expedition, on their way to Michigan's Upper Peninsula, or UP as he'd heard it called.

He watched the scenery go by outside the window, wishing he knew more about where they were going, their route. Ideally, he would have liked to have made his getaway with Tasha before they arrived at Roman's place. The man claimed the house was well fortified against intruders.

Harder to get into also meant harder to get out of.

He didn't want to make any rash moves, though. Once they'd gotten out of the last airport, Kolyakev and Gregor and their pals Petsky and Slavatsky pulled their fully registered and legal—if you believed the fake paperwork—.454

Magnums out of their checked luggage and stuffed them under their jackets. Two more cars showed up with two men in each, who Levi assumed were equally well armed, to escort them en route.

Levi might be a little crazy from being cooped up under Roman's watchful eye on the boat for so long, but he wasn't completely insane. Any escape attempt would have to wait until they reached the house.

He leaned forward to talk to Roman, who sat in the passenger seat in front of him. Hopefully a little conversation would both help pass time and give him a jump on his escape planning. "So what's this house of yours like?"

Roman turned his head to talk over his shoulder, but not far enough to actually look at Levi. "It's an estate really. Fifty acres."

"Wow. Has it been in your family long?"

"We don't keep property, Levi. We're forced to move around a lot so the others can't track us down."

"So it's pretty well secured?"

"The property is gated. Both the fence and the house are covered by floodlights, motion sensors, cameras. The usual."

Great.

"What about the waterfront. You said it was a lake house."

"The shoreline is a concern, yes, but we post guards, and there are several trained dogs on the property."

By trained dogs, Levi assumed Roman meant dogs that bite.

Levi sat back. "Sounds nice." *Nice like Alcatraz.*

By the time someone got the bright idea to stop for gas, Tasha had her lips pinched, her hands clenched in her lap and her legs crossed. Then crossed again at the ankles. She made a beeline for the ladies' room before the driver had even shut off the truck's engine.

Three minutes later, feeling much better, she washed her hands at the stainless steel sink, fluffed her hair in the mirror and checked her teeth to make sure she wasn't still carrying around any of the Cheetos she'd eaten in the car since Roman didn't want to stop at an actual restaurant for fear of being attacked.

Satisfied her teeth were clean, she pulled open the door, and all hell broke loose.

Three cars screeched into the gas station lot, sliding to a stop in front of the Expeditions and blocking them in. Men in masks piled out of the cars, firing in the air and shouting. Some bright lightbulb managed to put a round into one of the pumps, and fire broke out. Pretty soon, things were going to go *boom*.

Unarmed, there wasn't much Tasha could do but watch in horror from the corner of the building. One of the bad guys had Petsky on the ground at gunpoint, arms spread. The other didn't waste the energy on Slavatsky. He put a bullet through the Russian's head and moved on. Roman's men from the first escort car seemed to be down, too. The guys from the trailing car were laying down cover fire for Kolyakev and Gregor, who were trying to flank the masked men who had pinned them down. Behind the hood of Roman's Expedition, she saw Levi had acquired himself a weapon somewhere and was crouched down just waiting for a target to shoot at.

The two baddies farthest from the action crept wide. They looked like they were going to try to sneak up behind Roman and Levi's position. Of course, the two of them would be the bad guy's targets.

She opened her mouth to shout a warning, but her words

were lost in the explosion of the gas pump. The two bad guys sailed backward, hit the ground hard and didn't get up. The remaining two, the ones in the firefight with Gregor and Kolyakev, retreated to their car. As they burned rubber out of the parking lot, Tasha heaved a sigh of relief.

They'd narrowly escaped another one.

She took a step toward the cars but was pulled back before she cleared the corner of the Quick Mart. A gloved hand clamped over her mouth, and another around her waist, swinging her off her feet and spiriting her away to a car waiting around back with the engine idling.

TWENTY-SEVEN

"Nathan."

Rachel said his name so quietly he thought she might have been mumbling in her sleep. She sat in an overstuffed chair with a book on her lap and her head bowed. He thought she'd been napping, but now he wasn't so sure. He knew that vacant expression.

He was at her side before he drew his next breath.

"It's Levi," she said.

Nathan cursed out loud. "How the hell could he do that? We cast the protections."

"He's very strong," she said, her voice still barely above a whisper. "And he's very . . . upset."

His heart skipped a beat. Several beats. "Shut your mind down, Rachel. Block him. I know you can do it." He squeezed her hand, found her fingers cold.

"No. He needs me."

"Dammit, Rachel. You know what happened the last

time your little brother got *upset*. He nearly killed me. Block him!"

"I can feel his anger. It's . . . vivid. Powerful. But he's not hurting me." She licked her lips, frowned in concentration. "He's . . . showing me. He and Roman are in a car. Or were in a car. With Tasha and some others. They were attacked."

"By who?"

She shook her head. "Don't know. They fought them off, but Tasha . . ."

"What? What happened to her?"

"Tasha's gone."

A moment later, Rachel jolted and sucked in a breath of surprise. "He's gone."

Then the satellite pager she always carried, the one only one person had been given the number to, chirped and vibrated in her pocket.

She pulled it out and opened the cover.

Did U take her?

She showed the message to Nathan and then typed in the answer and hit the send button.

No.

Within moments, the text message question came back.

R U sure?
Yes.
Who took her?

Looking at Nathan, Rachel shook her head and typed text message lingo for *I don't know.*

IDK

A minute or more passed before the next message arrived.

Good-bye

"Christ." Nathan took the satellite pager from her. His fingers bobbed over the miniature keyboard.

We can help

Even longer passed before the final message arrived.

No

Levi was going to go crazy, and he was going to take every single person in this house with him. "We've got to go back. We've got to find her."

"We looked, Levi; there was no sign of her." Roman had told him the same thing five minutes ago, and five minutes before that, and so on. "I've sent more of our men to keep searching, but we had to move on."

"Why would they take her? What could they possibly want with her?"

"I doubt it's her they want."

Levi paused. "Me?"

"Possibly both of us. We are strongest together. They'll use her to bait a trap, draw us in."

"Then she's probably still alive. They need her alive."

"Probably." Roman turned and walked off into the next room.

Relief washed cool and swift through his veins. As long

as Tasha was alive, he had a chance to get her back. But he was going to need help.

Dammit, in the few hours he'd been on Roman's UP estate, he'd already seen several possibilities for getting out. But he couldn't leave now. Regardless of who had her, Roman was his best chance of finding her and getting her back.

He could try the locating rituals on his own. Her mind was certainly familiar enough for him to find. But if he tried alone and screwed up, the consequences were too drastic. He couldn't take the chance.

Roman stood in front of a bay window that looked out over Lake Superior. On another day, the view would be impressive. Today, all Levi could see was Tasha's face, in the glass, on the surface of the water, in the light clouds. Levi stepped up beside his teacher, the taste of desperation bitter on his tongue.

"What can I do for you?" Roman asked.

He had to know what Levi wanted, but the bastard was going to make him say it. "You know what I need."

Roman faced him, hands clasped behind him. "You want me to help you find Natasha. I thought you didn't want any part of ritual magic."

"I've changed my mind."

"Mmm. Funny how that happens when it's suddenly one's own loved ones whose lives are on the line, not a bunch of strangers."

Levi didn't bite on the dangling guilt trip. His priority right now had to be Tasha. "Are you going to help me or not?"

Roman strolled over to a massive wooden desk, sat in the leather chair behind it and propped his feet up. Behind him, cold sunlight poured through the window in white shafts. "If I do you this favor, Levi, will you help me the next time I need it? Or will you turn your back on me again as soon as your girlfriend is once again warming your bed for you?"

His eyes narrowed at Roman's tone. He didn't take well to emotional extortion, but he bit his tongue. "I'll help you."

Roman dropped his feet to the floor. "Good. Then let's get started."

Tasha woke up in the middle of her worst nightmare: handcuffed to the bed in a maternity ward. My God, she couldn't think of anything more grotesque than the thought of a bunch of screaming women spitting out babies from between their legs.

Until the man she immediately nicknamed the Beast Master walked into her room, that is. He was as ugly a person as she'd ever seen. At about three hundred and fifty pounds, this man should not be wearing leather pants.

The hair on the back of his neck—which she'd be willing to bet extended all the way down to his buttocks—was thicker than that on his head. His teeth were crooked and his breath smelled of fish.

"You's awake."

She tried for a smile, didn't get much. "Looks that way."

He grunted. "Sorry we's had to give you that shot in the car. You's was putting up quite a ruckus."

"A ruckus. Yeah."

A man as thin and neatly dressed as the Beast Master was fat and sloppy poked his head in the door, a clipboard tucked under one arm. "She's awake."

"Looks that way," Beast Master said. "You want I should take her downstairs for you?"

"No, she's not for the breeding group. At least not yet."

Tasha's cuffs rattled against the metal headboard. *Breeding group?* What the hell kind of insane asylum was this place?

"She'll go fast when they put her up for bid," Thin Man said. "She's a strong one."

"Put up for bid?" Okay, if she hadn't been seriously freaked out by being kidnapped, drugged and handcuffed to a hospital bed—in the maternity ward yet—this discussion was pushing her over the edge. "Wh—what is this? Some kind of white slavery ring?"

Thin Man shrugged and moved on down the hall while Beast Master patted her ankle as if having him touch her anywhere was comforting. "Don't you worry 'bout that. That's not for you."

"Then what is for me? What am I doing here? What are you going to do with me?"

"You's going to be our guest for a little while is all."

"Oh, well in that case, can I get a cheeseburger and fries from room service, and maybe a set of handcuff keys on the side?" She yanked on the cuffs again and the metal dug into her wrist. "Ouch."

"Ouch," he repeated, wincing. "Da quieter you lay there, the better it'll be for you. If you's get too riled up, we'll have to give you another shot."

A shot of what? she wondered. Because honestly, unconsciousness sounded pretty appealing right now. Except that she needed to be figuring out how to get out of this friggin' place.

She sweetened her voice. "So, handsome. You want to tell me where I am?"

He smiled at the compliment. Dufus. "In Michigan. Upper Peninsula."

"What is this place?"

He looked around as if it should be obvious. "It's a hospital. For womens."

"Womens?"

He nodded. "Womens and babies."

"Jerry, there you are." A man in a white coat with a stethoscope around his neck stopped in the doorway.

Jerry the Beast Master smiled. "Here I ams."

"You need to go sweep the front hall, Jerry."

"Going."

The new man came in as Jerry walked out. "I'm Doctor Smith. I hope Jerry wasn't bothering you."

"No." She'd belatedly realized that Jerry was a few cans short of a six pack, and she was feeling a tad guilty about judging him the way she had. Then she realized she'd been kidnapped and decided she could think any damn way she wanted about all of them.

The doctor took her wrist and settled two fingers over the pulse point. "Are you feeling okay?"

"Actually my wrist is really sore. I don't suppose you could loosen these cuffs. Just a little?"

"Nice try." He let go of her arm and headed for the door, talking without looking back, as if women handcuffed to beds were commonplace in his practice. "There's a bedpan on the shelf of the nightstand if you need it. You should be able to reach. Dinner is at five o'clock. Have a nice evening."

TWENTY-EIGHT

Roman set up the altar quickly and dispatched the welcome and calling of the quarters. "You know her mind well, Levi. Search for it."

"Where?"

"They would not take her far, not if they are laying a trap for us. She won't be far."

He reached out with his senses, let them travel over land and water, across treetops, over roads and buildings. It was tiring work, especially when his whole body buzzed with the need for action, not meditation, but he couldn't afford to rest, to lose focus.

He concentrated on the mind he knew so well, thinking about the pathways to pleasure and pain, joy and despair he knew so well. There were dark places there, too. Paths he'd never traveled, areas she shut out, never allowed him to travel. He searched for all the contours of her mind.

"I'm not sensing anything." The knot of worry in his gut pulled tighter.

"Keep trying. Reach out a little farther."

"I found her!" His breath hitched as he recognized the pattern to her thoughts. The irreverent mind-set.

"Good. That didn't take too long. Now guide me to where she is. I'll help you do what needs to be done."

A moment later, Levi felt the strength of another mind—a very powerful one—join his. Roman had arrived.

"She's . . . on a bed." Yes, he could see her clearly now, sheets mussed, legs akimbo. It was a hospital bed, he saw. "God, is she hurt?"

"She is only asleep. Wake her. Just nudge her mind with yours."

That part was easy. Her eyes flew open and he recognized the shape of his name on her lips, though he couldn't hear her.

"She knows it's me. Us."

"Levi," she said again, and this time looked pointedly at her right wrist and rattled the handcuffs locked around the metal frame.

"Do you know this place, Roman? I have to get there, get her out."

Roman picked up his cell phone, punched in a quick message. "I have men nearby already. They're on their way. But you can do more from here."

Maybe he could, but he was afraid. If he couldn't control his power when a boy he'd only met a few hours before had been killed, how would he ever expect to master the rage if someone hurt Tasha? God knew what kind of damage he could do, how many innocent people might be hurt this time.

On the other hand, the same held true if he went to this place in person, wherever it was. If he walked in there with a gun, and found someone had hurt her, he wouldn't hesitate to fire, would he?

"All right," he said. "Let's start with the handcuffs."

"Look into the lock with your mind. See the tumblers."

Suddenly the parlor tricks he'd practiced seemed very propitious. The lock was more delicate than the other objects he'd manipulated with magic, but no more difficult. The silver bracelet clicked open, and Tasha rubbed her wrist.

"Now to get her out of there." A sweat broke on Levi's forehead. He'd never held a connection this intense, this draining, for this long.

"There is a guard at the end of the hall, to the left outside her door. Make him sleep."

Levi wasn't sure how to do that, so he just thought sleep, and the man's head nodded to the side. He showed Tasha a picture of the empty hall, and she peeked out her door, and then darted out.

"Slow her down," Roman commanded. "We've got to stay ahead of her, find her a route. We can't have her crashing into a night watchman or a doctor on rounds."

Levi dredged up images of a slow stroll on the beach and flung them at her. She stopped, seemed to think a minute, then stepped out slowly.

Roman and Levi guided her through the maze of corridors to the stairwell, then down to the ground floor and out into a service hall. She came to a T intersection, and he projected the image of the hallway going left to Tasha.

She shook her head and pointed right, toward a set of glass double doors that exited into the parking lot.

"No," Roman said. "There are others out there. Make her go left."

Levi projected left, and Tasha jabbed her finger right.

"Damn stubborn woman." Losing his patience, Levi grabbed her shoulders with his mind and spun her left.

Roman chuckled. "That's it. Now hurry her up a bit. Someone is coming."

Levi gave her a little shove. She stumbled but caught her balance and moved out.

They had her almost out of the building when they hit trouble. She was halfway down a long narrow service hall when the elevator door chimed and opened right in front of her. Two men in scrubs, probably orderlies, startled at the sight of her, then apparently realized she shouldn't be there, and started after her.

Without thinking, Levi flung one against the tile wall. *Too hard, too hard,* he thought, but the guy got up, shaking his head groggily, and stumbled away.

He didn't know these people, didn't know who was involved in what. He didn't want to hurt anyone, he just wanted Tasha out of there.

She had run toward the doors, and the second orderly was giving chase. Picturing his own foot, Levi stuck it out and tripped the man just as he reached for the back of Tasha's shirt. She must have heard him fall, and she stopped to look back, breathing hard.

A big man in leather pants stepped out of a supply closet and bumped right into her. Levi recoiled to push him off her, but Tasha held her palm out in a *stop* signal.

She smiled and said something to the man. He ambled back into the closet to get a broom and then headed toward the front hall.

Looked like Tasha was working a little magic of her own tonight.

She pushed open the door and scurried outside, past the trash containers and heat and air-conditioning units, down the alley to the street where Roman's men waited. The door to the Expedition opened, and she jumped inside.

Levi let go of the vision, drained but relieved. "That was easy enough."

Too easy, a niggling vibe in the back of his mind told him, but he didn't have time to dwell.

He was waiting out in the drive when the black Expedition pulled up. He'd thought she would have jumped out and into his arms, but he should have known better. Tasha Cole wouldn't show the goon squad clustered around watching that much weakness. She wouldn't let them think she needed to be held—even if he really needed to hold her right now.

He settled for taking her hand and leading her inside. Not until they were in their room, a plush suite with a king-sized four-poster bed and a Jacuzzi tub did he drag her into his arms.

"Are you all right?"

Her breath shuddered a little bit, but she claimed yes. "You were unbelievable, guiding me around like that. It was like you were standing right there next to me telling me which way to go."

"Thanks." He rubbed her shoulders. "Roman helped, too."

"What?" she spat.

He'd guessed her reaction was going to be something like that. "I didn't know where you were or who had you. I wasn't sure I could pull it off by myself."

"So you asked that snake to help?"

"Pretty much, yeah."

"And he agreed, just like that?"

"Not exactly like that. He's been pretty pissed off at me, you know."

She narrowed her eyes. "What did he get from you?"

He shrugged. "Just a promise to help him next time. You know, when he needs it."

"In a ritual."

"Probably."

"Where he no doubt plans to take on this mysterious group of others that are trying to destroy the good, honest Gargoyles like him."

"Guess I'll find out."

She wrapped her arms around him. "Levi, you shouldn't have done it."

"I had to. Your life was at stake. I couldn't afford to screw up." He stroked her back, resting his chin on her shoulder. "Guess this is what people mean when they say they sold their souls to the devil, huh?"

Two floors up from where Levi and Tasha were having their reunion, Roman held up his wineglass and saluted himself in the gilded mirror above his dresser. In truth, he should probably have made the escape a bit more difficult. His men didn't put up much of a fight. But he hadn't thought it worth the effort. All he'd wanted was Levi in his debt once again, and he'd gotten it.

TWENTY-NINE

Tasha's head rolled back on her neck as Levi lifted her out of the bubbling water and set her on the edge of the Jacuzzi tub. She leaned back on her palms. He spread her legs and lowered his head.

The pleasure that coursed through her was caused by more than just good tongue. It came from the possessive way he'd carried her into the bathroom, the reverent way he'd touched her as he'd undressed her. The sacrifices he'd made for her.

It was getting harder and harder to remember the time when they'd been business partners and bed partners, nothing more. When their hearts had been so encased in their protective shields that they'd never dared admit to true feelings. Especially love.

Oh, God. She loved him, and she still hadn't told him.

"Levi?"

"Mmmm." The moan vibrated through her core. He

lifted his head and put two fingers inside her, slid them out and back again. "What?"

Sensation overload nearly strangled her. "Never mind."

In the middle of sex was not a good time for serious conversation, she decided. Later.

She curled up, leaned over Levi and wrapped her arms around his head, tunneling her fingers through his hair and kissing his temples. She eased him back into the Jacuzzi and sank down over his hips, taking the length of him inside.

Now his head fell back.

"So good. God, that's so good, Tash."

She clenched her inner muscles and slowly lifted her hips, gripping him the whole way, then relaxed and sank back down.

"Oh, baby. Do that again."

She did. Several times.

She couldn't project images the way he could, at least not without performing a ritual. She only hoped he could feel in her body what she hadn't been able to say in words yet.

The tension built. Jets of hot water tingled the skin in sensitive places. Bubbles frothed around them. Tasha gave herself over to the rhythm, the song playing between their bodies, the beautiful music.

His body bucked beneath her, increasing the tempo. He punched upward with short staccato strokes, his cock tapping her walls with every note. All the blood in her body seemed to rush down as he pushed up. She heard him cry out, a guttural sound ripped from the heart, and then her own voice joined his in celebration.

When the world came back into focus, she realized she was lying on top of Levi, holding him underwater. She popped back up, and he came after her.

"I thought I drowned you."

He grinned. "Nah. I'm good in the water, remember?"

She flicked droplets at his face with her fingers. "You're very good in the water."

The next morning, Levi led Tasha on a stroll around the grounds of Roman's lakeside estate, his arm draped over her shoulder and his hip bumping hers with every step. A dozen pigeons followed them like a line of ducklings, stopped every few feet to peck at the crumbs Tasha threw from a piece of bread she'd brought with her.

"Much as I love the sea," Levi told her, "it feels good to be off the boat."

"Mmm. No doubt. Even if we are being watched every second by a dozen guards and God knows how many cameras." She looked up at him. "You don't think he has the rooms bugged, do you? I mean the guy is a little paranoid."

"I doubt it," Levi said, but he couldn't help but rewind and replay all that had been said between them overnight. And if the bathrooms were monitored, well, the person watching the cameras last night was probably blinded for life by what he'd seen.

They strolled along a walking path that wound around the perimeter of the grounds for almost an hour, chatting about the difference in the lake air and ocean air, the ten-foot-tall red-tipped photinias that lined the fences, inside and out, on the grounds, almost hiding the razor wire on top but not quite, and whether or not the legitimate lobster fishermen in St. George's strait had noticed an increase in their haul since *The White Whale* was out of the picture.

When they ran out of conversation, they walked in companionable silence. Levi pondered the oddity of hearing the twitter of little birds rather than the harsh caw of the seagulls and the rustle of the breeze in the leaves overhead instead of waves slapping the hull of a boat. It was a nice change, though, he decided. He liked putting his feet down on terra firma every now and then, even if his heart would always belong to the sea.

All the while he walked, hoping he and Tasha appeared as nothing more than lovers out for a breath of air, he studied the security features around the lakeside estate. He memorized camera positions, guards' patrol patterns, and made note of a few motion sensors barely noticeable at the base of the shrubs near the fence. He also took special notice of the location of the dog kennels, where three beautiful but more-than-a-little-intimidating German shepherd dogs paced anxiously while they waited to go on duty.

He also took a close look at the exterior of the house, searching for possible escape routes, and mapped out the location of garden sheds, garages and outbuildings that might provide cover.

At some point during his ruminating, he noticed that while he was studying the estate, Tasha was studying him.

"I thought you were off on another planet or something there for a while," she said when he tilted his head at her in question.

"Just thinking."

"Trying to figure a way out of here?"

"Bingo."

"So how's it going?"

He jammed the fingers of his free hand into the front pocket of his jeans. "I think I'm ready to reconsider that idea you had about sprouting wings."

She winced. "That bad, huh?"

"This place is like freaking Fort Knox. And if what we

can see just by walking around is this good, you can bet he's got some other tricks that we don't know about. Not to mention he's probably cast all kinds of protective spells and warnings."

"I'm beginning to hate magic."

"I'm way past beginning."

He plucked a leaf off a holly bush as he passed. "Actually, I do have a couple of possibilities."

She looked up expectantly.

"I figure simple is best. Steal one of those big Fords and crash the gate or steal the speedboat tied up at the dock and make a break across the water."

"Does sound simple."

"Yeah, well . . . there's the little matter of keys. I could probably hotwire them, but it would take too long. Increase the risk of getting caught."

"Keys have got to be in the house somewhere. I can do a little snooping this afternoon."

He squeezed her waist. "You sound entirely too happy about that."

"Some girls are born to shop. I was born to snoop."

They'd finished the loop around the property and found themselves back on the garden path where they'd started. Winter still had a grip on the weather, so only a few hardy petunias and the evergreens were showing color.

"I'm sorry this didn't work out differently for you," Tasha said.

"Sorry what didn't work out differently?"

"Everything." She shrugged and gestured at nothing.

He knew what she meant. Damn if he wasn't sorry, too. "It's strange, you know, living your whole life with this big secret on your shoulders, no one you can share it with. Well, except you, of course," he corrected. "Then suddenly you find out there's a whole bunch of people like you, and you find out your secret doesn't have to be a secret anymore. You can talk about it and laugh about it and, I don't know, cry about it if you want."

She smiled. "I haven't noticed you crying yourself to sleep lately."

Giving her a look of chagrin, he continued, digging deep to find the words. "I guess it's like an alcoholic who's kept his addiction a secret, then all of a sudden someone gets him in AA, and he has people just like him he can talk to about it, so his problem doesn't seem so bad anymore.

"I thought it would be like that with Roman and his friends. Maybe not exactly like that, but you know what I mean."

"Yeah, I have a pretty fair understanding of what keeping a secret can cost you." She avoided his gaze. The pigeons who had been following them skittered away, seeming to realize there'd be no more treats today.

He looked her up and down, recognized the stiffness in her neck, the convulsive bob of her throat. "You have something you want to share?"

She tried. Actually thought about telling him. It wasn't such a big thing, really. Tiny compared to being Gargoyle. But her secret lay buried deep inside her, and it wasn't ready to be unearthed.

She ripped her gaze away from his and bowed her head. "Things are never going to be the way they were between us, are they?"

"Probably not."

"Is that what you want?

He paused so long she didn't think he was going to answer. "I don't know, Tash. I thought I wanted to know more about my people, myself. That hasn't turned out so well. I'm not sure about much of anything right now."

She was. She was sure what she wanted—who she wanted.

She just didn't know how to go about getting him.

"You'll figure it out."

She hoped she would, too.

THIRTY

"So you know what to do, right?"

Counting to three before answering in order to keep the sting out of her reply, Tasha nodded. He was just nervous, as was she.

"You're going to keep Roman occupied," she recited, "to be sure he's not spying on us with his mind tricks, and I'm going to snoop."

He put his hands on his hips. "You're going to wander around and get a feel for the place. And if you happen to see where they keep the boat and car keys, that's even better. But you're *not* going poking around in places that will get you in trouble looking for them. Got that?"

"Aye, aye, Captain." She saluted for good measure.

"All right," he grumbled. His hands fell to his sides in a more relaxed posture. "You be careful."

She stood on her tiptoes and touched her lips to his cheek. "You, too."

He left. She stayed behind, claiming she just wanted to run a comb through her hair. As soon as he was gone, she peeled off her heavy sweater and pulled on an old jersey of Levi's. It was oversized, and the neck fell to the side on her, baring one shoulder.

Perfect.

She knew how to get in places she wasn't supposed to be, and it wasn't by wandering around pretending she was looking for the bathroom. She decided to start with the garage.

A couple of guys sitting around the table drinking coffee and reading the sports pages locked on to her with long looks as she walked through the kitchen, but she ignored them. They weren't the ones she might need to con.

On her way through the pantry and mud room, she scanned the walls for cabinets or hooks that might hold keys. She checked a drawer under a phone nook outside the dining room but found it only held old pens and a pad of yellow Post-it notes.

If she had the layout of the house right in her mind, the next door would lead directly into the garage. She tried the knob and found it unlocked. On the other side, three shiny black Ford Expeditions sat in the four-car garage along with a golf cart and a BMW with a vanity plate that read "ROMAN 1."

Geez, the guy had an ego.

She stepped down three wooden steps onto the cement floor of the garage. The lights were off, but enough sun streamed through windows on the overhead doors that visibility was not a problem. No one seemed to be around.

Trying not to make too much noise in a room that was bound to echo every sound, she went to the first vehicle and opened the driver's side door. She ran her hand under the seat and over the visor, and checked the center console.

No keys. She supposed that would have been too easy.

Tasha didn't own a car. Her life had been *The White Whale* and she'd lived aboard. Everything she needed that she didn't have on her boat had been within walking distance of the marina.

She remembered when she had owned one, though, and had locked the keys inside. What a pain in the ass that had been. A lot of people kept spare keys in little magnetic boxes under the wheel wells or bumper for just such an emergency, she knew.

On her knees, she crept around the perimeter of the car, feeling beneath the running boards and chrome bumpers, ducking her head down to look under the wheel wells, but found nothing.

Opening the car back up, she popped the hood and checked around the edges of the engine compartment.

Still no magnetic box, dammit.

If there weren't any keys around for one Expedition, there probably weren't any laying around for the others, but she was nothing if not thorough, so she checked.

She was on the last vehicle when she heard the door to the house open and shut behind her and heavy feet clomp down the steps. Straightening, she made a show out of slamming the truck door and cursing out loud.

If you were going to get caught, better to make a show out of it and make some noise than to give the impression that you were sneaking around.

The man in black slacks and T-shirt stopped across the garage. "Ma'am?"

Hmm. A polite Gargoyle. She hadn't met many of those, Levi aside.

"God damn it," she repeated, planting her hands on her hips. "That was my favorite pair of earrings, and now I've lost one of them. I'm pretty sure I dropped it in the car the

night you guys came and rescued me—thanks for that by
the way—but I can't find it anywhere. Do you know who
cleans these cars? I mean, they don't have so much as a fin-
gerprint on the door handle. Somebody must clean them.
Do you think whoever cleans them might have found my
earring?"

She paused, out of breath. The polite Gargoyle wore that
dazed expression men get when women take off on a tirade
they know nothing about and care nothing about.

"No, ma'am. I don't know who cleans the cars. But I'm
sure if they found your earring, they would return it."

"Are you sure, because they were genuine cubic zirco-
nia. I paid a lot of money for those earrings at J.C. Penney."
She talked even faster than before. "I got a ten percent dis-
count for signing up for a credit card that day, but it was
still a lot of money, you know, and I work hard for my
money. I bet you work hard for your money, too. You look
like a hardworking guy. It took me two months to pay off
the credit card, and you know what rip-offs credit cards
are, with that twenty-one percent interest—"

"Ma'am," he interrupted, backing away like he'd just
come face-to-face with a great white shark. "I'll ask around
about your earring. If anyone found it, I'll let you know."

He backed up the stairs.

"You do that," she started. "Because if someone finds it,
I'd be really, really grate—"

He was gone. She smiled, licked the tip of her index
finger and flicked it in a downward slash in the air.

Score one for the good guys.

She did a quick search of the BMW—that one would
be a lot more difficult to explain if she got caught poking
around—with equally disappointing results.

Ironically, she noticed as she walked out of the garage
that the keys were in the ignition of the golf cart. Some

getaway car that would make. Maybe if this were a Three Stooges movie . . .

Where else would people keep car keys?

On their dressers and in their pockets came to mind, but she really hoped that wasn't the case. She didn't have time to search every room, and she sure wasn't going to play pocket pool with a bunch of Gargoyles to see if they were carrying.

Presumably the trucks were shared. There had to be a central place to keep the keys. Some kind of office.

She sauntered back through the kitchen, ignoring the looks again, and wandered around the ground floor. She found a billiards room and a library. Several sitting rooms. Assorted bathrooms and supply closets.

But no office.

Inspiration struck. She walked back to the kitchen and leaned on the entryway so that Levi's shirt slid farther down her arm.

"Excuse me?" All four heads at the table looked up. All eight eyes locked on her bare shoulder.

"Do you know where I could find a pad of paper and some pens?" She tugged the collar of her shirt up and shrugged so that it fell down the other shoulder. "I write poetry, you know, and I'm feeling inspired this morning."

Two of the men stood. One stared the other down. "I'll get it," he said, though he didn't sound happy about it.

She followed him through the library to a little reading nook tucked into a corner and partially walled off for privacy. There stood another door that couldn't be seen from the rest of the room, and inside she hit pay dirt.

Against the far wall, a computer, printer and fax machine sat atop a maple wood desk scattered with papers. Matching file cabinets flanked each side of the desk, and above one of them hung a pegboard sporting a dozen or more sets of tagged keys.

The man who had led her there pulled open the desk drawer and grabbed two pens, then picked up a legal pad from the top of the desk. "Here you go."

"Thank you so much." She smiled sweetly. "I would never have found this place without you."

"Glad to be of help."

Little did he know just how much help he had been.

She followed him out of the room and they split up. He headed back to the kitchen and she was supposedly going to her room to write. As soon as he was out of sight, she hurried back to the office.

If she got caught, she'd just explain that she'd decided to see if she could find some different color pens. She was a woman, after all, and a poet, prone to flights of fancy like that. Not that they'd notice if she dropped her shirt a little farther off her shoulder.

Easing the door shut behind her, she quickly checked the tags on the keys and found the rings for all three Expeditions. Nothing for the BMW though, darn it. She supposed that was Roman's private vehicle. No boat, either.

Oh well, she'd keep looking for those.

She was about to leave when the fax machine clicked on. She heard the ring tones and modem tones, and soon enough a page began to print.

She couldn't resist looking. Snooping really was in her blood.

It was a list of names, all female, and dates. There were two boxes after the dates, one marked "M," and one marked "F." On each row, one or the other of the boxes was checked.

She scanned the names, recognizing none, then fear-ing her time had run out and someone might be expecting that fax, she set it back on the machine and made for the door.

Time to pay the piper. Or at least make a down payment.

Levi sat in a satin settee in a small parlor off Roman's office, waiting quietly while Roman gathered the tools they'd need for today's ritual.

He'd promised to help Roman, and it hadn't taken long for the debt to be called. Levi didn't mind, though. The lesson Roman had summoned him for fit nicely into his and Tasha's plan. He would keep Roman occupied so that he couldn't spy on her with his magic tricks and she would work on finding a way out of this place.

And then what?

Tasha's affirmation that things would never be the way they had once been between them echoed in his mind. He could never go back to the man he was before he learned he wasn't a man at all. The question was, could she accept anything else?

His reasons for living life on the fringe as he had were clear. He knew why he chose life at sea, and claimed few men—and only one woman—as friends. But what were her reasons? Why did she choose to live like that?

Why had he never asked?

Because he hadn't wanted to know, he realized. She'd been convenient. She offered no explanations for herself and expected none from him. It was the only kind of relationship, if you could even call it a relationship, he could accept.

And it now felt so hollow, so shallow, that he was ashamed. She deserved more. A lot more.

"You must focus, Levi." The edge of impatience in Roman's voice was unmistakable.

He shifted restlessly. "All right. What did you want to show me?"

"Our enemies are many. They've grown strong in numbers over the years while our ranks have dwindled."

"Why is that?"

"The why is unimportant." If words were insects, those would have stung. "The matter at hand is that we need more. More soldiers to fight the fight."

Levi turned that over in his mind. "More Gargoyles? Like the Russian guys you smuggled in?"

"I recruit when I can, but it is not enough." Roman looked up from placing the ritual objects, and his cheeks looked feverish. Red veins crisscrossed the whites of his eyes, adding to the look of madness. "We must create more."

"Create?" A pit formed in Levi's stomach. "As in . . . *make* more Gargoyles?"

"That is beyond my power. Beyond your power now. Many factors joined together when we were made. The magic was strong; the ritual circle was created by the deities themselves. No, we cannot create more Gargoyles."

"Then what the hell are you talking about?"

Roman lifted a canvas cover off of a small wire cage. Within, a white mouse with pink paws and nose stopped chewing on a pellet long enough to twitch its whiskers and glance nervously at each man.

"We are a blend, Levi. A combination of human and animal souls. Our forefathers were the townsmen of Rouen . . . and the creatures of the forest."

The pit in Levi's stomach grew harder. Colder.

"Even with our power combined, we cannot blend the souls. But we can manipulate the bodies."

Roman quickly sealed the ritual circle, with the mouse and a covered silver plate inside, called the quarters and offered a dark welcome. The light in the room faded as if it had been sucked out. The air in the room seemed to roll in waves. Undulating.

Levi's heart rate kicked up a notch. Dropping the coveted pellet, the mouse skittered to the corner of his cage and cowered as the waves grew strong with each of Roman's requests to the deities. The creature's skin rippled as if something inside were trying to get out.

"Lords of man and beast, hear your son who is both. Let the power of earth and sky, water and fire fill the creature. Raise him up to serve. Raise him up to slay the enemy. Raise him up to shed the blood of those who would ruin us. Raise him up so that his own blood may be shed if need be."

The mouse's eyes grew wide. He sat up on his hind legs and chattered, tiny white teeth clicking. Then he grew. And grew. His body rounded, his bones lengthened. He panicked, running himself into the bars of his cage until finally he grew so big the wire gave way and his body popped out of confinement.

Instinctively, Levi reared back.

Roman cackled. "Fear not. For he is half of you. He will die for you. He will kill for you."

The mouse expanded like a balloon being blown up. Overfilled. His whiskers reached as long as fingers now. In a game of cat and mouse with this one, the cat wouldn't have a chance.

"Stop," Levi called out. "Stop this."

The bigger the thing got, the more the features of his face showed his horror, his rage. Red rimmed light eyes, giving him the look of a devil. What had been dainty little paws grew to claws that could kill with a swipe. In mere moments, the giant mouse stood taller than Levi. It reared its head back and gnashed its teeth, snarling like a feral dog cornered by the dogcatcher.

Roman lifted the lid on the covered plate, picked up a hunk of raw meat the size of a bowling ball and tossed it to the creature—Levi couldn't bring himself to call it a mouse any longer.

The creature tore into the flesh with claws and teeth, spitting and growling and swallowing without bothering to chew.

"Behold, the new soldier, Levi. Together, you and I will create an army of crusaders."

My God, the man had truly gone insane.

In moments, the roast was gone and the creature stood on its hindquarters again, eyes wild and blood dripping from its mouth, and studied Levi with the intensity of a predator sizing up its prey.

It took a step forward. Levi lurched to his feet.

Again Roman cackled, then he pulled a .45 caliber pistol from beneath his robe and shot the abomination of nature in the head. By the time it hit the ground, it was once again small enough to fit in the palm of a man's hand.

Bile rose in Levi's throat. He dragged a shaking hand through his hair. "You have lost it, man. Gone totally off the fucking grid."

"You promised me, Levi. You swore you would help me defeat our enemies when the time came."

"All bets are off, old man."

"I don't think so."

Levi tried to leave the circle, just managing not to run. Pain like none he'd felt before knifed through his skull, driving him to his knees. He grabbed his head with both hands, stifling a moan. His stomach heaved.

"My magic is powerful, Levi, and I collect what I am owed. Think about that until we talk again. Soon."

The pain disappeared as fast as it had stricken him. He lurched to his feet, fist already airborne and looking for contact with the old man's face.

But Roman DuValle was nowhere to be seen.

Levi could have sworn he heard a laugh from the empty room as he stalked out the door.

THIRTY-ONE

❧

Tasha was waiting for Levi in their room after he'd finished "distracting" Roman for the day—and nearly losing his lunch on the insane asylum carpet—and gaining the headache to prove it.

Roman had been causing Levi's headaches. He'd suspected before, but now he was sure. And he had a head that felt like a coconut someone had cracked with a hammer to prove it.

She was sitting in a wicker chair with flower print cushions, her feet propped up on the sill, staring outside and chewing on her thumbnail.

He set the bottle of water he'd been drinking on the dresser and steadied himself. He hadn't decided how much of what had happened to tell her. "You okay?"

"Fine. Just thinking."

"That's some mighty deep thinking judging by the look

on your face." And not all entirely pleasant. "How did it go today?"

"Good." She dropped her feet to the floor and her expression perked up. "No luck yet with the boat, but I found the keys to the trucks. They're in an office just off the library."

"Excellent. We need to get out of here. The sooner the better."

She lifted her chin and frowned as soon as she saw his face. "What's wrong? What happened?"

So much for keeping anything to himself. He gave her a brief overview of Roman's little experiment.

"My God. And he thinks you're going to help him?"

"He saved your life."

"So he says."

"Don't worry. I'm not helping him. And if you think I would even consider it, you don't know me as well as you think."

She got up and dug a bottle of Advil out of the dresser drawer for him. A peace offering, he figured.

"I found something else interesting in the office," she said. "A fax came in while I was there. It had the address of the building where I was taken on the top, but no name."

He popped the pills in his mouth and slugged down some water, thinking about that. "You saying there's some connection between that place and someone here?"

"I don't know. The paper was a list of names, all women. I told you the guy in that place told me it was a hospital for women and babies."

"You also said that guy was mentally handicapped."

"He seemed pretty sure of himself. Have you noticed that the guys at the cottage at Cape Sim, and some of the guys around here, talk about kids, but there are no women around?"

"So you think this place, this hospital, is where they stash their wives and kids?"

"I'm not so sure they are wives." She chewed her fingernail again. "But it makes sense. If Roman was worried that there was going to be an attack on his men, he'd want somewhere safe to keep the women and children."

"That place didn't have half the security this place does."

"You're right about that." She plopped down on the edge of the bed.

"Besides, if that place was connected to this one, that would mean that someone here was responsible for kidnapping—" It struck him what he was saying.

Someone here was responsible for kidnapping Tasha.

He knew that escape had been too easy.

"It got me to go crawling back to Roman for help. To promise to help him with his fight."

She blew out a noisy breath, full of meaning. "But some of Roman's men were killed at that gas station when they took me. You think he's capable of killing his own men just to manipulate you?"

He chose his words carefully. "I think we have no idea what Roman DuValle is really capable of." But Levi was beginning to. "That still doesn't explain the list. Why fax over the names if they're the women who belong to the men here?"

"It wasn't just names. There were dates by each name, and boxes to checkmark 'M' and 'F.'"

"Male and female."

"Womens and babies, Jerry said. And—oh! I just remembered. He said something about me not being part of the breeding group! I remember it sounded like the ant farm I made for a science fair in fifth grade. What the *hell* is a breeding group?"

"You remember what I told you Roman said about the

priest that created *Les Gargouillen*? That he wanted them to propagate?"

"Yes." She smiled. "Explains your magnificent sex drive."

He didn't laugh. This was going to be a tough one to explain. "He also said that the priest gave them some incentive. You know we reincarnate."

"Gargoyle one-oh-one."

"Well, apparently, we only get another life if we produce at least one son in this one."

Her face twisted. "What? That's . . . that's just . . ."

"Sick? Crazy?"

"Screwed up."

"You remember what Calvin's dad said about not all women being as understanding about our differences as you are? And how it was hard for a boy to get a girlfriend?"

"So what, you think these guys keep their own harem downtown? Sex slaves imported from . . . wherever they import them from?"

"I don't know." He turned it over in his mind, didn't like where it landed. "You remember any of those names?"

"Sure."

"Shoot." He pulled the satellite pager out of his desk drawer, punched in Rachel's number and the message as she called out the names.

Need 411
RE: Mary Sellers, Kathy Blocken, Shirlaine
Justin, Florence Gerot

"What are you doing?" Tasha asked.

He hit send, closed the pager and handed it to her. "Me? I'm taking a shower. You hold on to this. Let me know if we get an answer."

* * *

He'd been dreaming of blue skies and open seas when the pager chirped, waking him. He cracked one eyelid open and checked his watch. Three A.M.

He opened the pager, hit the backlight button so he could read it in the dark. Tasha curled over his shoulder, trying to see. "What?" she asked sleepily.

He held the screen up where she could see.

411
RE: Mary Sellers (missing, Detroit, 11/08), Kathy Blocken (missing, Chicago, 12/08), Shirlaine Justin (missing Indianapolis, 2/09), Florence Gerot (no info)

"Oh my God," Tasha breathed.

His mouth dry as if he'd eaten a pound of sand, Levi pulled the device back down and typed in the address of the "hospital" and a simple message.

HELP THEM

Tash grabbed the pager from him, scanned to see what he'd sent. "You believe me now. You trust them."

"No."

"Then why—?"

He shrugged. "If they're the ones behind whatever is happening to those women, they already have the address, so no harm done. If they're not, then they'll help."

She chewed her lip, considering, then thumbed in another message on the pager and handed it back.

He read the screen.

PS—DON'T HURT JERRY. LEATHER PANTS.

"Oh Jesus H. Christ in a poppy field, not another breeding facility."

Connor Rihyad took the printout of the satellite pager messages from his wife's hand as her rosy complexion faded to gray.

"It looks that way," he said.

"We have to get those women out. We have to help them, and soon."

He understood her sense of urgency. Not so long ago she'd been held in a place like the one Levi Tremaine—or Tasha Cole, they really weren't sure who had sent the messages— had informed them of. A place where Romanus's merry band of Gargoyles-gone-bad held kidnapped women and forced them to have their babies so Romanus would have fresh troops for his army and the Gargoyles would be ensured another life after this one.

If he hadn't been undercover in that place, she would have been forced into the same life of sexual slavery the women in this place they'd just found out about were probably suffering.

She'd been lucky.

So had he, since now she was his wife.

He ran his hand over the top of her head, down the soft nape of her neck.

He'd been very lucky, Connor realized. "Nathan is gathering the council to talk about the plan. We should head downstairs."

The Council of Elders of the Chicago congregation of *Les Gargouillen* met in a basement with half-empty cans of paint that had dried out long ago on metal shelves along the walls, and a furnace rumbling and blowing behind the dais.

It was a far cry from the hallowed days of old, when they'd met in ornate cathedrals and vaunted castle keeps. Times had changed, but their traditions remained the same. As much as possible.

The seven elders stood on a platform at the front of the room. Before each one was a carved lectern displaying their Gargoyle form. Some of the carvings showed the Gargoyle in battle with evil beings. Others showed them pulling children from a raging river or holding back a boulder threatening to crush a young family's cart as it passed by a bluff.

The elders wore robes of rich colors, woven with gold and silver strands which caught what little light shone in the basement like tinsel on a Christmas tree.

The rest of the audience, the congregation, stood before the elders. There were no chairs in the room, no sitting allowed. The elders found that decisions were made more quickly if no one was allowed to sit until the choices were made.

Teryn, the Wizenot of the congregation and therefore council leader, called the meeting to order and dove into the issue without preamble.

"We have new information," he said. "About another abomination on humanity, perpetrated by Romanus and his minions." He trailed his gaze across the room, allowing the weight of his words to settle. "Romanus has abducted a number of young women, and holds them in a place in Michigan where they are forced to bear the children of their captors against their will."

The crowd had fallen quiet as soon as Teryn had begun speaking. Now they hardly seemed to be breathing, so silent was the room.

"We are here to decide what action to take against this abomination. And to accept volunteers to carry out whatever course is set."

A middle-aged man wearing glasses stepped forward. "What is the source of this information?"

Teryn acknowledged the question. "A text page. From someone inside Romanus's organization."

Another of the congregation spoke up. "Is it true this inside man is Levi Tremaine, son of one of the Old Ones and brother to Rachel Cross?"

Teryn bowed his head slightly. "This is true."

Murmurs rippled through the crowd.

The man continued. "And that Tremaine is working with Romanus now?"

Nathan raised his hand for quiet, and looked to Teryn for permission to speak. "We don't know exactly what the relationship is between Levi and Romanus. We know that Levi was not raised among *Les Gargouillen*, and that Romanus found him before we could and may have lied to him about his heritage. But Levi has contacted us several times. I don't believe his soul is lost to Romanus yet."

"But it could be a trap," someone shouted out. "Romanus could be using Levi to lure us in, knowing we will trust him." The speaker nodded toward Nathan's wife. "Sorry, Rachel."

Connor let go of Mara's hand and stepped up next to Nathan. "Every time we leave this building, we could be walking into one of Romanus's traps. We cannot abandon our directive, to protect humans, because we are afraid."

Mara moved to his side. "You all know that I have been in one of these facilities. I have witnessed firsthand what goes on there. Teryn is right when he calls it an abomination. It must be stopped."

Connor's chest warmed with pride. And how far his congregation had come. Not long ago, a woman wouldn't have been allowed to attend this meeting, much less speak. Nathan Cross and his wife Rachel had changed that.

At first Connor had vehemently opposed those changes. Modern human women could not accept what Gargoyles were and how they lived. For *Les Gargouillen* to expose themselves to a woman was to invite the end of the race.

As Rachel had proven him wrong in her love for Nathan, Mara had proven him wrong in her love for him. They still had to be very careful treading on this new ground of lasting, honest relationships. It was dangerous territory. But it was an area they needed to explore if they were to survive. The alternative, what Romanus's men were doing, was too atrocious to contemplate.

"What about Tremaine?" one of the elders asked. "Are we to leave a son of one of the Old Ones in enemy hands?"

Teryn cast a sorrow-filled glance at Rachel before speaking. "I'm afraid there is nothing we can do for him at the moment. We don't know where he is."

Connor turned to his Wizenot. "Actually, we do."

The congregation leader raised one eyebrow and waited.

"I did an online search for the coordinates—"

"You what?"

Connor smiled. His congregation was coming into the modern ages in their relationships with women, but technology still evaded some of them. "Google Earth. It's a website where anyone can print out satellite photography of any location in the country. I went in to print out pictures of this building Levi told us about. I also got some original blueprints from the city records home page, you know, for our guys to use as intelligence before they go in. So I started thinking, Levi sent us that address by satellite text message. You see there are twelve satellites in synchronous—"

"Connor," Teryn warned.

"Yeah, sorry." He took a deep breath and thought about how to explain without all the technobabble. "Max works for the telecom company that serves the pager the message was sent from. That's how we got the pager. So I had him hack their database and get me the coordinates the message was sent from. I overlaid those coordinates on a map of the earth and zoomed in until I could swat the fly on the mailbox if I wanted to."

No one else in the room seemed to appreciate his humor. He cleared his throat and continued. "I've got the address and more pictures. The facility is well fortified, but it's not large. I believe Nathan and I have come up with a plan to get the women to safety and to get Tremaine out of Romanus's clutches."

They discussed the specifics for a few moments, the needs for personnel and specific skills, then Teryn called the question. "All those who abide by the decision to carry out an action on this place, say 'aye.'"

The *ayes* were resounding.

"All those who disagree, say 'nay.'"

The group of men, and two women, looked around for any who might dare speak up. No one did.

"It is decided. Those who wish to volunteer, please stay behind. For everyone else, the Council of Elders is adjourned."

About twenty men remained in the room. Plenty for their needs. Nathan briefed them, then turned to Connor. "Give us two hours to get everything together, then have them bring the cars around. We've got quite a drive ahead of us."

Not to mention quite a battle.

THIRTY-TWO

Levi crawled out of Lake Superior in sea monster form, then changed himself back into a man and shook the water from his hair. He disliked fresh water as a rule, but the swim had been bracing. And necessary.

Most of the guards were out watching him—leaving Tasha and the house, with its car keys, unattended.

Mission accomplished.

He grabbed a banana as a midmorning snack on his way through the kitchen and set off in search of her. He didn't like being too far away from her these days. If he thought they would have had half a chance, he would have grabbed Tasha and made his break for it right after he left Roman's last lesson with the monster mouse.

They wouldn't have had any chance at freedom, though. Roman would have been expecting something, and security was watching them too closely. No, he had to play down what had happened, and hope he didn't puke just thinking about it.

He had to wait until the time was right.

He turned down the hall that led to the exercise room and nearly ran face-first into Roman. The man's cheeks were ruddy and his eyes a little wild.

"Where the hell have you been?" he spurted. "I've been looking all over for you."

Hmm. His blocking technique must be improving, since Roman would have searched with his mind, not his feet. "I went for a swim," he explained, but Roman was already turning for the stairs.

"Come with me. Hurry."

"What's going on?" Levi nearly had to jog to keep up.

"One of our facilities is about to be attacked." He heard seething in the older man's tone, and wondered, if he could see him from the front, if there would actually be specks of foam at the corners of his mouth. "It's a place where we house our children. They're after our sons."

Nathan Cross.

This had to be the result of the message he'd sent the Chicago congregation. Had his communication been a mistake? As he'd come to believe in Roman's deceit, he'd had to believe that the Chicagoans, including his sister and her husband, were honorable.

All the Gargoyles in the world couldn't be bad guys, could they?

But if Levi was wrong . . . God, he didn't want to think about what would happen to those women and children.

He picked up his pace behind Roman. "What do you want me to do?"

"We need to form a circle, now. Lay protective spells. And stop those bastards!"

Levi had never seen Roman form a circle so fast. Within seconds a fabric ring had been rolled out. The altar was set, the tools in place, including tools of violence this time—a dagger with a wavy, but very sharp-looking blade, and a heavy bat.

What the hell did the old man intend to do with those?

He took his place on the floor. Roman stood over him with his arms spread wide and up, making an impassioned plea. He spoke the welcome, called the quarters and summoned his favorite deities with a voice full of emotion. "Oh gods and goddesses, come to us on this darkest day, in this darkest hour, for the protection of our children, our future. We ask that you grant us the power of the ages, the power of the earth and the stars, the wind and the sea, fire and ice."

Wow, that was a lot of power he was asking for.

"Grant us all that we need," Roman continued, "to protect those who sprang forth from us at your grace, to be your army, your eyes, your hands, your voice, your spears."

Weapons, in other words, Levi thought. The man thought of his children as nothing more than organic weapons.

Roman sat on the floor across from Nathan, folding his legs beneath him. "Let us begin." He bowed his head.

Levi followed suit, closing his eyes.

"Look into my mind," Roman instructed. "Follow where it leads."

Soon he was traveling, moving so fast that everything around him blurred. There was no sound but the rush of wind. Then as suddenly as the movement had begun, it stopped. When his vision cleared, he saw a building. The same building where Tasha had been held prisoner.

Across the street a group of men split into smaller teams and dispersed in different directions. Levi recognized the leader of the group coming his way—his brother-in-law, Nathan Cross.

Nathan and three others approached a door marked "Employees Only."

"Bind the doors!" Roman ordered. "Bar them with your mind."

Levi wasn't so sure he wanted to do that, but he needed time to figure out what to do about this whole situation, so he imagined all the doors of the building sealed shut. He felt Roman doing the same, their strength merging to an impenetrable weld.

"The windows, too," Roman said. "They'll try those next."

He was right, but again their binding worked.

The Chicagoans tried prying the doors, breaking the windows. Nothing worked.

While the stalemate lasted, Levi cut away a part of his attention to Roman himself. Cautiously he drew closer to the well of Roman's power, closer to his mind. His thoughts breathed like a living thing. He couldn't hear them, but he could feel their force, the strength of the old man's magic.

But Levi had magic of his own. In his mind, he whispered an enchantment for insight and for secrecy. In his concentration over the attack by the Chicagoans, Roman didn't seem to notice the stealthy intrusion.

Random images flashed in Levi's mind's eye. Touring Roman's mind was like flipping through a history book. He saw the dark ages and the feudal violence of the middle ages. He watched as kingdoms fell and fiefdoms rose. He rode horses clad in armor and sailed in ships powered by slaves with long-handled oars.

His attention was called back to the present by Roman's voice. "Damn it, they're casting spells of their own. We need to call forth the creatures, Levi."

"What creatures?"

"There are many in the city. Rats and pigeons and blackbirds. Spiders. We must call them all."

"No." He was nuts. Those things killed indiscriminately.

They would slaughter everyone, including the women and babies, and Roman knew it.

Levi looked into the building again. Within moments he felt them. The others. They were strong, these Gargoyles of Chicago. Perhaps not as strong as he and Roman together, but a force nonetheless. The doors on the building began to quiver, then shake. The frames rattled. Levi increased his focus, holding the entrances shut, then smiled to himself as a new idea came to him, and let go.

That should keep Roman busy for a while.

The Chicagoans rushed in.

Roman roared. "No!" He glared at Levi.

"Sorry. I couldn't hold them." He breathed hard to make it look as if he'd put out a valiant effort.

"Help the guards," Roman said, and bowed his head again.

Levi watched the confrontations inside the building, looking for one man in particular, his brother-in-law But he didn't find Nathan Cross.

The strike team worked like practiced soldiers. They used strategy to their favor, and quickly overpowered the first two guard stations without shedding a drop of blood.

At the third, one of the security force drew a gun, and a fight broke out. Levi made sure the weapon slid out of anyone's reach. He threw a couple of invisible punches to make it seem as if he were trying to help Roman's men, then went back to his real reason for being there.

Back to Roman's mind.

Only he couldn't find the connection. Another image kept forming behind his closed eyes. The wall in front of the estate.

What the hell?

He squeezed his eyes shut and tried again, forcing himself into Roman's mind. He didn't have much time, and there were things he needed to know. Truths to be uncovered.

But the same image of the outside of the estate popped into his head—and then he understood why.

There, crouched outside the stone and wrought iron fence, hidden behind the red-tipped photinias, hid three men.

Nathan Cross, the older man Levi had seen him with in visions and another man Levi didn't know.

How had they found him?

Nathan looked up as if he felt Levi's presence observing him. He made a hand signal. Up and over. He and his partners were coming in. But why?

Nathan flashed him an image of Tasha.

Levi's defenses unfurled. *No.*

The image blinked in Levi's mind again, brighter this time, almost painfully so.

No.

No reaction from Nathan. Levi forgot—he had to think the action, not the word. He visualized himself between Nathan and Tash.

Cross rolled his eyes. He sent images of Levi and Tasha running through the estate, climbing the stairs to a third floor landing with a big bay window and tossing the antique desk there through the glass. He showed Levi an image of Tasha astride the back of a giant owl, flying to safety while Roman and the other Gargoyles were distracted with the attack on the hospital. He showed an image of Levi himself climbing onto the back of the gryphon.

So that was Nathan's shape.

Not just no, but *hell* no. He wasn't flying anywhere. Besides, he still didn't know if the Chicagoans were here to rescue him and Tash, or kidnap and kill them.

Who knew? Maybe Romanus and his crew weren't the

only evil empire in the Midwest. A moment of panic froze his chest. Maybe all of his people were evil. Maybe they really were monsters.

Regardless, he and Tasha couldn't stay here. He said a quick veiling chant to blind Roman. It wouldn't hold long, but he needed only a few minutes. He jumped to his feet, gave one glance back over his shoulder to check that Roman was oblivious to his movement, and sent a mental image to Tasha of her meeting him at the staircase, praying his skills were strong enough to hold the veiling spell and get through to her at the same ti—

He needn't have worried.

The door to his right opened so fast it slammed into the wall behind hin. Tasha rushed in, breathless. "Levi, there's some kind of attack going on—"

Halfway across the room, just outside the edge of the ritual circle, she caught herself and skidded to a halt. "Oh."

Her gaze trailed over the circle, the candles, the chalice, and finally landed on the oblivious Roman. She tiptoed to his side and waved a hand before his eyes. He didn't flinch.

"What did you do to him?"

"Veiling spell."

"Cool!"

He took her hand. "We have to get out of here. Now."

She squeezed his fingers. "That's what I came to tell you." He was already dragging her out the door and toward the steps. "I got this image in my head. Just pop, there it was. It was weird, but I think it's from Nathan. He wants us to go to the third-floor landing."

Levi turned down the staircase and pulled her behind him. "We're going to get the car and crash our way out."

Tasha dug in her heels, yanking him to a stop. "But Nathan . . ."

"We can outrun him in the car."

"I don't want to outrun him. He's here to help us!"

"You don't know that."

She tugged her hand out of his. "No, *you* don't know that. Or at least you don't believe it. I do."

She ran up the stairs to the third floor. He jogged behind her. "Tash. Wait."

She never slowed down. "Please, Levi. Don't do this."

"I don't trust them. Hell, I don't even know them."

She stopped on the landing, table in hand to break the glass, just as Nathan's vision had instructed. Outside, someone shouted. Boots pounded pavement in rushed steps.

They were almost out of time.

"Then trust me," Tash whispered and heaved the table into the glass. Broken shards tinkled onto the concrete below. Heavy wings beat the air outside with an audible thump.

A moment later a giant owl swept away the jagged edges of the glass and poked its head inside, its claws hooked on the windowsill for support. Its beak was long as a shovel and as sharp as a pickax.

Tasha's eyes went wide a moment, then the great bird maneuvered one wing inside as if offering her a ramp to climb onto its back.

She glanced back at him once. "Please." And then she climbed aboard and was gone.

"No!" As if he'd just woken, he suddenly found his feet and rushed forward. He leaned on the sill, ignoring the spread of warm blood when a piece of glass impaled the heel of his hand. "No, God damn it. If you hurt her . . ."

"We're not here to hurt either one of you, you idiot. We're here to rescue you."

Levi spun.

Nathan Cross.

"How did you get in here?"

"Through the French doors in the adjoining room. I figured you weren't going to leave without a struggle. We'd need to do some talking first. Look, I don't know what Romanus has told you, but—"

"Romanus?"

"The man who brought you here." *Roman*. But somehow Romanus sounded right to Levi. Without knowing how he knew, he knew Cross wasn't lying about that, at least.

"He's probably filled your mind with a lot of crap. Put a bunch of spells on you to hide the truth. We can help you sort it all out."

"I can sort it out myself. All I need is to get away from all of you."

Nathan looked out the window to where the owl perched on a second-story window treatment, waiting with Tasha straddling his back. "What about her? Do you need to get away from her?"

Levi's fists balled. "Leave her out of this."

"She's already in it. Come with me, I'll take you where she's going."

Cross's body changed. Arms sprouted feathers and legs sprouted lethal talons. His face took on the shape of an eagle, black eyes shining with intelligence, and his body rippled with the muscle of a lion.

They both turned at the sound of feet pounding up the stairs.

The gryphon squawked and flapped a wing impatiently. Levi tried to move but could hardly drag his feet across the floor. He knew the feel of magic weighing him down.

Roman/Romanus had broken through the veiling spell and was working a few tricks of his own.

The shouts from below increased in number and urgency, but everything seemed to be happening in slow motion to Levi. Even the sounds dragged out, syllables stretched and pitch dropped low, like a recording playing out below its recorded speed. A single shot reverberated for seconds. The next even longer.

Cross shrieked and turned his head. Levi lifted his heavy gaze in time to see the owl take flight. The draft off his wings brushed Levi's face like a touch. Tasha turned her head toward him. Her mouth moved, but it took too long to make out what she was saying.

Behind you.

She looked beyond him, over his shoulder. Her arms contracted to her body. Her head jerked and chest heaved. She was going to have a seizure.

No.

She let go of her feathered handhold just as a third shot rang out. The owl pitched hard left with one wing partially folded and held at an odd angle. He dove, took out two gun-wielding guards on the ground before raising his head and flapping the one good wing harder, valiantly trying to gain altitude to clear the wall around the estate. Tasha slipped to the side, her limbs thrashing uncontrollably, then fell. Her crumpled form twitched and writhed on the ground in the throes of a full-blown seizure.

The owl glided over the wall, then went into a nosedive and never came up.

The gryphon shrieked, then lunged toward Levi, one wing taking on the partial shape of an arm, scooping him closer.

But out of the corner of his eye, Levi watched as Roman/Romanus leveled the gun at his chest and pulled the trigger.

THIRTY-THREE

Romanus stared down the yellow and black striped barrel of his Taser, across the thin wires connecting the gun to Levi Tremaine and the leads buried deep in Levi's chest and shoulder to meet his young student's wide eyes, and pulled the trigger again, sending another million watts of electricity through his body just for spite. He laughed as Levi's back arched up off the floor, his face twisted in pain and his hands grabbed at nothing to stop the pain as his chest seized.

He let the trigger go and watched the impertinent boy go limp.

Levi turned his head toward the Gargoyle Cross who reached for him from the window. He tried to pull himself over, to crawl to him, so Romanus hit Levi again.

The gryphon roared, but this time when he let up the trigger, there was no movement from Levi. Just a matte-finish gaze in his brown eyes and a single word whispered to Cross through still lips.

"Go."

If Levi's plea wasn't enough to convince Cross, the guard who showed up behind Romanus with a rifle was. A shot cracked out, missed as Nathan swooped toward the ground then gained altitude with a great flap of his wings.

On the lawn below, the woman's body had gone still, her fit passed. Alive or dead, Roman didn't know. Didn't care.

At the edge of the property, the gryphon dove again, this time coming up carrying the body of another, limp as a rag doll.

Levi swallowed convulsively, his gaze fixed on the woman. Her hand flopped.

So, still alive.

"Get her," Romanus ordered his guard, then when Levi managed to turn his head and look at him, zapped until those brown eyes closed.

Tasha ached from the roots of her hair to her toenails. The fall from the sky put the pain in her bones, she thought, while the seizure left her muscles feeling like elastic that had been overstretched and lost its resiliency. Her mouth felt like someone had stuffed it with cotton, and her eyelids ground across her eyes like sandpaper when she tried to open them.

The ground jolted beneath her, sending new waves of agony zinging from her spine down her limbs.

No, not the ground. She lay on her side. Beneath her shoulder and hip she felt the vibration of an engine. Beneath her ear she heard the hum of tires. She was in a vehicle . . . and one of the reasons she hurt so bad was her wrists were bound, her arms twisted painfully behind her. Her legs were also secured, her feet numb from loss of circulation.

Gritting her teeth, she cracked one eye open.

Yes, it was a vehicle. A van of some kind, and she was on the floor. Outside the cargo windows, telephone poles whizzed by every second or two. She struggled to raise her head, to see where she was going, who had taken her, but she was too weak. Her mind and her body felt disconnected. She remembered the effect from a surgery she'd had a few years back.

She'd been drugged.

A wave of nausea hit her, and for a moment she panicked, afraid she would vomit behind the gag over her mouth and choke, but the urge to throw up passed, and gradually she was able to open her eyes again. Both of them, this time.

Her breath hitched at the sight of Romanus's cold gray eyes looming over her. He tapped her cheek as he leered. "Wakey, wakey."

She tried to slow her breathing, inhale through her nose, but she wasn't getting enough air. Romanus tugged the gag down over her chin and she gulped in a deep breath.

"Where are we? Where are we going?"

"Tsk, tsk. So many questions."

He trailed the pad of his index finger up her jaw and down her neck to her collarbone. She shuddered. "Doesn't it bother Levi, you asking questions all the time? I should think he wouldn't put up with that."

He was still touching her, now tracing the neckline of her blouse, and she fought the urge to squirm, bile rising again in her throat. At least now she wasn't gagged. If she vomited, she would spew it in his face.

"Bastard. Where is Levi?"

"Now don't fret." He talked to her like a father would talk to a small child, but his touch was anything but parental. "He's right there."

He jerked his chin to the space on the floorboard above

and behind her. She craned her neck and just made out the back of his head, his tousled shaggy hair unmistakable. But he wasn't moving.

"Oh. Oh, God. Is he dead?"

Romanus pulled his hand away from her chest and tapped his lips with his finger as if trying to remember an inconsequential piece of trivia. "You know, I'm just not sure. Maybe he is. Maybe he isn't."

"Levi?" She squirmed toward Levi, pushing with her numb legs and scraping her hip and shoulder over the floor-board. *"Levi?"*

Romanus grabbed her ankle and dragged her back. "Of course he's alive, bitch. What good is he to me dead? You, on the other hand, are entirely dispensable. So if you want to keep breathing, you'll shut your trap and do as you're told."

He pulled the gag back over her mouth and reached into the seat in front of him, coming back with a syringe. He uncapped the needle with his teeth and tapped the air bubbles out of the injection.

"No. Don't." She tried to pull back, but who was she kidding? She wasn't going anywhere.

The prick of the needle burned in her shoulder. The warm heat of the drug in her veins dragged her under a sea of indifference to her predicament. There was only the hum and vibration of the tires. Her eyelids sagged. Before they closed completely, she saw Romanus touch her again, this time intimately. Odd that she saw it but didn't feel it. Her nerve endings had all gone to sleep already.

"If you're a good girl, once I'm done with Levi Tremaine, I might just keep you alive anyway." He touched himself through his pants and smiled. "I'm sure I can find some use for you."

Despite the drugs in her system, her skin crawled as if

ants were marching over her. Once Roman had climbed back into his seat in front of her, she scooted herself up close to Levi.

Not dead, her foggy brain reported just before she lost consciousness again. Not dead.

Warm.

She pressed herself closer and gave in to the darkness.

Nathan Cross paced the threadbare carpet in the Holy Saints emergency room, his cell phone to his ear. "Dammit, Rach. We nearly had them; we nearly had them both."

"We'll get them again." Her words placated, but he heard the strain in her voice. This couldn't be good for the baby. "You're sure he was alive, though. And Natasha, too."

He looked at the clock again, automatically calculated the time since Teryn had been taken into surgery for a gunshot wound to the chest and fractures of the collarbone, humerus and several ribs. Two hours. Two freaking hours.

"Nathan?"

"Sorry. Yeah, he was alive. It was a Taser, and Romanus was pumping him good with it, but he was alive. The girl, I couldn't tell, but I think so. She had some kind of seizure."

His wife's worried sigh spoke right to his heart.

"We'll find them again. Levi was ready to come with me. He was trying to get to me. We'll find them, and this time we'll get them."

His reassurances didn't sound any more convincing than hers had.

"How long until Teryn is out of surgery?"

"It's only been two hours."

"Two hours, twelve minutes."

He didn't tell Rachel that every minute the doctor didn't come out of surgery was a victory. The man hadn't given his patient stellar chances for survival, but Rachel didn't need to know that. Not yet.

He glanced at the clock again. She was right, as usual. "The nurse said three or four hours, at least. What about the women Romanus's goons were holding?"

"Our teams got them all out, and the two babies as well. Everyone is fine, but Mara is going to have her hands full with this batch."

"How many?"

"Six altogether, but we're pretty sure three aren't pregnant yet, so we should be able to put them into a regular victim support program."

Nathan nodded, and then realized Rachel couldn't see his assent. "That's good. We'll work it out with the others. Somehow."

"Mara's shelter is the best place they could be." Who else could understand the needs of women who had been kidnapped, forcibly impregnated and bore babies who would grow up to be not quite human—if they were males, that is?

"What are we going to do now, Nathan?"

He paced faster, turned sharper. "Unless we can figure out where Romanus might have taken them, we're going to have to wait for him to make the next move. He'll make a move against us before long, and we'll be ready. We don't have much choice unless Levi or Tasha can find a way to contact us again."

That wasn't likely to happen. Romanus knew that he no longer had Levi in his camp. Not willingly, at least. He wouldn't let them out if his sight.

Nathan said good-bye to his wife and made himself stop pacing, sit. For about four seconds. Then he was up and walking again. Damned plastic chairs would ruin his back anyway.

Two hours and twenty-eight minutes.

Come on, old man. Don't give up on me now.

*Levi drifted through the murky depths of unconscious-*ness toward the light. Toward awareness. As he rose, he thought he saw dark shapes pass by him, ominous in their lack of identity. He heard murmurs, gurgles. Speech? But the words meant nothing to him. He felt nothing. His body was uncharted territory to him. His mind was almost as foreign, as he couldn't string together two coherent thoughts. There was just rage. Hate. And fear, not for himself, but for . . .

"Tasha!"

Levi groaned at the fire speaking had ignited in his throat. His senses returned in a rush. Pain. Thirst. Dried blood and sweat. His eyes snapped open, and he automatically jerked his arms in toward his body, protecting himself, gathering himself for a fight. But his hands were snapped back when he hit the limits of the chains which held down his arms and legs.

He lay spread-eagle on his back. The effort to suppress the urge to struggle, to fight until he ripped his arms and legs free at any physical cost, stole his breath. He forced his head back to the floor, his arms and legs to go still. Though *still* was not entirely possible. His muscles still quivered spontaneously, feeling gelatinous after taking multiple high-voltage Taser bursts.

He eased his head left and right, studying his surroundings. He was on the floor, all right. A piece of hemp lay strung out a few feet away. He lifted his head just enough to trace it, and saw the complete circle around him.

Levi's head thunked back to the floor. It was a ritual circle. He was staked out like a lamb for slaughter inside one of Roman's damned ritual setups. The candles set around the room on stands of different heights and around the edge of the circle added to the mood. All he needed was some chanting monks in hooded robes and a man in black carrying a scythe and he could be playing a role in a B horror movie.

"It's about time you woke up."

Levi turned to see Roman stroll into the room in khaki pants, loafers and an off-white cable-knit sweater as if he were walking into his club for a drink and a game of backgammon.

Levi scowled. He couldn't help it; he pulled at the chains one more time. "What the hell is going on?"

With a quick blessing of the dark deities, Roman entered the circle and squatted next to Levi. "The endgame, my boy. The fulfillment of all my plans."

"What plans?

"The usual." He picked at a hangnail. "Excessive wealth. World domination. The extermination of all Gargoyles who won't follow my rule. Especially the Chicago congregation." He spat the last as if the words tasted bad.

"*Extermination*?"

"Of course. Why else do you think I've been training you all this time. With your power and my skill, we can finally rid *Les Gargouillen* of the weak. We can take our rightful place, not as *protectors* of the human race, but as *masters* of it."

"Like hell." Levi's heart thundered, rocking his chest. "I'll never help you."

"No?" He sighed. "My boy you are so tiresome. Just like your father."

"You said you were my father."

"Of course that was a lie."

Of course. Levi had figured that out some time ago. At least he'd hoped it was a lie. The thought of being born of someone like Roman, or Romanus—whoever the hell he was—it would put a burden of self-loathing on him he wasn't sure he could carry.

"Your father was a meddlesome, troublesome sort. Always wanting to talk things out. To take the responsible course. He urged the townsmen of Rouen to reject my offer. But in the end, the villagers were more afraid of the dragon terrorizing their homes and stealing their children than they were of me."

"So you struck a deal. You offered to slay the dragon if they would convert to Christianity, earning you favor with the powerful church at the time. Not to mention a fair ransom. Only they didn't know, did they?" Levi had pieced that much together from his dreams. From the panic as they began to change without understanding what was happening to them or why, much as he had changed with the same ignorance as a teenager. "They didn't know what you were going to do to them."

"Of course not. They would never have consented to that, weak-minded cowering fishermen and farmers. But look at what I made them. Look at the power I gave them!"

"You used them. They slayed the dragon, not your prayer, as you promised."

"It was my prayer, my cast, that created them. Their human selves couldn't have killed that beast. Therefore I was responsible for the dragon's demise, just as I had promised I would be."

The man had truly lost his mind. If he'd ever had one.

"So if you're so powerful," Levi said. "If you're so god-like, if you can create Gargoyles, how come you can't kill them as easily as you created them? Why do you need me?"

"Ah, my boy. You don't understand. I had little power at that time. What I have now I've studied for centuries to develop. Lifetimes. There was more magic in the world in those times. We were closer to the days of the deities. There were artifacts of great influence to be found. Casts to be learned from the bards. One needn't be born with power to use it."

"In other words, you bastardized the people of Rouen's own religion for your gain. You used their beliefs and their history against them."

"I used their very Gods against them. And it worked. Too well. I hadn't intended myself to be caught in the cast." He laughed. "Imagine my surprise when I found myself growing fur and a tail."

Levi remembered the wolf form Roman had first appeared to him in. That wolf had looked pretty comfortable in its skin. Apparently Romanus had adapted. But then, he'd had plenty of time to.

"I still won't help you."

Roman smiled and looked toward the door he'd entered. "Bring her in."

Kolyakev dragged Tasha into the room. She squirmed and tried to kick her captor, only to be pushed and tripped for her trouble. Her hair was in wild disarray, the spiky peaks pointing every direction. Dark circles sagged under her eyes. Her clothes were rumpled, and she was cursing like the crusty sailor she was.

She'd never looked more beautiful to him.

Kolyakev pushed her against the wall beyond Levi's feet, where he could see her without craning his head sideways or back. She spit in the Russian's face and he slapped her. Hard.

"Fuck off. Knock that the fuck off!" Levi rattled his chains knowing escape from them was impossible. "I'll kill you!"

Roman called off his dog. "Kolya." He threw the man a set of keys, which Kolyakev used to secure Tasha's handcuffed wrists to a ring in the wall.

For a second, Levi's gaze met Tasha's. More was said in that look that they'd said in the two years they'd lived together on *The White Whale*. More truth exchanged.

"I'm sorry, Tash," he said, because he knew what had to come next, and he was right.

Roman walked up to her, took her chin in his hand and turned her face away from Levi, toward himself. He clamped his fingers over her jaw so she couldn't spit on him.

"You will help me, Levi," he said without looking back. "You will help me, or I will kill her in the most elongated, painful way I can devise. And you will watch."

THIRTY-FOUR

Romanus lowered his binoculars and turned away from the window. "It's almost dawn. I can see the building now, their building. Soon we'll begin. I want to see my enemies die. I want to hear their screams, their pleas. I'll kill her, Levi. A horrible and painful death. You will help me. It's time."

"Son of a bitch!" Levi yanked at the chains around his wrists until blood ran into his palms. "If you touch her, I'll kill you!"

Romanus's gray eyes glinted pure white in the candle-light. "You will help me."

Pain shot through Levi's head like a stiletto through one eye. "Never."

Romanus laughed. He turned Tasha, held her head steady by the jaw and looked into her eyes. His thumb rubbed her bottom lip in a lover's gesture.

She tried to bite him but couldn't quite reach.

He laughed again. "Look at her, Levi. So full of life. She doesn't want to die, do you my dear?"

"Kill him, Levi! Kill him now!"

Levi tried. He tried with every fiber of his being. He tried with every skill he'd learned over the last weeks. He tried by sheer power of will. But every attempt to cite a cast, to draw on his powers, only made the pain in his head worse.

He moaned, writhed and tried again. A bomb exploded in his head. White light and fire. Chanting helped him focus on anger instead of pain. *"Sonofabitch, sonofabitch, sonofabitch."*

"You can't turn on me, Levi. It will only cause you harm. You're in pain now—it's nothing compared to what you will feel. The more you resist me, the worse it will get, as it has since I cast the first veil over you before we ever met. You are in my control, Levi. You always have been."

"No!" The pain that single syllable incited caused him to cry out loud in agony. He bit his tongue until he tasted blood. "I *will* kill you."

"That's it, my boy. Use your rage. I have already cast the spell. I need only your power to give it strength. To bring it to life. My skill, your power. Feed it. Feed me. Power." Romanus lifted both his hands above his head.

Pain. So much pain. His neck arched back. Levi could feel the column of his throat jutting up, closing.

Electricity darted out of his body and zinged around the room. Miniature lightning bolts that crackled and struck.

Bastard. It was as if Romanus was drawing the power from him forcibly.

"That's it!" Romanus stretched his arms higher. "This building is old. Abandoned, but full of life. Feel the life around you. It's in the walls, behind the floorboards, in the rafters. Feel each life force and help it grow. I will send them on their errand of destruction."

Christ. That was his plan. Levi's head hurt so badly he could hardly piece together the thought, but he understood. The wild life forms in the building. Romanus was going to use him to create abominations like he had with the mouse. Hundreds of them. Maybe thousands. An army of unstoppable monsters. The he would unleash them on the Chicago congregation.

"Why do you hate them so much, Romanus? Why this particular congregation?"

"They defy me. They've dared to attack me. They think they can stop me." His hands, still above his head, clenched to fists. "They will learn—just before they die."

"That's not it. *Ahhhhh*." Levi's face contorted with a new level of pain that traveled from his head down his spine to every nerve ending in his body. "You're afraid of them. They're powerful. They're *good*, and you are afraid of that."

Now Romanus's face contorted. Not in pain, but in rage. He pulled a long knife with a serrated edge from his sleeve and laid it alongside Tasha's neck. A thin line of blood marked the edge of the blade on her skin.

"No!"

He pressed the knife deeper. Levi yanked uselessly on the chains.

"Feel your fury, Levi. Feed it to the beasts around us. They crave the anger, the violence. Let them feel your rage. Let them take it inside themselves. Let them *be* your rage."

Levi couldn't take his eyes off Tasha, off that thin line of blood. His control slipped and he felt the beings Romanus spoke of. He felt the lives, the beating of their hearts, the scuttling of paws and shuffle of wings. He felt them change subtly. A shift of their life force. They were coming.

"No, Levi." Tasha spoke carefully, wary of the blade at her throat. "Be strong. Don't help this poor excuse for a shit bag, no matter what. He's trying to use you to kill innocent people, Levi. Your people. Your true family."

He concentrated on her eyes, her pretty mouth. It gave him strength. He pushed back on Romanus's power and paid a high price in pain. He felt as if his brain were turning to mush from the effort, and felt a trickle of blood run from his nose, and another from his ear. "Trying . . . Tash."

"Keep trying," she said. "Try harder!"

He managed to nod. His body couldn't hold out much longer. And he couldn't die without saying one thing, no matter who was listening in. "Love . . . you . . . Tash."

"I love you, too," she choked. He could just make out the shimmer of tears in her eyes through his agony and the veil of blood in his eyes.

"Enough of this!" Romanus roared. "Use your power. Use it now!" Romanus pulled the knife from her neck, flipped it in his hand so that the blade pointed up and punched her in the face with his fist.

Levi's body convulsed as if he'd been the one struck. He couldn't leash his anger any longer. The fury, the need for violence within him was like a powerful river breaking through a dam. The barrier between him and the full strength of his mind crumbled and was washed away in the current of rage.

Levi felt the creatures again. They were coming closer, growing larger. He felt his rage pour into them. Heard them gnashing their teeth, snapping at each other even, as they approached. He felt the sharpness of their claws and nails and teeth. Felt the blood in their eyes.

No.

His whole body arched off the ground. His fists clenched and his toes curled. He tried to hold back, to stop the flow of power, but it was too late.

Romanus's army—thousands of soldiers foaming at the mouth with a need to kill—was born.

Nathan Cross sat in a hard plastic chair next to the bed of the man who was both a father figure to him and a son, of sorts, in the complex way of *Les Gargouillen*'s reincarnation genealogy. His breath stuttered a little waiting for each next beep of the heart monitor, each raspy sigh of the ventilator. The bullet Romanus's goon had put in him had missed his heart by half an inch, but it had still done plenty of damage. The fall from thirty feet, a spiraling, plummeting descent designed no doubt to protect the woman he'd carried on his back at the expense of his own bones, hadn't helped, either. He had a broken collarbone, a broken arm and a ruptured disk in his back.

But he was alive, and for that Nathan was thankful. Someday he would take over from Teryn as Wizenot of the Chicago congregation, but today was not that day. He had more to learn from the old man. And he had a son to raise, a wife to love. He wasn't ready for Teryn to die.

He cupped his palm over the old man's hand, wrapped his fingers round Teryn's bony knuckles. "I'm not ready, you hear me?"

He felt a movement, and a weak squeeze.

He jumped up. "Teryn?"

Another squeeze, longer this time.

"I'll get the doctor."

He turned, but the fingers grabbed on. He could easily have pulled away but understood the message to stay.

Teryn's head shifted. His eyelashes flickered, eyelids opened, then slid shut again. His throat convulsed.

"No, don't try to talk. You're on a ventilator. Just relax and let it do the breathing."

The old man's mouth moved. His throat jerked, and Nathan thought he might choke. He started to ease his hand out of Teryn's and go for the doctor anyway when an image flashed in his mind, shocking in its violence. The feeling of evil it brought lingered even after the picture faded.

Teryn was trying to tell him something. Unable to speak around the tube in his mouth, he'd used pictures.

"What? What are you trying to tell me?"

Another image leaped into total clarity. The woman, Natasha, eyes wide with panic and chained to a wall. Candlelight. Levi on the floor in front of her, writhing. The sight shocked him, but what made the hairs on the back of his neck stand up was what he couldn't see. What he heard. What he felt. The click of claws on the old floor, the snuffling breaths. The blood.

Death approached.

"Levi and Natasha? They're in danger. Where are they? You want me to send help to them?"

Teryn's head swung pitifully side to side as far as he could move without pulling at the tubes and wires.

"What then? What are you trying to tell me?"

An even more shocking image splashed across his mind with a spatter of blood and human tissue. The growling was loud as a raging river. Screams. The smell of heavy copper in the air. Glowing, inhuman eyes.

Nathan saw the walls of his home, St. Michael's. He saw people he knew being slaughtered. His congregation. His family.

His blood went cold. *God, Rachel.* Rachel was at St. Michael's.

"These . . . things. These creatures. Romanus is going to use them to attack St. Michael's." Statement, not question.

Nathan had no idea how Teryn knew this—even they couldn't see the future at will. But he knew better than to question. If Teryn saw this, then Nathan believed it.

"He's in Chicago? Somewhere nearby."

Teryn nodded. Gurgled.

"He would want to watch."

Another nod.

He squeezed the old man's hand one more time. "Don't worry. You rest. He won't win."

If only he believed it.

Leaving Teryn was one of the hardest things he'd ever done. Wondering if he'd ever see him again. Wishing he'd said good-bye.

But he strode out of the room, flipping his cell phone open, without time for so much as a look back.

"Hey, Rach. Put Connor on—fast."

Tasha tried to kick Roman in the balls, but he blocked the blow with his knee. Over his shoulder, Levi still lay on the floor. Speech was past him. He moaned occasionally. He writhed constantly, choppy jerks not unlike her seizures.

"Fight it, Levi. Fight it."

She kicked out again, missed again.

"He can't fight it, bitch. It is who he is. What he is. It is his destiny."

His destiny? To destroy the very people he longed so much to find. She'd been blind for so long. She'd thought he was happy on her little boat, with her. But Levi needed more, he needed to belong. He needed his people—the good ones.

"No. He won't give in. Don't give up, Levi!"

Levi's eyes stared blindly at the ceiling. She doubted he could hear her any longer. Knew he couldn't see her. The sight of blood flowing freely from his nose and ears, one corner of his mouth, frightened her. But not as much as what was behind him. What came creeping out of the dark corridors and passages of the abandoned tenement.

Their whispers grew louder. Their mewls and growls. Dozens of paws and wings shuffling by the door, eerie eyes occasionally poking in on over-sized heads, giant whiskers twitching, became hundreds.

"Levi, please!"

"It's too late, bitch."

Levi stiffened. His neck arched and blood gurgled in his throat. Amazingly, he found his voice. "No!" and another single word. A command. "Turn."

She couldn't fathom what he meant.

He scrunched his face and screamed hoarsely, "Turn!"

Roman rocked off the wall he'd been leaning on. "What are you doing?" He focused his gaze on Levi. The power that passed between them was nearly visible in its strength. Levi howled in agony. Gritted his bloody teeth.

"Circle of Darkness," Levi said.

"Stop it!"

"Become Circle of Light"

Romanus entered the circle around Levi and kicked him in the head.

Levi's hands fisted so tight his knuckles turned white. "Turn around; abandon the fight."

The creatures passing in the hall stopped. One by one, they hopped, slunk, skittered or flew through the doorway until the far half of the room was filled with heaving, furry bodies. Bats the size of men clung to the ceiling. Rats with bloodred eyes jostled and crowded each other, biting and clawing for position at the front of the pack.

Tasha's heart pounded so hard she wasn't sure her chest would contain it. Her mouth tasted of bile, and her body broke into a cold sweat. The atrocities of nature before her made her stomach roil, but she couldn't look away. Madness shone in their eyes. Violence.

"No!" Strain etched deep lines on Romanus's face. "Your mission is at St. Michael's. You know the place. I've given you the knowledge."

The beasts crept closer, licking their lips in anticipation of a blood feast. They moved until their ranks almost closed around the circle.

Romanus's muscles shook. He reached for his knife, lifted it in two hands over Levi's chest, blade pointed down. "You can't do this. You don't have the skill."

Levi smiled sickly. Blood coated his teeth as he spoke the final verse to his cast. "End the one who started this blight."

Romanus screamed in rage. He plunged the knife down. A man-bat swooped down from the ceiling, flew over Levi just in time to take the blade into his own body. It crumpled onto Levi, collapsed back to its original tiny shape and scuttled away, dragging one wing.

The knife clattered to the floor. Muttering unintelligible curses to himself, Romanus backed out of the one small opening left in the circle. He jumped back to Tasha, unchained her and took her in a headlock.

"Stop them, or I'll kill her."

She struggled, lifting her feet off the floor and kicking. Romanus's hold on her throat tightened until she wheezed and her vision filled with black spots.

"Don't do it, Levi. Kill him. Kill him!"

The creatures advanced, filing around the edge of the

circle, growling and snapping their teeth. Suddenly an image appeared in her mind, and she knew what Levi was going to do. Knew what she had to do.

She stomped hard on Romanus's insole. Turned and kneed him even harder in the balls. The movement wrenched her neck, but he loosened his chokehold enough for her to tuck her chin and duck out of his grasp. His hand caught on her necklace, and the chain came off in his hand.

She dove into the circle, crouched near Levi and held his head in her lap.

The creatures moved in on Romanus. He pressed himself back against the wall, lips quivering. "It won't matter," he said in a voice full of false bravado. "I have the key now." He held up Tasha's necklace, the one with the strange symbol pendant Levi had given her.

"With this, I don't need you. I have many sons in this life and I've shown them the key. I'll reincarnate." Romanus made himself even smaller as the beasts moved in for the kill. "I'll be back."

"So will I."

Levi closed his eyes, and the creatures leaped on Romanus. Blood spouted as if from a fountain. Body tissue and screams flew.

THIRTY-FIVE

The first sensation Levi could put a word to was warmth. For the first time in a very long time, he felt warm. Specifically on his left cheek and his right hand.

The second was that he had to pee.

He shifted in bed. Wires and tubes pulled at him in very sensitive places, including beneath the cover laying over him.

Hell. He hated catheters.

He heard footsteps around him, murmured voices, and opened one sluggish eyelid, not sure where he was or how he had gotten here. The last thing he remembered—

Shit!

He bolted upright, or nearly upright, more tubes pinching him and an alarming beep suddenly shrieking from a machine behind him before gentle hands eased him back to the mattress.

He managed to get a second eye open. Half open.

"It's okay. You're okay." Tasha leaned over him, smoothed his hair. The beeping machine settled back into its complacent rhythm.

"What happened? Romanus—"

"He's dead. His . . . creations tore him apart."

"Damn lucky they did, or they'd have been tearing our people apart."

Levi tracked the male voice to a brown-haired man slouching in a chair in the corner by the door.

Tasha glanced over her shoulder. "Luck had nothing to do with it."

"Yeah, I know." The man rose, walked toward the bed. "Connor Rihyad." He nodded instead of extending his hand, since Levi's were poked and taped and strapped. "You stopped them. Must've been a hell of a mental battle of wills."

Levi frowned. "I don't remember very much."

Tasha squeezed his hand. "You were stronger than even Romanus knew. You were able to turn his magic around, turn it on him. But you had a brain aneurism doing it. I thought I'd lost you."

The man who'd introduced himself as Connor jingled change in his pocket. "You've been unconscious for three days."

Three days? It didn't seem possible, but when he studied the mark Romanus's fist had left on Tasha's cheek, he could see it had faded from purple to yellowish green, and the cut on her neck had sealed over.

"Doc says there's no brain damage, though. You were lucky."

He didn't feel lucky. He ached everywhere. And he still had to pee. He pushed himself up a little higher in the bed. "Where am I?"

"Chicago Medical Center," Tasha explained. "They moved you out of intensive care yesterday."

"A hospital? I don't think that's such a good idea—"

"Don't worry." Connor smiled. "They won't find anything strange about your physiology. It's magic that makes us, not science. Once we're back in this form, we're as human as anyone else. Besides." He winked. "Your doctor, Ethan Neville, is one of us."

"So you're . . ."

Connor waggled his eyebrows. "A Gargoyle? Of course. Who do you think dragged your butt out of that tenement while Romanus's little pets tore him to shreds?"

"How did you know? I tried to send an image to the other guy, Cross, or Rachel, but I couldn't. Romanus had shielded the circle. I couldn't use any skills except the one he wanted me to—to help him create those creatures."

"Guess he never thought you'd be able to turn them against him."

"So how did you know?"

"Tasha told us. Actually Tasha told Teryn, who told Nathan, once he was out of surgery—Teryn that is, not Nathan—and Nathan called me from Michigan."

This was all going too fast. Making Levi's head spin.

"Once we knew there was an attack coming, we evacuated St. Michael's, and most of our people were out. So even if you hadn't been able to turn the beasties, we wouldn't have been slaughtered into extinction. But there would have been losses. Not to mention the fact that Romanus would have killed you and Tasha when he was through."

Levi struggled to piece all the information together. He turned to Tash's deep green eyes. "How did you know?"

She ducked her head. "Yeah, we need to talk about that someti—"

The door swung open, and Levi's very pregnant sister bumped it back with her hip while holding two steaming disposable cups steady. "I found some green tea, Tasha, I hope you li—"

Both cups bounced off the floor. Hot tea splashed onto cold tile.

"You're awake!"

"That or this is a very weird dream," Levi answered. All of this attention was making him squirm. Well, that and the peeing thing.

Tasha stepped back, and Rachel took her place next to the bed. She held his hand. Her fingers were warm and smooth and soft. He couldn't remember ever holding hands with someone he wasn't having sex with. The sensation was odd, but somehow comforting.

"You have to tell me everything," his sister said. "Where you've been, what you've done. What your life has been like."

He nodded toward her belly, his discomfort with the closeness easing a bit. "I don't think some of those things are suitable for little ears."

She laughed, and he realized what a nice smile she had. In a brotherly way.

"Okay, then. Just the highlights. Connor, would you go get Nathan? He'll want to know Levi is awake." She turned back to him. "He's down the hall in Teryn's room. They brought him down from Michigan by private ambulance as soon as he was stable."

"Nathan?"

"No, Teryn." Enlightenment dawned. "He is the leader of our congregation here. He went to Michigan with Nathan to try to get the two of you away from Romanus."

"The owl."

"Yes."

"That's when Tasha told Teryn an attack was coming, and where we would find you."

"But that was before we even went to—"

Tasha threw him a pleading *later* look. Reluctantly, he acceded.

Nathan Cross strode into the room, strode up behind Rachel and locked two arms around his wife and child. "It's good to see you, Levi."

"Now I can't wait to get you home." Rachel swung her gaze to Tasha. "Both of you."

Home. The word sent a ripple through Levi's stomach. Was that what this was? He wasn't sure he would ever truly have a home, not even with his own people. Not after all that had happened.

"I almost got you all killed," he said.

Cross's eyes narrowed. "You saved us all, and nearly got yourself killed doing it."

"Hey, no serious talk, no guilt and no blame. This is a victory celebration, and a family reunion, remember?"

Rachel's blatant attempt to lighten the mood was mostly successful. But more details of the final scene with Romanus were flashing through Levi's mind, rapid-fire.

"He said he'd be back," he told the group.

"And so he will. Our kind reincarnate—he told you that, didn't he?" Cross shifted his wife to his side, one arm still holding her close.

"Yes. But he said when he came back, he wouldn't need me any longer. That he had the key."

Cross's expression darkened. "What key?"

"He took Tasha's necklace, he held it up and said I'd given him the key."

"What did the necklace look like?"

Tasha spoke up. "It was just a symbol. I tried to look for something like it on the Internet once and couldn't find it. I didn't think it meant anything."

"What did it look like?"

She picked up a notepad and pencil from the bedside table. "I can draw it."

When she'd finished, she held the sketch out for Nathan, Rachel and Connor to see.

"Doesn't mean anything to me," Rachel said.

"Me, either." Nathan took the drawing. "Let me take this down the hall to Teryn. If anyone knows what it is, it will be him."

Rachel patted Levi on the knee, noting the looks passing between him and Tasha. "Let's all go see Teryn. I think Levi and Tasha could use a few minutes for a reunion of their own, anyway."

When the door closed behind the others, Tasha eased one hip down on the edge of his bed and took his hand again. He studied their linked fingers, knowing more than their bodies were joined at that moment. Somehow their hearts had been bound together.

Even so, he saw dread in her eyes when he looked up at her. "Is it so bad?" he asked.

She lowered her gaze. "Maybe."

"Tell me."

"Can't it wait? Just until you're feeling better?"

He nudged her with their joined hands. "Spill it. Just do it quick, like ripping off a bandage."

"I've had seizures and migraines since I was a kid. Mostly just petit mal—kind of like spacing out for a few seconds, but sometimes worse."

"That much I know."

She blew out a deep breath. "They usually happen when I get bombarded—sensory overload."

"Overload from what?"

"People."

He waited for her to explain. More questions weren't necessary.

"When I'm around people, especially crowds, strangers who are highly emotional, like angry or sad or even really, really happy . . . I get glimpses of their lives."

"The future?"

"No."

"Then how—"

She quieted him with a look. "Sometimes I just feel their emotions very strongly. Sometimes I hear words, like arguments between husbands and wives. Sometimes I even see the scene. But it's not necessarily the real scene. So if a person is daydreaming or something, or planning something, I might see what they are seeing—mentally seeing—even if that thing is in the future. I can't control it or stop it. It just happens," she added defensively.

"So you're psychic."

She shrugged. "I prefer the term sensitive."

"And you *saw* Romanus thinking about taking us to that building in Chicago, using me to kill Nathan and his bunch."

She nodded. "Every detail. The candles, the circle, the knife, the . . . monsters. I even saw the view out the window, which is how I was able to tell Teryn which building. When I was flying with him, I told him. I thought it was our only hope."

"But he got shot and wasn't able to tell his people until it was almost too late. How come you never told me about this before?"

Now at least he understood her isolation. Why she lived so remotely, with so few friends. Away from the crowds of the mainland.

"It's not something I talk about."

"You're talking about it now."

"That's how we ended up together, you know. When you first came by the boat looking for work, I was going send you away, but I got an image of . . . the other you. You were beautiful and scary and I was intrigued. So I followed you, and that was the day I caught you coming out of the water. I saw you."

"You're changing the subject."

She slapped his forearm lightly. "It was romantic, you dope."

"We'll get to romantic when I get out of this damned hospital and get you home. Now tell my why you've kept your gift a secret."

He could see it in her eyes. There was a story there, and a painful one.

She swallowed hard, twined her fingers in her lap. "My mom was freaked out by it. She definitely didn't consider it a gift. She accused me of spying on her all the time, because I would know things about her. She just told everyone I had epilepsy, and she warned me not to say more."

"That's not it. That's not all there is to it."

She shook her head. "I loved to go on the boat with my father—he taught me everything I know. But during the school year, I usually had to stay home. Mom started . . . when I was about thirteen she started seeing this guy, the guy who delivered our home heating oil. I knew what they were doing while Dad was gone. I could feel it, I could smell it, in my mind. I could see it. It made me want to puke."

"God, you had visions of your own mother fooling around?"

"I warned her to stop, and she cracked me one across the face and told me to stop spying on her and John. So I told Dad when he got home. He didn't believe me at first, but then his next trip, he didn't really leave port. He came home, parked down the street and watched the house. When John came over, he confronted him. They got into a big fight."

Tears welled in her eyes. Not good. His Tasha was not a cryer.

"John pulled a knife and killed my Dad."

"Oh, God, honey." He rolled up on one elbow and managed to pull her into a half hug. She lingered with her head on his shoulder a moment, then straightened and sniffed.

"I snuck behind him and grabbed the knife and tried to kill the son of a bitch myself afterward."

He rubbed a thumb across her cheek. "That's my Tasha."

Her fist went to her chest. The scar on her chest. Levi knew what had to come next.

"He cut me, too, but the police came before he could do more. I'd called 911. When my Dad was buried and John was in jail, my mom took me to the mall one day and dropped me off. She said I'd ruined her life. I knew when she drove away that she wasn't coming back."

Her lips quivered, but she didn't cry again.

"You were alone at thirteen."

"I walked away and never looked back. The bitch didn't deserve her life. A few years later I tracked down Paddy, who used to crew with my dad, and we schemed our way into getting a boat. The rest is history, but I never told anyone what I saw again."

"Until three days ago."

She smiled, wobbly, but a smile. "Some things are worth breaking rules for. And some people."

He pulled her into a hug again. "You did it for me?"

"He was going to kill you."

"He was going to kill both of us."

"I knew you wouldn't let that happen."

"Humph. You have too much faith."

"Never been accused of that before."

He pulled back, looked her in the eye. "That's because you're a different person now. We both are."

"Things are never going to be the same between us, are they?"

"Is that what you want?"

She picked at the blanket while his heart nearly bounced up his throat. He didn't think either of them could go back. The question was, could they go forward . . . together.

"No," she finally said.

Relief washed through him. "We can go away again. It won't be like before. It'll be better. Between us. But we don't have to be around so many other people. If it bothers you, we'll sail out, just the two of us—"

"You can't leave. You've just found your family. Your real family."

He shook his head. "They might be the blood relatives. But *you* are my real family. You always have been, you always will be."

To his surprise, she finally let go of a tear. It slipped down her face to his palm, where he caught it and brought it to his heart.

"And you're mine. But it's not so bad here. I've been to their place, this St. Michael's. Even though there's lots of people, most of them are . . . well, they're Gargoyles, like you, and their minds are more disciplined than normal people. I don't get bombarded so much around them. It's been such a long time since I've been around people. I'd like to give it a go. Stay awhile, if we could."

She was lying through her teeth and he knew it, but she was doing it for him and he loved her all the more for it.

"And St. Michael's is real close to Lake Michigan, so you can get away and do your thing when you need to. So are we staying?"

He smiled, nodded. "One condition. We get a little sailboat, and when *you* need to get away, we put out. No explanations necessary."

"Deal."

She leaned down to give him a peck on the lips, but he caught her behind the neck, drew her in for a much deeper, more meaningful kiss to seal their pact.

The door opened behind them, and Rachel stopped in the threshold, shielded her eyes. "Uh-oh. Maybe we should come back later."

Tasha and Levi ended their kiss. "No. Your timing is perfect."

Levi held Tasha's hand, looked around the room first at his lover, whom he planned to marry just as soon as he could stand up long enough to get through the ceremony, then at the sister he thought he'd lost, the brother-in-law he'd recently gained and the bulge of a nephew on his way.

Maybe fate had dealt him a pretty good hand after all.

"Sex incarnate," the women and men around her whispered. "Half incubus."

Aislinn didn't know if it was true, but she did know the man was Unseelie in a Seelie Court. That didn't happen very often, so she stared just like everyone else as he passed down the corridor.

Dressed head to toe in black, wearing heavy boots and a long coat over a thin crewneck sweater that defined his muscular chest, he seemed to possess every inch of the hallway he tread. He walked with such confidence it gave the illusion he took up more space than was physically possible. Seelie nobles shrank in his wake though they tried to stand firm and proud. Not even the most powerful ones were immune. Others postured and drew up straighter, offering challenge to some imaginary threat in their midst. Not even the gold and rose bedecked Imperial Guard was immune from his passing, like they sensed a marauder in their midst.

And maybe this man was a marauder.

No one knew anything about him other than that the dark magick running through his Unseelie veins was both lethal and sexual in nature. The court buzzed with the news of his arrival and his meeting with the Summer Queen, High Royal of the Seelie Tuatha Dé Danann.

According to gossip, Gabriel Cionaodh Marcus Mac Braire had been welcomed past the threshold of the gleaming rose quartz tower of the Seelie Court because he was petitioning the Summer Queen for permanent residence, a subject that had received a huge amount of attention from Seelie nobles. Predictably, most of the people against it were men.

Gabriel, it was said, held Seelie blood in his veins, but the incubus Unseelie part of him overshadowed it. The rumors went that he was catnip to females and—when his special brand of magick was wielded at full force between the sheets—he possessed the power to enslave a woman. The afflicted female would become addicted to him. She'd stop eating and sleeping, wanting nothing more than his touch until she finally died from longing and self-neglect.

Just the thought made Aislinn shudder, yet it didn't seem to deter his female admirers. Maybe that was because no one had ever heard of any woman who'd suffered that fate. If this man could use sex like a deadly weapon, apparently he never did.

Yet some kind of sexual magick did seem to pour from him. Something intangible, subtle and seductive.

Watching him now, so self-assured and beautiful, Aislinn could see the allure. His long black coat melded with his shoulder-length dark hair until she wasn't sure where one began and the other ended. A gorgeous fallen angel whose every movement promised a night filled with the darkest, most dangerous erotic pleasure? There was nothing to find uninteresting. Even herself, jaded and pride-pricked by "love" as she currently was, could see the attraction.

That attraction, of course, was the stock and trade of an incubus and Gabriel was at least half, if court gossip was to be believed. But for all his dark beauty and lethal charm, and despite that odd, subtle magick, he didn't entice Aislinn. To her, he screamed danger. Perhaps that was because of the very humbling public breakup she'd just endured. All men, *especially* attractive ones, looked like trouble to her now.

"Wow," said her friend Carina, coming to stand beside her. "I see what everyone was talking about. He's really . . ." she trailed off, her eyebrows rising into her ebony hairline.

"He's really what?" Carina's husband growled, coming up from behind them to twine his arms around his wife's waist.

"Really potent," Carina answered. "That man's magick is so strong that even standing in his wake a woman feels a little intoxicated, but it's false." She turned and embraced Drem. "My attraction to you is completely real." Her voice, low and honey soft, convinced everyone within hearing range of her honesty.

"Do you think he's *potent*, Aislinn?" Drem asked, curving his thin lips into a teasing smile.

She watched the man disappear through the ornate gold and rose double doors leading into the throne room at the end of the hallway. The last thing she saw was the edge of his coat. Behind him scurried a cameraman and a slick, well-heeled commentator from *Faemous*, the annoying human twenty-four hour "news" coverage of the Seelie Court that the Summer Queen found so amusing. "A woman would have to be dead not to see his virility, but if he's got any special sex magick, it's not affecting me."

Drem shifted his green eyes from her to stare at the end of the hallway where the man had disappeared. "So detached and cool, Aislinn?"

She shrugged. "He doesn't make me hot."

"You're the only one," Carina muttered. Her husband gave her a playful swat on her butt for punishment. She gasped in surprise and then laughed. "Look over there. He's the reason no men are making you hot right now."

Aislinn followed Carina's gaze to see Kendal in all his glittering blond glory. He stood with a couple friends—people who used to be *her* friends—in the meet and greet area to socialize outside the court doors.

Ugh.

Kendal locked gazes with her, but Aislinn merely looked away as though she hadn't noticed him. She'd wasted too much time on him already. She could hardly believe she'd ever thought she'd loved him. Kendal was a social climber, nothing more. He'd used her to further his position at court, for the prestige of dating one of the queen's favorites, and then tossed her aside.

"I have nothing to say to him," Aislinn said in the coolest tone she could manage.

Carina stared at him, her jaw set. "Well, I do." She began to walk across the corridor toward him.

Aislinn caught her hand and squeezed. "No, please, don't. Thank you for being furious with him on my account, but Kendal isn't deserving of the attention. Anyway, that's what he wants. It feeds his ego."

"I can tell you what that weasel *is* deserving of."

Aislinn laughed. "You're a good friend, Carina."

The doors at the end of the corridor opened and a male hobgoblin court attendant stepped out dressed in the gold and rose livery of the Rose Tower. "The Queen requests the presence of Aislinn Christiana Guinevere Finvarra."

Aislinn frowned and stilled, looking toward the doors at the end of the corridor through which Gabriel Cionaodh Marcus Mac Braire had recently disappeared. Why would the queen wish to see her?

Carina pushed her forward, breaking her momentary paralysis. Aislinn moved down the corridor amid the hush of voices around her. She'd grown used to being the topic of court gossip lately. The Seelie nobles didn't have much to do besides get into each other's business. Magick wasn't a valuable commodity here, practiced and perfected, like it was in the Unseelie Court.

She entered the throne room and the heavy double doors closed behind her with a loud thump. Caoilainn Elspeth Muirgheal, the High Queen of the Seelie Tuatha Dé Danann, sat on her throne. Gabriel stood before her, his back to Aislinn. The Imperial Guard, men and women of less pure Seelie Tuatha Dé blood, lined the room, all standing at attention in their gleaming gold and rose helms and hauberks.

It always gave her shivers to stand in the throne room before the queen. Arched ceilings hand painted with frescoes of *Cath Maige Tuired*, depicting the fae taking over Ireland from the Firbolg, humans in their less-evolved and more animalistic form, instilled a sense of awe in all who entered. Gold veined marble floors stretched under her shoes, reaching to rose quartz pillars and walls. It was a cold place despite the warm colors, full of power, designed to intimidate and control.

The Unseelie, Gabriel, seemed utterly unaffected. In fact, the way he stood—feet slightly apart, head held high and a small, secretive smile playing over his lips—made him seem almost insolent.

The Faemous film crew stood near a far wall, the light of the camera trained on the Summer Queen and Gabriel.

Though now the camera turned to record Aislinn's entrance. The silver-haired female commentator—Aislinn thought her name was Holly something—whispered into her mike, describing the goings-on.

Ignoring the film crew, as she always did, she halted near the incubus, yet kept a good distance away. The last thing she was going to do was fawn like most women. Out of the corner of her eye, she saw him do a slow upward appraisal of her, the kind men do when they're clearly wondering what a woman looks like without her clothes. He wasn't even trying to hide it. Maybe he was so arrogantly presumptuous with women that he felt he didn't have to hide it.

Aislinn was seriously beginning to dislike this man.

She curtsied deeply to the queen, difficult in her tight Rock & Republic jeans. If she had known she was going to be called into court, she would have worn something a little looser . . . and a bit more formal. Today she was wearing a gray v-neck sweater and wedge-heeled black boots with her jeans. She'd twisted her hair up and only dashed on makeup. This was not an event she'd planned for.

The queen, as always, was dressed in heavy brocade, silk and lace. Today her color theme was a rich burgundy and cream, her skirts pooling at her feet like a bloody ocean. The Royal's long pale hair was done up in a series of intricate braids and heavy ruby jewelry glittered at her ears and nestled at the base of her slender, pale throat. She wore no makeup because she didn't need it. Her beauty was flawless and chilly.

Caoilainn Elspeth Muirgheal gestured with a slim hand, the light catching on her many rings. "Aislinn, please meet Gabriel Mac Braire. He is petitioning the Seelie Court for residency, in case you hadn't already heard. It seems word has spread through court about it. I am still considering his case. As you know, we don't often grant such requests."

Yes, but there were precedents. Take Ronan Quinn, for example. He was a part blood druid and Unseelie mage. He'd successfully petitioned the Summer Queen for residency in the Rose Tower over thirty years ago because he'd fallen in love with Bella, Aislinn's best friend. Ronan had lost Bella, fallen into a state of reckless despondency and pulled some mysterious job for the Phaendir that had nearly gotten him beheaded by the Summer Queen. In the end, Ronan had retained his life and won Bella back—but both had been banished from the Rose Tower as punishment for Ronan's transgressions. Aislinn didn't know where they were now.

She missed Bella every single day. Bella had been the only one to know her deepest and darkest secrets. Without her presence, she felt utterly alone.

That entire story aside, Ronan Quinn was one example of an Unseelie male who'd managed to find a place in the Rose. Ronan, like Gabriel, was exceedingly good looking. That would weigh heavily in Gabriel's favor. The queen couldn't resist a virile, highly-magicked man.

"He'll be staying here for the next week and I have decided you shall be his guide and general helpmeet while he's here."

"Me?" Aislinn blinked. "Why me?" The question came out of her mouth before she could think it through and she instantly regretted it. One did not question Caoilainn Elspeth Muirgheal; one simply obeyed.

The Summer Queen lifted one pale, perfectly arched brow. "Why *not* you?"

"With all respect due you, my queen, I think—"

"Do you have a problem with my judgment?"

Oh, this was getting more and more dangerous with every word the queen uttered. The room had chilled a bit too, a result of the Seelie Royal's mood affecting her magick. Aislinn shivered. "N-no, my queen."

Gabriel glanced over at her with a mocking smile playing on his sensual, luscious lips.

Nope, she didn't like him one bit even if he did have sensual, luscious lips.

"That's a good answer, Aislinn. Do you have a problem with Gabriel? Most women would kill to spend time with him." The queen gestured airily with one hand. "I thought I was doing you a favor after your . . . unfortunate incident with Kendal."

Oh, sweet lady Danu. Aislinn gritted her teeth before answering. "I don't have a problem with him, my queen."

The queen clapped her hands together, making Aislinn jump. "Good, that's all settled then. You're both dismissed."

Aislinn turned immediately and walked out of the throne room, Gabriel following. Aislinn didn't like having him behind her. It made her feel like a gazelle being stalked by a lion. He'd soon find out this gazelle had fight. There was no way she was going to lay down and show him her vulnerable, soft stomach . . . or any other part of her body.

The corridor was thronged with curious onlookers as they exited. Carina, partway down the hall with Drem, made a move to walk to Aislinn, but Aislinn held up a hand to stop her. All eyes were on her and Gabriel. She didn't want to linger here and she really didn't want anyone listening in on their conversation and using it to weave rumor. They could watch Faemous for the juicy details, just like everyone else.

Gabriel surveyed the scene and ran a hand over his stubble-dusted, clefted chin. "Is it always like this over here?" His voice was deep and low, and reminded her of dark chocolate.

"Like what?" she snapped in annoyance.

He encompassed the thronged corridor with a sweep of his hand as they made their way down. "Is this is all the Seelie nobles have to do? Stand around and gossip?" He glanced at her stern expression and sobered. "Never mind. Forget I said that."

"Insulting my home is not a good way to start things off, Mac Braire."

"Call me Gabriel, and I wasn't insulting it. I was making an observation. I want to make this my home, remember? That's why I'm here."

"Sounded like an insult to me," she muttered, high tailing it away from the clumps of Seelie nobles doing exactly what he'd just accused them of. Though he walked faster than she did. She had to fight to keep up with the strides of his longer legs.

"I apologize."

"How does the Shadow King feel about your defection from the Black? He can't be very happy."

Gabriel gave a low laugh. "He's not. I'm taking a huge gamble. If the Summer Queen rejects me and I lose the protection of the Seelie Court, I may lose my head too."

"You don't seem all that nervous about it."

"Life is too short to spend in fear. Anyway, I've lived so long that I'm a thrill seeker. Anything to break up the monotony. Anything for change, Aislinn."

The way he pronounced her name sent a shiver down her spine. He rolled it on his tongue like a French kiss, smooth and sweet as melting candy.

It made her miss a step and deepened her annoyance.

She picked up her pace and matched his strides once more. "Listen, I don't know why the queen selected me for this job, but the last thing I want to do right now is babysit you."

Ouch. That had been harsh.

She winced as the words echoed through her head. He hadn't done anything to her and she wasn't sure why she was feeling so hostile. It had to be because of her recent breakup with Kendal. Gabriel reminded her of him.

Every man reminded her of him.

She still felt so raw and vulnerable. She needed time alone to lick her wounds and heal. The last thing she wanted was to be forced into spending time with an obvious womanizer who could wield sex as a weapon. Literally. Perhaps she was using this man as a scapegoat for her wounded pride and broken heart. If so, that was wrong . . . yet she couldn't seem to help herself.

"Whoa. Look, Aislinn, if you feel so strongly about it, I'm sure I can find someone else to *babysit* me."

She winced again. She was being a bitch and needed to rein it in. Maybe she'd misjudged him and he was a great guy. After all, he bore nothing but a passing resemblance to Kendal. That wasn't his fault. Regret pinched her and she opened her mouth to apologize.

"It's too bad you don't want to spend time with me, though, since I have news of Bella and Ronan. They've been anxious to get back into contact with you."

Danu. She nearly tripped and fell. Bella and Ronan? So they were at the Unseelie Court, after all. Aislinn had assumed they'd gone there, but wasn't sure whether or not the Shadow King had allowed them residence in the Black Tower.

The Seelie Court was called the Rose Tower because it was constructed of rose quartz. The Unseelie Court was referred to as the Black Tower because—never to be outdone—it was made from black quartz. The delivery of large quantities of each had been allowed by human society and the Phaendir, and magick had been employed to make it useable as a construction material.

Gabriel walked ahead of her, intending to leave her in the dust. Damn the man! He'd tossed that last bit out and then left to punish her. He knew she'd chase him. Clearly her first impulse to dislike the man had been dead on.

"Hey." She took a couple running steps to catch up with him. "I'm sorry. I've been unfair to you. You're all alone and could clearly use a friend"—although she was sure he'd end up with plenty of "friends" here soon enough—"and someone to show you around. Let's start over."

He stopped, turned toward her and lifted a dark brow. "Ah, so you do want word of Bella and Ronan."

"No." She shook her head. "I mean, yes, but I didn't say that just to have news of them. This is about me being fair and giving you the benefit of the doubt."

"Benefit of the doubt? What movie about me have you made in your head, sweet Aislinn? And without even knowing me."

"That you're a dangerous, arrogant, superficial man with piles of discarded, heartbroken female bodies to each side of the path you tread."

They'd stopped in large open area with a huge fountain in the shape of a swan in a pool. There were less people here. For a moment all was silent except for the sound of running water and the clicking heels of the few passersby.

He studied her with hard, glittering dark blue eyes. "Your honesty is very refreshing. I'm sorry that's your first impression of me. Perhaps I can change it."

"Maybe you can."

"A little too honest, that's my first impression of you." He narrowed his eyes. "And perhaps a bit jaded about men at the moment." He loosely shrugged one shoulder. "Just a guess."

Good guess. Time to change the subject. "Why do you wish to change courts anyway?"

"I'm surprised a pure blood Seelie Tuatha Dé would ask such a question. I thought everyone here believed the Rose Tower superior in all ways. There should be no question why I wish to defect from the Black."

Aislinn didn't understand the twist to his words. It was almost—but not quite—mockery. An odd attitude to have when he seemed to want to join those he mocked for the rest of his very long life.

"Apparently Bella and Ronan have gone to the Unseelie Court. It can't be that bad."

Gabriel smiled. "Well, there's no Faemous film crew there." No. Apparently the film crew the Shadow King had allowed in years ago had been eaten. "And the nobles aren't as . . . prissy."

She raised her eyebrows. "Prissy?"

He nodded. "The Unseelie Court is darker and you have to watch your step."

"So I've heard. Magick cast, blood spilled."

"Sometimes. The magick is stronger, more violent and held in higher regard. You know that. The laws are different there and you must be careful. You don't want to make enemies of some of them."

Fear niggled. "How are Bella and Ronan?"

"Very well. They've adjusted to life in the Black. They said to tell you they're fine, but Bella misses you. They say to tell you they're happy."

She studied him for lies. It was what she wanted to hear, of course, and Gabriel seemed the type to tell you what you wanted to hear. But she *so* wanted to believe what he'd said. She'd lost more than one night's sleep worrying about her friends. The memory of watching them walk away into Piefferburg Square on Yule Eve, forever banished from Seelie by the Summer Queen, still made her heart ache.

Though the crime that Ronan had committed—taking

work from the Phaendir—normally would have held the punishment of death. He'd been lucky. They both had. The Phaendir, a guild of powerful immortal druids, were the sworn enemy of the fae—Seelie and Unseelie alike.

There was good reason.

The Phaendir, with the full support of the humans, had created and controlled the borders of Piefferburg with powerful warding. They called it a "resettlement area."

Piefferburg's inhabitants called it prison.

If one wanted to be philosophical about it, the fate of the fae was poetic punishment for the horrible fae race wars of the early 1600s that had decimated their population and left them easy prey to their common enemy, the Phaendir. The wars had forced the fae from the underground, and the humans had panicked in the face of the truth—the fae were real.

On top of the wars, a mysterious sickness called Watt Syndrome had also befallen them. Some thought the illness had been created by the Phaendir. However it had come about, the result was the same—it had further weakened them.

The two events had been a perfect storm of misfortune, leading to their downfall. When the fae had been at their most vulnerable, the Phaendir had allied with the humans to imprison them in an area of what had then been the New World, founded by a human named Jules Piefferburg.

These days the sects of fae who'd warred in the 1600s had reached an uneasy peace. They were united against the Phaendir because the old human saying was true—the enemy of my enemy is my friend.

Aislinn cleared her throat against a sudden rush of emotion. Bella had been the only one in the court who'd carried the weight of Aislinn's secret. Really, Bella had been more of a sister than a friend. "Come with me. I'll give you a tour before dinner."

"Sounds good."

They walked the length and breadth of the Rose Tower, which was enormous and completely self-sufficient. She showed him all the floors and how they were graduated in terms of court ranking. The higher floors, the floors closest to the Queen's penthouse apartment, were where the purest blood Seelie Tuatha Dé resided. She showed him the courtyard in the solarium where the families with children lived so they could have yards to play in. The school. The restaurants on premise where the nobles dined. The ballroom, the numerous gathering areas and the banquet halls.

Most of the residents never really left the building for much beyond shopping or to have a night of dining out. Some of the more adventurous slummed it at a few of Pief-ferburg's nightclubs, but the Summer Queen discouraged the Seelie Tuatha Dé from mixing with the trooping fae—those fae who didn't belong to either court and weren't wildings or water-dwelling.

While social contact with the trooping fae was discouraged, unchaperoned and unapproved contact with the Unseelie Tuatha Dé was strictly forbidden. Aislinn suspected more of the illicit sort went on than was widely known. After all, she suspected her own mother of it. There was no other way to explain away certain . . . oddities . . . in Aislinn's magickal abilities.

She and Gabriel ended up at her front door. A good thing since she wanted her slippers, a cup of hot cocoa and her own company for the rest of the evening.

Gabriel grabbed her hand before she could snatch it away. "Thank you for spending time with me today," he murmured in Old Maejian, the words rolling soft and smooth like good whiskey from his tongue. He bent to kiss her hand in the old custom, his gaze fastened on hers. At the last moment, he flipped her hand palm up and laid his lips to her wrist. All the while his thumb stroked her palm back and forth.

That callused rasp in conjunction with his warm, silky lips sent shivers through her. Made her think about his hands and lips on other parts of her body, which made her think of his long, muscled length naked against her between the sheets of her bed.

In a sweaty tangle.

Limbs entwined . . .

Bad incubus. She snatched her hand back.

He stood for a moment, bent over, hand still in kissing position. Then he grinned in a half mocking, half mischievous way, straightened, and walked down the corridor, all sex wrapped in black and adorned with a swagger.

She supposed the Summer Queen thought spending time with Gabriel would be good for her after her break up with Kendal. A little meaningless fling to get her back on the dating horse? But Aislinn did not do meaningless flings.

And she was definitely unappreciative of being saddled with a man like Gabriel Mac Braire.

Sweet Danu, what had the Queen thrown her into?

FROM *NEW YORK TIMES* BESTSELLING AUTHOR

Angela Knight

WARRIOR

First in the Time Hunters series

In the twenty-third century, anyone can leap through time at will. Galar Arvid is a genetically altered warlord and Temporal Enforcement police agent who's been sent back to 2008 to save a pretty Atlanta artist from a Xeran time traveler who intends to kill her for profit. What Galar doesn't count on is the powerful desire Jessica Kelly ignites in him. Can their romance work with a three-hundred-year chasm between them and a maniacal killer on their tails?

M389T1208